When Good Things Happen to Bad Boys

When Good Things Happen to Bad Boys

Lori Foster
Erin McCarthy
HelenKay Dimon

BRAVA

KENSINGTON PUBLISHING CORP.

BRAVA BOOKS are published by

Kensington Publishing Corp.
850 Third Avenue
New York, NY 10022

ISBN:0-7394-6648-8
ISBN:978-0-7394-6648-3

Printed in the United States of America

CONTENTS

PLAYING DOCTOR

Lori Foster

One

Trying to be inconspicuous, Libby Preston glanced over her shoulder—and found that sexy, dark brown gaze still following her every move. He had a way of looking that felt like touching. Warm and gentle, but bold. Brazen, but complimentary.

She wanted to fan herself, but that'd be giving too much away, so instead she pretended not to notice and continued setting out more food on the buffet table.

They'd been at the stupid party for hours now and he'd done little more than watch her, smiling occasionally, giving her that sensual once-over that made chills race up her arms. He was a devil all right, and very sexy. She'd be smart to steer clear of him.

But really, what choice did she even have? Doctors and not-quite nurses didn't mix very often. Her uncle hadn't given her the job of playing waitress for his party so that she could flirt. No, it was one more way to pay him back for all she owed him, and she'd do well to remember that. And to remember her place: a lowly nobody among esteemed physicians.

The man eating her with his eyes probably thought her part of the catering crew. And that suited her fine.

Whatever he thought, he kept her keenly aware of him.

Anytime she looked up, he was looking back, even while speaking with others, even while asking for a drink or munching on the fancy snacks.

Unlike the other docs attending the benefit, he didn't wear a tie. Or a jacket. He'd unbuttoned his silky, coffee-colored dress shirt at the throat, showing a sprinkling of dark chest hair that intrigued her. He had his sleeves rolled up, and she couldn't help but notice the thickness of his wrists, the size of his capable hands, and more black hair on his forearms. The shirt tucked into black dress slacks, emphasizing the contrast of his wide shoulders against a flat abdomen and trim hips.

Restless fingers had rumpled his midnight black hair, and beard shadow colored his jaw. He was unlike any other man in the room.

He was unlike any man she'd ever seen.

More than one woman had noticed him. But strangely enough, he paid little attention to the finely dressed female physicians flirting with him, vying for his attention. Instead, he leaned against the wall, at his leisure, sipping his drink and . . . watching her.

Whoa. Libby pulled herself together and finished emptying her tray of hors d'oeuvres on the linen-covered table. Giving the man her back, she retreated to the kitchen.

Her uncle stood in idle conversation with a touted surgeon. As the chief of staff at their local hospital, he knew everyone. Uncle Elwood could give her the name of the man—but no, she wouldn't ask. Not only would it be unforgivable to interrupt, but questions on doctors would only earn her a lecture.

When her mother died, Uncle Elwood had grudgingly taken her in, but he made a point of reminding her that if his sister hadn't been such a frivolous partier, she'd have been the one to raise Libby instead of foisting her off on him. In his eyes, the apple didn't fall far from the tree. He often claimed Libby was the exact image of his sister, in looks and temperament. Therefore, at least in his mind, she could be no different.

Libby knew she had a lot to prove to her uncle. And she would—then she'd leave his life with a big fat *thank you*, owing him nothing, not a dime, not gratitude, nada, zip.

With everything currently in order, Libby helped herself to a small glass of punch. She'd just gotten the icy drink to her lips when Uncle Elwood harrumphed behind her.

Wincing, Libby turned, raising one eyebrow in inquiry.

"The sun has long set and you haven't yet lit the torches along the garden path."

"Oh." Libby glanced out the enormous window behind the kitchen sink. "Yeah, I'll get right on that." She upended her glass and guzzled down the spiked punch in one long gulp, then covered her mouth with a hand to muffle her delicate burp.

Much aggrieved, her uncle sighed. "Please try to behave yourself, Libby. These are my esteemed colleagues. As chief of staff at the hospital, they expect much decorum from me. You mustn't—"

Well used to the lectures, Libby cut him off by patting the front of his rich suit jacket. "I won't shame you, Uncle Elwood, have no fear." She set her glass in the sink and dug in the drawer for matches. "What do I do after I light the torches?"

As if hoping to think of something more, he glanced around, but as Libby already knew, organization ruled. "I suppose you could circulate, make sure everyone has a fresh drink, that the buffet table stays full, things of that nature."

Sounded to Libby like she'd be twiddling her thumbs a lot. She winked at Uncle Elwood. "Sure thing." Waving the box of matches in the air, she headed out of the kitchen. "I'll go take care of the gardens right now."

At mid-April, the evenings remained too cool for most people to venture out, but she wouldn't mind the breath of fresh air. The stuffy nabobs her uncle deemed friends were enough to curdle her blood. She'd been hustling for hours and had worked up a dewy sweat. With any luck, she could linger outdoors and catch a breather, with no one the wiser.

The second she reentered the room, Mr. Sexy Brown Eyes tracked her, following as she crossed the room to the double sliding doors. Libby did her utmost to stay impervious. Since her mother's death right before her fifteenth birthday, there'd been no time in her life for guys. Until she became a full-fledged nurse and gained financial and emotional independence from her uncle, nothing would change.

She could wish it different, but for tonight at least, Brown Eyes would just have to entertain himself.

With an indulgent smile, Axel Dean watched the young lady exit the room of suffocating, overbearing people. Damn, she was sweet on the eyes. Tall, nearly as tall as he was, with raven black hair and piercing blue eyes and an air of negligence that dared him, calling on his baser instincts, stripping away the façade of civility he tried to don in polite company.

Her straight hair skimmed her shoulders, darker than his own, blue black without a single hint of red. It was so silky it looked fluid, moving when she moved, shimmering with highlights from the glow of candles. The white catering shirt and black slacks didn't do much for her figure, which he guessed to be slim and toned. She didn't have the lush curves he usually favored, but what she lacked in body she made up for in attitude.

And attitude, as he well knew, made a huge difference in bed.

As a waiter passed, Axel plunked his empty glass down onto the tray and headed for the sliding doors. He hated up-tight, formal affairs, but being a doctor often obligated him to attend. That didn't mean he had to linger. That didn't mean he had to mingle.

Especially when more enlivening entertainment waited outside.

Making certain no one paid him any mind, he slipped

through the doors and onto a wide balcony lit by twinkle lights that mirrored the stars in the evening sky. He waited, saying a silent prayer that no one followed him. Every time he attended a gathering, women hit on him. And that'd be okay, fine and dandy by him, given that he adored women, but not within his professional circle.

He absolutely never, ever, dated anyone in his field. Not even anyone related to someone in his field.

Despite the marital bliss of both his brother and his best friend, he had no intention of settling down any time soon. That being the case, it wouldn't be wise to get involved with relatives, friends, or associates of the people he worked with. Walking away could cause a scene, and then the entire situation would get sticky and uncomfortable.

There were plenty of women who weren't interested in medicine, like secretaries, lawyers . . . or caterers.

He'd been prepared to be bored spitless tonight. Then he'd seen her hustling around the crowded room with robust energy. At first he'd assumed her to be a mere waitress for the catering company, but given how she performed each and every job, from putting out food to collecting empty dishes to directing the others, she might actually be the one in charge. Given her air of command and confidence, he figured her to be late twenties, maybe early thirties. Sexy. Mature. Flirtatious.

His heartbeat sped up, just imagining how the night might end.

When no one followed, Axel went down the curving wooden stairs to the garden paths behind Elwood's home. The pompous ass loved to flaunt his money, and why not? He had plenty to flaunt.

Spring had brought a profusion of blooming flowers to fill the air with heady scents. The chilly evening breeze didn't faze Axel as he searched the darkness for her. Then he saw a flare of light, realized it was a match, and made his way silently toward her.

She had her back to him, going on tiptoe to reach the top of an ornate torch anchored to the ground and surrounded by evergreens. Just as the wick caught, Axel said, "Hello."

She went perfectly still, poised on tiptoes, arms reaching up to the top of the torch. Slowly, in an oh-so-aware way, she relaxed and turned to face him.

Insufficient moonlight left long shadows everywhere, and with the torch behind her, silhouetting her frame, Axel couldn't read her features.

She cleared her throat. "You're not enjoying the party."

A statement, not a question. He put his hands in his pockets, his mood already improved. "I never do."

"Then why attend?"

He took one step closer to her and reached for her hand. Her fingers were chilled and felt very small in his light grip. He shrugged one shoulder. "You never know when something'll happen to make it worthwhile." Using his thumb, he stroked her knuckles. "Like this."

"This?"

She didn't pull away, but wariness had entered her husky tone, cautioning him to go slowly. "You're a smart woman. You feel it."

Her teeth shone briefly in a quick smile. "What I've felt is you watching me."

"Mmmm. Watching—and wishing." He tugged her a bit closer. "Wishing for a private moment, just like this."

Sexual tension hung in the air between them. Axel counted the heavy beats of his heart, tried to judge her response . . .

She turned away, saying lightly, "I have other torches to light." Her hand remained held in his.

"I'll keep you company." Axel followed along, trailing her as she wove her way into the gardens. Elwood owned ten acres, all of it wooded but meticulously manicured. The acreage closest to his home was especially lush with ornate landscaping.

"The path leads down to the pond," she explained. "It's not a quick jaunt."

Filling his words with innuendo, Axel murmured, "Quick is overrated. I prefer going slow." The scent of her heated skin carried back to him on the breeze, more delectable than the sweet fragrance of the flowers. He breathed deeply, and his gut clenched with need.

She made a sound that could have been a chuckle or exasperation. "It's deeper into the woods."

Grinning to himself, Axel growled, "I can go deep."

Now *that* was a laugh. She glanced over her shoulder, eyes twinkling, white teeth showing in a grin. "I meant that there might be mosquitoes."

"It's too early in the season." His thumb pressed her palm. "The bugs won't be biting—but I might."

Another husky chuckle, then: "You're pretty outrageous, you know that?"

He loved the sound of her voice, playful and not at all shy. "Just trying to make headway with a beautiful woman."

"Trying for a one-night stand, you mean."

His fingers tightened on hers, pulling her to a halt beside a gurgling fountain of marble nymphs, flanked by benches and a profusion of flowers. Small colored lights within the fountain sent a rainbow of subtle color to dance in the air.

She stared at him, her gaze level, even challenging.

Lifting a hand, Axel touched the cool velvet of her cheek, trailed his fingers into the warmer silk of her hair. Damn, but he loved how women felt, and he especially loved the feel of this particular woman. "Is that a problem?"

Her lips parted. Her eyes almost closed. Then she snapped them open and cleared her throat. "You are a temptation. But if I succumbed—the key word being *if*—then no, one night is all I could spare, believe me."

The way she said that . . . "You're married?" God, he hoped not. His disappointment at the thought was extreme, far too exaggerated for the brief time he'd known her. He didn't confine himself to many rules, but dallying with married broads headed his personal list of taboos.

"Hardly."

She made it sound as if marriage were a heinous act, a sentiment he shared. He used both hands to cup her face. Her softness seemed addictive, sending his mind into a tailspin of erotic images, making him wonder just how soft she might be in other, more carnal places.

Those thoughts brought about a semi-erection, urging him to clear the way, and quickly. "Engaged then?" *Let her say no.*

She licked her lips. "No."

Thank God. He eased her closer, and it struck him how well she fit his body, her height aligning her mouth just below his, her belly to his groin, her slender thighs bumping his thicker, more muscular legs.

They had traveled enough distance from the house that no one could possibly see them. He stared at her mouth, and could almost taste her.

Her hand flattened on his chest just over his heart. "Not so fast, Romeo. What about you?"

"What about me?"

"Involved?"

"No." And with more vehemence, "Hell no. Not married, not engaged, and definitely not looking to be either."

Seconds ticked by while she stared at him, and Axel prayed she'd come to an agreeable conclusion.

Finally, on a long sigh, she said, "I think I have to kiss you. I'll never forgive myself if I don't."

Something tightened inside him—anticipation. Something loosened at the same time—relief.

He tilted up her chin. "We can't have you berating yourself later, now can we?" His mouth curled in a smile of welcome. She wanted to kiss him? Then by all means, he'd make it easy on her. "Make it any kind of kiss you want. Just make it soon, before I forget my manners and take charge."

She snorted. "I doubt you have any manners, but with an invitation like that . . ." Still holding the box of matches, she braced her hands on his shoulders and leaned in. Her nose touched his, playfully nuzzled him while her warm breath teased his mouth and her breasts just barely skimmed his chest.

And then her lips were on him, scalding hot, damp, so sweet that he actually groaned out loud.

She eased back with a smile. "What was that?"

Axel caught her waist—a damn narrow waist—and brought her back in close again. His breath was labored, his boner now full-fledged and throbbing. "Lust, darlin'. Pure, unadulterated lust." His voice dropped to a husky growl, and he ordered, "Now kiss me again."

Two

Instead of obeying, her fingers covered his mouth. "I don't know," she fretted. "This feels very dangerous."

"So live dangerously." Axel nipped the tip of her finger, sucked it into the warmth of his mouth, and her lips parted on a whispered, *"Oh."*

Satisfaction roared through him. He licked the center of her palm and rumbled, "Better yet, I'll kiss you." He didn't give her time to think about it or to deny him. He took her mouth with the verve of a sexually starved man, when in fact he never stayed celibate for more than a week. But somehow, this felt different. Hotter, more exciting.

He had to have her. No other option would do.

Her lips parted to the prod of his tongue and he sank in, tasting her deeply, slanting his head and bending her back so she'd feel his power, his greed. This time she groaned. The box of matches hit the ground with a quiet rustle and her nails sank into his shoulders, giving him a quick thrill that burned down to the core of his masculine being.

Usually, he calculated his every move, timing himself for the best reaction, aware of the woman's every response and countering it in a way to ensure success. This time, he acted solely on instinct and his own escalating need. Before he had time to consider it, his hand was over her breast, carefully because she felt so small and delicate, so completely female. She might have gasped, but with his tongue in her mouth, their breath soughing together, it was hard to tell.

With his free arm around her back, he arched her into his body, holding her snug, pressing his dick into the soft seam of her thighs. Oh yeah, that felt good, too good.

She pulled her mouth free, dropping her head back on a shuddering moan.

Axel looked at her, the moonlight playing over her face, her lashes sending long feathery shadows over her cheeks. She looked young and aroused and ripe.

He stared down at the sight of his dark hand covering her chest over the white shirt. Her heartbeat galloped and heat poured off, filling his nose with feminine spice.

He bent his head to her throat, deliberately sucking her skin in against his teeth to mark her while plucking her buttons open, one by one, all the way to the waistband of her black slacks.

Both her hands sank into his hair. "This is insane," she all but wailed—but she didn't shove him away.

With her shirt gaping open, Axel slipped his hand inside, under her bra, and cupped silky bare flesh.

Their gazes met and held.

Her stiff little nipple prodded his palm.

Keeping her eyes locked with his, Axel pushed the material aside, easing her shirt over her shoulder and down her arm, tugging the lacy bra low. He captured her nipple between fingers and thumb, and tugged.

A near silent moan shuddered past her parted lips and her lashes fluttered.

Neither of them said a word. The fountain gurgled, music floated on the air from the live band at the party, leaves rustled and crickets chirped. All Axel could hear was the rushing of blood in his ears and his own resounding heartbeat.

His attention dipped to her breast. Beautiful. Small, but

round and firm, and her nipple looked darkly flushed in the dim light. Her pale flesh made a striking contrast to her inky black hair. He pictured her white thighs open, the black curls between, and wanted her now, right here in the gardens.

His arm around her waist pressed her upward an inch, and he bent to suck her nipple into his mouth.

"Oh God." She half laughed, half groaned, then whispered in amazement, "What *am* I doing?"

"We're having fun." He insinuated his leg between hers, immobilizing her. "And we've only just started."

"But—"

He sucked her nipple again, effectively cutting off her breath and ending whatever protestations she might have made. And while she was quiet . . . He smoothed his hand down her ribs, over the slight, delectable roundness of her belly, and pressed it between her legs.

She jumped in surprise. "Oh wow."

Axel could feel the heat of her through her slacks. "Why couldn't you be wearing a skirt?" he complained. He lifted his head and smiled at her while gently stroking, petting. His voice dark and low, he teased, "I'd much rather be touching you instead of stiff cotton."

She hung in his grasp, panting, flushed and ready, and then she whispered, "They unzip."

His knees nearly gave out. If ever permission had been granted, that was it. Scooping her up, Axel took three steps to a marble bench, stopping in front of it and standing her back on her feet. When she swayed, he caught her, steadying her then seating himself in front of her.

"Let's take care of the rest of these buttons first." In rapid order he pulled her shirt free of her pants, opened the last button, and dropped the shirt to the ground. One side of her bra was down, showing her breast. He expertly opened the front clasp and the cups parted.

A small sound escaped her, and again she swayed.

"Beautiful." He could have looked at her for hours, but

now wasn't the time, not with a party going on behind them and his dick so hard he hurt with needing her.

When she started to cover herself, Axel caught her hands and put them on his shoulders. "Hold on to me."

Again, her short nails bit into his flesh, proving that she felt some of the same urgency that gripped him. To ease her into things, Axel forced himself to be content with her breasts for a time, sucking, licking, going from one nipple to the other.

When she trembled all over, he opened the top button of her slacks.

She kept squirming, making all those soft female sounds guaranteed to drive a man into a frenzy. He dragged the zipper down, and finally her slacks opened over a pale belly. Without hesitation, Axel tugged the pants down her hips, all the way to her knees.

She gasped, stumbling back out of reach.

Axel stared up at her. "Come back here."

Hands folded around her middle, she made an enticing, adorable picture. Her knees peeked at him above the lowered waistband of her slacks. Her open bra framed her modest breasts and tightly puckered nipples. Moonlight glowed on her startled face, showing her uncertainty and the arousal she couldn't hide.

"You don't have to be afraid," Axel soothed. "I know this is fast. Mach speed fast. And believe me, I'm not in the habit of fucking in the garden."

Her mouth firmed at his crude language.

"Still, you can call a halt at any time."

She watched him, keeping a scant distance that wouldn't do her any good at all if he were the type to force a woman, which he wasn't.

"You'd stop right now?"

It'd kill him, but . . . "If you said stop, of course I would." He waited, but she kept quiet, relieving him and firing him at the same time. "You should know, from the moment I saw you, I wanted you. Deny it if you have to, but I think you felt the same."

Again he waited, giving her time to adjust, and little by little her shoulders relaxed.

She bit her lip, then said, "This is so strange."

"But exciting?"

"Yes."

Axel couldn't keep his gaze on her face, not with her body almost bare. He alternated between perusing her breasts, her belly, her thighs, and those incredible blue eyes filled with turmoil. "If you come over here," he promised, "I'll kiss you again. Everywhere."

She briefly closed her eyes, fighting some internal battle, before searching his face in the darkness. "Everywhere?"

His chest labored. "Yeah." Saying it made him feel it, the texture of her flesh on his tongue, the richer scent of her in private places. His nostrils flared, his muscles clenched. "Your mouth," he told her. "Your nipples. Your belly." He reached out one long arm and hooked his fingers in the top of her slacks between her knees. "If you let me get your panties down, I'll kiss you there, too, until you can't stand it anymore."

Breathing hard, she allowed herself to be tugged forward.

"You'd like that," Axel told her in a coaxing whisper. He wrapped his arms around her ass and nuzzled her soft belly, inching his lips lower, to the front of her lace undies. "Right here." His tongue pressed, and he could barely taste her through the lace.

Her knees threatened to give out, which was answer enough for Axel. Almost.

She seemed so timid that his oft nonexistent conscience prickled. He pulled her into his lap and kissed her again, long and deep until she went limp, then began clutching at him. Finally, when her reserves had been stripped away, he said, "Sorry to press you, but I need to know you're okay with this. I need to know you won't have regrets."

Her soft sigh thrilled him, as did the quiet, "No regrets," that she murmured against his mouth.

Heart pounding, Axel looked at her body curled on his lap. Her breasts were entirely bare. Her belly trembled with each shallow, fast breath. And when he slipped his hand into her panties, her thighs opened without his instruction.

Soft, springy curls tangled around his fingers. He simply cupped her, not moving, giving her time to get used to that. She turned her face into his chest and tenderness rolled over him, taking him by surprise.

It suddenly dawned on him that she could be risking her job with the catering company, that she could end up humiliated if they got caught.

He glanced up at the house, and presumed they weren't missed. No one hovered on the deck, searching through the darkness for them. Through the glass doors and windows, he watched people milling around and he could hear the drone of conversation mingled with music. She'd only lit a few torches before he'd distracted her, leaving the grounds dark enough to conceal them.

He kissed the top of her head, down to her ear. "Give me your mouth."

She lifted her face and he covered her lips in a long, soft, deep, eating kiss. She clung to him, kissing him back, taking his tongue and sucking on it. And when her hips lifted, silently urging him on, he parted her gently and pressed one finger in, encountering wet heat that sent his heart into a race.

Growling, he deepened the kiss even more. Insane, wanting a woman so much when he didn't even know her name. But now wasn't the time to ask. No way in hell would he interrupt the moment.

She was so damn small and tight, squeezing his finger while little purring sounds escaped her and she squirmed on his lap.

Axel pulled out, then inserted another finger, amazed that he was actually stretching her and that she groaned in excitement even as she stilled in discomfort.

"Easy," he whispered, a little awed, a little overwhelmed. "Am I hurting you?"

"Don't talk," she said. "Please."

He should have been offended, but at the moment he just didn't give a damn. He kissed her ear, dipping his tongue inside, then licking her throat, and finally down to her breasts, suckling while gently fingering her, thrusting, teasing, taking her higher and higher.

He gauged her reaction, registering each shudder, each heated sound, the way she tautened, more and more and more . . .

Raising his face to watch her, he put his thumb to her clitoris. Her eyes squeezed shut and her teeth locked. He circled, rubbed, again and again.

"Oh God." Her thighs stiffened, her back arched, her face contorted, unself-conscious and real, and then she cried out, one hand knotted in the front of his shirt, the other fisted against his back.

Quickly, Axel covered her mouth with his own to muffle the sound of her unrestrained pleasure. Hips moving against his hand, body drowning in heat, she rode out the climax until finally she went utterly lax against him. If he hadn't kept a tight hold on her, she'd have poured right off his lap to the leaf-covered ground.

Axel cradled her close, hugging her, kissing her throat. He always enjoyed a woman's pleasure, but somehow this seemed different. She was so honest in her climax, so open, that he felt . . . moved.

"Very nice," he said, shaking off the odd sensation, anxious to get inside her.

"Yeah. Nice." Then she giggled.

Smiling, Axel lifted his head. "It's funny?"

"Astounding." She drew a deep breath and let it out, dropping her head back with a groan. "Man, I had no idea. You make it seem so easy."

Somewhat lost, Axel said, "It?"

She sat up a little and smiled, touched his face. "The whole sex thing. Especially the satisfaction part."

More confused by the second, he tilted his head. "I'm not following you."

She grinned, gave him a smooching kiss, and said, "That was my first. Orgasm, I mean."

Oh. Well . . . Pride swelled his chest. "You must have been out with some bozos, then."

Shaking her head, she said, "No, actually, I meant . . . well, I shouldn't admit this. It's sort of embarrassing."

No way in hell would he let her get away with *not* telling him now. "It's dark. It's just us." He smoothed back her hair, cradled her cheek. "No secrets."

She hesitated, then finally said, "I've never been with a guy."

Oh shit.

His stomach bottomed out and his heartbeat went into double time. Like every guy everywhere, some really awesome woman-on-woman sex scenes crowded his already turned-on brain. "You mean you're a . . . ?"

"No!" She laughed, swatted at him. "I'm not gay. I meant that I'm a virgin."

His blood ran cold. No, hell no. He pulled back, appalled. "Tell me you're making that up."

"Of course I'm not." Then, with a chilling frown and a stiffened spine: "Is that a problem?"

"Uh . . ." Hell yes, it was a problem. He avoided virgins almost as much as he avoided associates. Rather than answer, he asked another question. "How old are you?"

"Twenty-one."

Dear God, he was robbing the cradle. He had sweatshirts

older than her. Hell, he might even have underwear older than her.

As if she'd turned red-hot, he jerked his hands back and held them up. "I didn't realize. That is, you look older."

"What difference does it make?" She sat straight, perched on his lap, her breasts still bare, her pants still around her knees.

Oh God, oh God. "Could you, maybe . . ." Talk about awkward. "Get up?" He groaned. "And get dressed."

Clearly affronted, her chin tucked in. "You're kidding, right?"

"I wish." He couldn't believe that he, Axel Dean, sexual addict, known hedonist, had given such an order. Especially with his boner still prodding her sweet behind. His brother would laugh his ass off. Cary, his best friend, would faint from shock. But he absolutely could not do this.

The little darling on his lap didn't budge. "If this is because I'm a virgin—"

"And a baby."

"I am *not* a baby."

Proof positive right there. "You're defensive as only the young can be." He bodily lifted her from his lap and hastened to stand. His legs shook. Damn, he was horny. She'd given him a fantasy, then ripped it away with a cold dash of reality.

Women could be so cruel.

"Look," he said, starting to worry. "Let's forget this, okay? No need to tell anyone—"

"And you called me a baby?" She yanked her pants up so hard, she almost lifted herself off her feet. "You can relax, you . . . you . . . *tease*."

"Tease!"

She zipped and buttoned with undivided fury. "I have no intention of telling anyone that I was stupid enough, gullible enough, ridiculous enough to let you touch me."

Now he started to feel offended. "Gullible?"

"Exactly. I thought you had other intentions. You misled me."

Axel leaned close. "You ungrateful brat. I made you come."

"Ha! You pulled up short, that's what you did."

Oh, now she insulted his ability. Eyes narrowed, Axel accused, "You liked it."

Nose to nose with him, she said, "Prove it." Then she sneered, "Oh wait, you're *afraid* to. Virgins terrify you."

Heat and embarrassment reddened his face. Voice wooden, he snarled, "They don't terrify me. They just complicate things."

"If I hadn't told you, you wouldn't even have known."

"Bullshit. I knew." Sorta. He had noticed how tight she was, and that awe in her face when the orgasm took her spoke volumes, but . . .

"You had no idea until I stupidly spilled my guts. And here I'd figured you for an experienced man. I thought I could have a little fun, learn a few things, then never have to see you again."

Of all the outlandish plans. "You were going to *use* me?"

"Mutual use." She sniffed as she stabbed her shirt back into the waistband of her pants. "But you had to go and ruin everything."

"Not everything," Axel told her in a haze of anger. "You still don't ever have to see me again."

"Thank God for small favors." She turned her back and bent over.

Staring at that sexy, upturned rump, Axel sucked in his breath, caught between taking her after all, and giving her a swift swat for her rudeness.

She felt around on the ground until she located the matches, then straightened. "With any luck," she yelled, starting along the path again, "you'll be long gone before I return from lighting the torches."

"You can bet I will be," Axel hollered right back. Then he

realized he had yelled and drew himself up. Shit, he shouldn't be making so much noise. He glanced up at the house, but luckily he didn't see faces pressed to the glass, trying to determine the cause of the commotion.

He turned, stomping back toward the house, praying his erection would be gone before he reached it. But it was so dark out. And that stubborn little female was so small . . .

Guided by a conscience he hadn't known existed, he hung back, lingering in the shadows, watching her. He told himself he'd make sure she got back to the house safe. Yeah, it was gentlemanly concern that kept him watching her. That's all.

He sure as hell wasn't interested in a virginal post-teen.

He kept track of her as she lit each torch before stomping on to another. At the pond, she paused. Her head dropped forward and for one single instant, she covered her face, filling Axel with guilt.

Please don't let her cry, he prayed. He detested crying women.

In the next instant, she shook her fist at the sky, growled like a wild animal, and turned to plod up the path to the house.

Axel grinned despite himself. She really was in a temper, all because she wanted him. Cute.

No, scratch that.

She wasn't cute.

She was a catastrophe waiting to happen. A virgin on the loose, with experimenting on her mind. Luckily, he'd escaped her clutches in time.

Yeah, real lucky.

Shit.

He didn't bother going back to the house. Elwood wouldn't remember if he'd said good-bye or not. Axel dug his keys from his pocket and went around the house to the drive. He climbed into his BMW and slammed the door.

All the way home, he groused to himself. Even with the windows down and the cool wind in his face, he burned. He kept remembering the feel of her, how she tasted, the look on her face as she came.

And damn it, regardless of what common sense told him, he still wanted her.

Now maybe more than ever.

Three

Libby punched her pillow hard, shoved it this way and that, but it didn't help her get comfortable. And she knew why.

For three weeks now, she'd tried to forget the big lug and his compelling dark eyes. Her first foray into sexual matters had been less than awe-inspiring—if she ignored the way he'd made her feel. But she couldn't. She remembered it oh too well. Every single shiver and tremor and spark and gasp. It plagued her mind and left her achy and fidgety and . . . needy. She didn't like it. She didn't like him.

So *why* couldn't she get him out of her head?

Flopping to her back and throwing an arm over her face, Libby tried to block out the memory of how exciting he'd been, how sexy—up until the moment he'd turned into such a jerk.

He'd called her a baby. Now there was a laugh. Maturity was her middle name. Losing her mother so young had forced her to grow up quick, to plan her life long before most kids even thought about tomorrow, much less years down the road. She was mature all right—but given the tantrum she'd had on him, he'd never believe that now.

Of course, she'd never see him again, so what did his beliefs matter?

It mattered, blast him, because he'd gotten her all primed, showed her what she'd been missing, then turned as prim as a maiden aunt. All his suave, macho confidence had melted beneath sputtering incredulity.

All because she was a *little* younger than him.

How old was he anyway? Thirty-three or four? Certainly not old. Twelve years was no biggie. Not to her. Not to most men.

She'd considered asking Uncle Elwood about him, but luckily she'd snuffed out that idea before it had a chance to take root. Her uncle would have a complete conniption if he ever found out she'd been playing hanky-panky in his gardens. He wanted her to study, graduate nursing school, and remove herself from his responsibilities.

And she would, as fast as humanly possible.

This meant she needed to relegate good ole Brown Eyes to the status of an opportunity missed, and stop thinking of him. That should have been easy to do. Never before had she had a problem dismissing guys. First there'd been the grief for her mother. Then the uncertainty of living with Elwood. And her studies. Her determination.

Guys just hadn't factored into her priorities.

Before meeting *him*.

But now he had her so blasted curious, she thought she might implode. In one short, unsuccessful interlude, he'd managed to turn her into a sex maniac. She wanted to find out all there was to the whole intimacy game. Maybe the time had come for her to notice the masculine sex.

Other guys wouldn't mind her age or inexperience. She knew plenty of men, from college, from working, even from the hospital. When she smiled at them, they always smiled back. They seemed delighted by her attention. And a few of them even had dark brown eyes.

Not eyes like his, but . . .

Tough tootsies. Her choices were limited, so she'd have to make do. But first things first. She wasn't a dumb girl to mess up her life because of a little sexual exploration. She was a woman of the new millennium. A modern woman. If she intended to be sexually active—and she sort of did—then there were certain precautions to take.

She'd set an appointment first thing tomorrow. Not with a doctor at the hospital. Heaven forbid her uncle should get wind of her private plans! No, she'd hunt in the phone book, pick someone out of the way, and take care of business.

Then she'd find a guy who suited. There had to be one out there for her. And maybe looking would prove fun.

Mind made up, Libby punched her pillow one last time and settled in to sleep. But sometime during the night, dark brown eyes and a sensual smile invaded her dreams, and she knew in her heart that any man other than him would simply be a substitute.

Since she didn't even know Brown Eyes's name, a substitute was all she could have.

It'd been damn near a month. A *month* of celibacy and Axel couldn't take it. Since that fantasy-inspired interlude in the garden, he'd been turning women down. It was enough to curdle his blood. He was worse than a married man. At least they had wives at home. All he had was one super sexy young lady who had turned him inside out for reasons he couldn't begin to understand.

Letting her occupy his mind in his off hours was bad enough, but no way in hell would he let her affect his work. When in the office, he had only the well-being of each patient on his mind.

He snatched up a file on his desk, determined to read the medical history on the young lady he'd see next. A moment later, his thoughts back in order, he nodded. His newest patient appeared healthy as a horse. No history of serious medical problems. She only needed a routine exam to get a prescription for birth control.

Wearing his doctor face, Axel went down the hall to exam

room three. Along the way, Nora—who was both a nurse in his employ and his best friend's wife—fell into step beside him.

Nora said, "This one is a little skittish. I take it she's never seen a gynecologist before."

Axel nodded. "Thanks. We'll try to make her at ease." As he opened the door and drifted in, Nora on his heels, he was already saying, "Good afternoon, Ms. Preston. How are you to—"

Her screech of horror made his hair stand on end.

Axel back-stepped and bumped into Nora, who bumped into the hallway wall.

"What in the world?" Nora sputtered.

But Axel couldn't say a damn thing. There *she* was, on his exam table, buck naked except for a paper sheet. "Good Lord," he rasped, his aplomb thoroughly shot to hell.

"Get out!" she yelled, and then in utter horror, *"Shut the door."*

His brows came down in a snap. To Nora, Axel said, "I know her. Give us a moment, please." He did shut the door—but with him on the inside.

"Kindly lower your voice."

Wide-eyed and white-faced, a pulse wild in her throat, she stared at him. Her small hands clutched that paper sheet so tight, he could see every single curve beneath. Not good.

Turning his back, Axel drew in a calming breath. "My entire waiting room is probably agog with curiosity after that scream."

She said, "Ohmigod. Ohmigod, I'm sorry. Just . . . please. Get out."

Axel peeked at her over his shoulder. It wasn't easy. In fact, it was damn hard. But he kept his gaze on her face. "There's no reason to be so embarrassed."

Her mouth fell open. "No reason . . . You idiot, I'm *naked.*"

Don't go there. Don't go there. He resolutely cleared his mind of all sexual images. He was a doctor, a damn good doctor, a concerned, caring medical professional—who had never been in quite such a predicament.

He hadn't even had a chance to tell her to scoot down.

He swallowed a groan. "I'll step out," he assured her in a rush before she fainted, which she looked ready to do. "You can get dressed, and then we'll talk."

Her mouth dropped open again and just as quickly snapped shut. "We have absolutely *nothing* to say to each other. Nothing. Now *leave*."

The hell they didn't. She'd come to him to get on the pill, after claiming to be a virgin. Apparently she meant to remedy that awesome circumstance.

He faced her fully, crossed his arms over his requisite white coat, and glanced at her small bare feet. So dumb, but even that little glimpse at pink toes, for crying out loud, and his stomach muscles tightened.

"You came here for birth control. If you don't want me as your doctor—"

"Ha!" As if hunting for something to throw at him, she looked around his office. Holding the sheet tight with one hand, she stretched over to grab a metal tray.

Axel held up a hand. "I can recommend someone."

She froze in midreach. "Are you out of your mind?"

"Uh, no."

She clutched that stupid sheet tighter, and Axel prayed the paper wouldn't tear. He watched, just in case, but no, it didn't.

Her chin lifted. "That's such a generous offer," she sneered with a load of sarcasm, "but no thank you. I don't want your help. I don't need your help." And then she went one further, saying, "And I wouldn't trust one of your friends."

"Oh, that's low." He leaned back on the door. "I am a very good doctor, I'll have you know, and I would never recommend someone who wasn't highly qualified."

"That is just *sooo* kind." More and more sarcasm. "But if you'd simply remove yourself, I'll leave and handle my business entirely on my own."

Axel didn't budge. "You want birth control."

"Oh God." She rocked back and forth a little. "*Go. Away.*"

He wanted to stay and hash it out with her. He wanted to grab her and kiss her silly. He wanted . . . but no, he had no choice. He had to do as she asked. It was the only decent, professional thing to do. He grabbed the doorknob. "Get dressed and then come to my office."

"Yeah, sure, whatever."

Face stiff, Axel left the room, and a second later he heard the frantic rustle of paper as she all but leaped off the table. He could picture her dressing with the same frenzy she'd employed when dragging up her pants and closing her shirt after he'd given her a screaming orgasm in the chilly gardens of his host's party.

God. Not a good memory at the moment.

He detoured into his private rest room and closed the door. After splashing his face with cold water and giving her plenty of time to dress, he sauntered out and headed for his office. On the outside, he looked calm and in control. He hoped. Because on the inside, every single fiber of his masculinity stood on high alert.

His office door was open, the room empty.

Damn it. Axel strode to the window and jerked up the blinds just in time to see her jump into a beat-up old Ford Escort and gun the motor. She ground the gears, squealed the tires, and drove away as if wild dogs nipped at her heels.

He dropped the blinds with a clatter, so frustrated he wanted to—

"Would you like to tell me what's going on?"

Taken unaware, Axel spun around to see Nora standing in his doorway. He tried to wipe all expression from his face.

She smiled, closed the door, and leaned on it. "Come on, Axel. What's going on?"

"Nothing."

"Mmm hmmm." Her disbelief was palpable. "I'll just call Cary and see if he knows anything about—"

"No, don't tell him!" Frustration mounting, Axel ran a hand through his hair, then dropped into his leather chair. He had about two minutes before his next patient would expect him. His attempt at a lighthearted laugh fell flat. "It's really stupid."

"I expected no less of you."

He made a face. Nora had been married to his best friend for three years now. True, she'd seen both sides of him, the respected, serious doctor and the take-it-easy, live-life-to-the-fullest playboy. Never before had the two collided with quite so much fanfare.

Naturally, Nora would enjoy sharing his plight with others. She knew that he'd harassed Cary plenty when Cary fell in love with her, just as he'd done to his brother, Booker, when Booker had gone head over ass in love with Frances. Not that Axel intended to fall in love. Hell no.

He'd only just learned Libby's name!

But this little debacle could count as woman trouble, if either Cary or Booker wanted to stretch the facts. If they learned that a woman—a patient, no less—had screamed at the sight of him, they'd give him crap till the day he died.

"Ahem." Nora tapped her rubber-soled shoe. "I can have Cary on the phone in less than a minute."

Axel gave up with a groan. "She's . . . someone I met at a party."

"And?"

"We got mildly involved."

"Mildly involved? What does that mean, exactly?"

Axel leveled her with a look. "You really don't want details, now do you?"

"Oh." Nora drew back with a frown. "And she wanted you to be her gynecologist? How odd."

He could understand her astonishment. "It's not like that. She didn't know it was me."

Shaking her head, Nora said, "She didn't know what was you?"

Axel shoved to his feet to pace. "We never got to the name exchange, all right? We hit it off—sexually, that is. We just sort of went with it. Then things went wrong—and no, you don't want details about that either. We parted company, end of story."

And since then, he'd thought of her at least every other minute.

"But you never learned her name?"

He tapped the file on his desk. "I know it now. Libby Preston."

Nora slowly shook her head. "Lord, Axel, this is incredible, even for you."

"Yeah, I know." He rubbed his face. "When she screamed, I damn near had a heart attack."

Fighting a grin, Nora said, "I had a heck of a time explaining things to the women in the waiting room."

He could only imagine. "What'd you tell them?"

"That a sonogram had shown triplets."

Axel laughed. "Good thinking. That's enough to make any woman shout." He immediately sobered. "I wanted to talk to her."

"So talk to her."

"I can't." Remembering the way she'd laid rubber in the parking lot, he scowled. "She ran out on me."

"So now you have her name. You even have her phone number and address."

Removing temptation, Axel shoved the file toward Nora. "That'd be unethical in the extreme. Given her reaction here, I'd say she obviously doesn't want to see me."

"No!" Feigning shock, Nora gaped at him. "It can't be. A woman who'd reject you? I'll be disillusioned for life."

"Ha ha." But to set the record straight, Axel explained, "I sort of embarrassed her. By . . . sort of rejecting her first."

"Uh-huh. And?"

"She's only twenty-one."

"So?"

"I'm thirty-five, Nora. A sophisticated doctor. A seasoned womanizer."

Nora rudely laughed.

"I am, damn it." Hands shoved in his pockets, he muttered, "She's barely out of high school."

"I took her history, Axel. She's twenty-one, totally legal by anyone's standards. If you like her—"

"*Like* has nothing to do with it." Lust drove him, nothing more. Pure, unadulterated, unfulfilled lust. "In fact, I'm not sure I do. Like her, that is."

"Of course you don't."

Axel narrowed his eyes on Nora. Since marrying Cary, she'd gotten awfully cheeky. "The young lady has a temper that could flay a man alive. And she doesn't moderate what she says. And she's a . . ."

"A what?"

He pinched his mouth shut. Libby's sexual history, or rather lack of history, was listed on her file, but he wouldn't discuss it with anyone. "Never mind." And then, "Her name is Libby. A pretty name, huh?"

Nora rolled her eyes. "Mrs. Culligan is waiting on you. And if you've never waited naked in a paper sheet on a cold plastic table, then let me tell you, it's excruciating."

Axel knew that. He made it a point to be especially sensitive to the needs of his patients, and he went out of his way to make the ladies feel as comfortable with him as he could. He never kept them waiting, was always as gentle as humanly possible, and treated every woman with extreme respect.

Which meant his personal woes would have to go on the back burner for now. "Right. Let's go."

Nora shoved Libby's file back across his desk with deliberate provocation. "Take care of business. Finish out the day. Then *call her*. If she tells you to lose her number, then yes, calling again would be a breach of professionalism. But until you call, until you give it a shot, you just don't know." And with that instruction, Nora left the room.

Knowing he couldn't make a rational decision right now, Axel followed. And because he really did care about the women he treated, he succeeded in stifling all thoughts of Libby.

At least until his last patient left.

Then he sat down at his desk, picked up her file—and finally made up his mind on what to do.

At seven o'clock, with the sun still out and birds still singing, Libby curled into the corner of her open hide-a-bed, wearing a nightshirt, a rumpled sheet over her lap, only half watching the kick-ass movie she'd rented from the video store. She didn't want to go to bed yet, but she didn't really want to stay up either. She felt miserable. Cold on the outside, hot on the inside. Achy and mortified and mind-numb with the reality of what had happened.

Her toenails were now painted purple, she'd put intricate braids into her hair, and she'd given herself a facial. None of that had been distraction enough. An uneaten quart of cherry cordial ice cream sat on the end table, a soup spoon spiked into the middle. She'd meant to have a binge, but somehow, that didn't really appeal either.

Moving to Timbuktu appealed. Changing her name and her identity appealed. Raping one very delectable doctor . . . No. She detested him, and the embarrassment he'd caused her. She really, really did. Sort of.

Blast it, she was lonesome. And *soooo* mad.

But it was red-hot, unbearable humiliation that she suffered most of all.

Groaning aloud, she curled in on herself and for the millionth time relived that awful moment when Dr. Dean had stepped into the exam room. Her heart had shot into her throat and her stomach had bottomed out when those brown eyes she remembered so well had locked with hers—then skipped down her sheet-covered body.

Thank God her feet weren't in the stirrups.

She hadn't been sure about that part, if she was supposed to be ready when he came in or if he'd want to talk first. Luckily she'd decided to remain stiff and straight until instructed to do otherwise.

At first, he'd looked very much the doctor, professional but detached—then scorching recognition had flooded his expression. *After* she screamed.

She curled tighter, half laughing at herself, half moaning in tortured agony. She'd actually done that, screamed like a raving lunatic and ordered him out of his own office. Wearing no more than a sheet. Waiting for him to . . .

No! *No, no, no.* She was not going to keep thinking about it.

So she'd screamed. Big deal. Under the circumstances, screaming seemed a reasonable, perfectly understandable reaction to discovering his true identity.

Oh why oh why did he have to do *that* for a living? And why, out of all the docs in town, did she make an appointment at that one particular office? Once again, fate had dealt her a raw deal. She and fate were now on very bad terms.

There were no answers to the questions she'd already asked herself over and over again. She shoved back the sheet and padded barefoot toward the fridge to put the ice cream away before it melted. Halfway to her kitchenette, a knock sounded on her door. Never mind that it was Friday night. Never mind that she was a single woman at a very dateable age. She never got company, and she didn't want any now. She continued on and shoved the ice cream into the freezer.

But ignoring her unwelcome visitor did no good because the knock came again and again until she stomped across the floor and flung the door open.

A potent, dark brown gaze captured her. "Hello."

She actually stumbled back a step before forging forward again. "You!"

He leaned one shoulder on the doorframe and casually—like she wouldn't notice—stuck his big, booted foot in the doorway so she couldn't slam it on his handsome face.

"Yeah, me." He gave her a quick once-over, frowning at her braids before meeting her gaze with a look of accusation. "You left without saying good-bye."

Libby blinked at him in disbelief. He came to her dinky apartment because he felt slighted? What a buffoon.

What a sexy hunk of a buffoon.

She'd seen him at the party wearing a dress shirt and slacks, and at his office wearing the clichéd white coat and casual tie. Now he wore an ancient T-shirt with a football logo on the front and broken in, faded jeans that looked soft, comfortable, and casual.

No matter what he wore, he looked too delicious for words. "Trust me," she told him, ignoring his inviting appearance, "I was hardly in the mood for friendly conversation."

He looked her over again, slower this time, lingering in impolite places and making her wish she wore sweats and a thick housecoat. Suddenly he realized he was doing it and snapped his attention back to her face. "May I come in?"

"No. Anything else?"

His long, drawn out sigh fanned her face. "Could I at least apologize?"

Her eyes narrowed. "For what?"

Clearing his throat, he said, "Well, for making you scream." And in a lower, sincere voice, "I'm sorry you were embarrassed. If it's any consolation, I was plenty shocked, too."

No consolation at all. "You weren't naked and on a table."

"No." His mouth twitched. "But I'm a doctor. A professional. Despite our . . . association, I would have—"

Libby drilled his hard chest with her finger. "Not in this lifetime, bud."

A smile brought out golden lights in his dark eyes. "I understand. Again, I apologize. Now please, let me in. I want to talk to you."

"Are you done apologizing?"

Wary, he said, "No?"

"You don't know?"

He huffed. "All right. I'm sorry for calling you a baby, too. Obviously, despite the odd braids in your hair, you're a mature young lady. But you are young and it threw me. I figured you to be much older."

"Ignore the braids. I was bored. But on the inside, where it counts, I'm an old lady."

He didn't look like he believed her. "I haven't been with anyone your age since I was eighteen."

Exasperation exploded from her. "Oh, for heaven's sake. You're saying you're into older women?"

"Experienced women," he clarified. "Because I accept who and what I am—"

"And that is?"

"Not a conversation for your hallway." He stiffened, put out and fed up. "Now let me in."

Libby examined a fingernail. "You were apologizing?" she prompted.

Seconds ticked by while tension thickened in the air. "All right. I'm also sorry that I . . . well . . ."

"Left me hanging?" she offered, her temper flaring again at the awful memory. "Gave me a bite, but not the whole meal? Led me on? Implied false promises? Made—"

He bent and kissed her, hard and fast. "I get the point," he growled, "and yes, I'm sorry for that, too."

Libby went mute. Even that, a smacking kiss that lasted less than a nanosecond, and she was ready to invite him in.

Still leaning far too close to her mouth, he said, "It was a first for me, and it's plagued me ever since."

Libby licked her lips, and because he was close, she tasted his lips, as well. "Plagued you how?"

He stepped in, crowding her back with his big body and closing the door behind him. He smelled good, like after-shave and fresh air and hot male. His wind-rumpled hair made her fingers itch to touch it. His five o'clock shadow made her skin tingle, imagining how it'd feel.

He stared at her, filling her with the swelling warmth she remembered oh so well.

"In every way known to man." He leaned back on the door, his gaze level, probing, saying more than his words could. "I can't stop thinking about you. I can't stop thinking about what might have happened if I hadn't blundered so badly. And most of all, I can't stop thinking about how nice it likely would have been to make love to you."

"Oh." So maybe they were finally on the same track.

His hands closed over her shoulders, slowly dragging her closer. "And on that note . . . I'd like to help if I can."

Four

Damn, she was sweet, Axel thought, watching the way her thick eyelashes lowered over her blue eyes and her lips parted. Sweet and so damn ready. He'd never tortured himself before. It sucked. But he felt a vested interest in her now. In a way, he'd gotten things started and now he felt compelled to involve himself further. He owed her that much.

The feeling was odd because, other than sexual satisfaction, he'd never really felt he owed a woman before. He stuck with experienced women who knew the score and wanted no more than he offered. He avoided virgins and young hopefuls, and kept a clear conscience because of it.

But not this time.

Libby slowly went on tiptoes, putting her mouth level with his. She clasped her hands around his neck and in a husky, *take me* voice, said, "What do you suggest?"

Oh, he had suggestions, all right.

No. *Get a grip, Axel.*

He caught her elbows and moved her back, putting some necessary space between them. That spontaneous kiss he'd planted on her mulish mouth was unfortunate. Sure, it had shut her up real quick, but it also gave her the wrong idea.

"As I started to say earlier, I know who and what I am."

"So enlighten me."

He intended to. "I'm a man who enjoys his freedom, a man who takes his job seriously, but not much else, including commitment. I would make a lousy significant other and an even worse husband."

"Did I propose and forget about it?"

"No, but women your age—"

Her eyes narrowed, but he didn't let it put him off.

"—they tend to get emotionally involved in physical relationships."

"And naturally, you don't."

"No. Never. If you don't believe me, you could ask my brother, Booker, or my best friend, Cary. They both succumbed to marriage years ago, but I like variety—in women and in everything else."

"Bully for you. So what exactly is it you think to offer me?"

"Advice."

She blinked. "Come again?"

"I'd like to offer you some advice."

Her neck stiffened. Her shoulders went back—which drew his attention to her breasts, barely concealed by a cotton nightshirt with teddy bears decorating it. Christ, *teddy bears?*

"Advice on . . . ?"

Pacing away from her and her girlish—and somehow super sexy—nightwear—Axel finally noticed his surroundings. He stumbled to a halt. A bed. Right *there*, within easy reach. "Uh . . . Why do you have a bed in the middle of the floor?"

"It's where I sleep."

Had she been curled up, warm and cozy, when he knocked? He gulped. He glanced at his watch. "You were already in bed?"

With a shrug in her voice, she said, "Watching a movie." She gave an evil grin. "About a woman who beats up men."

Axel looked around and frowned.

"Yeah, I know, the place is small. The bed folds up to a loveseat, but since I never have company, I don't bother with it very often."

So she always had a bed, right there, in the middle of her floor? He cleared his throat and tried to put that cozy-looking nest of blankets from his mind. Facing Libby, he clasped his hands behind his back and tried to appear impersonal. "You came to me today for birth control. I assume that means you intend to become sexually active."

"Wow. You are *so* perceptive." Arms crossed and head tilted in a challenging way, she said, "So?"

Damn. She didn't even deny it. He struggled for the right words. How in hell did fathers handle this stupid talk? It was harder than he'd ever suspected. "Since, as you claimed, I gave you your first orgasm, I feel responsible."

Red-hot color flooded her face. "Good grief, you're ballsy!"

"I know." He shrugged, not really repentant since it was true. "But you did tell me it was your first—"

"I told you that when I thought things were going to happen between us. Since they're not . . . They're not, right?"

Say no, say no . . . Axel rubbed the back of his neck and spouted his well-rehearsed speech. "Young virgins have a way of assimilating sex with love. Since, like I explained, I'm not in the market for anything serious, I don't want to mislead you."

Disgust washed away her embarrassment. "Yeah, don't mislead the poor dumb virginal child." She turned away, heading for the door as if she thought he'd follow. "Rest assured, my private business is no business of yours. You owe me nothing. But in case you've forgotten, I already told you I wasn't in the market for serious involvement either. I've got my life all planned out and some bozo with overcharged hormones doesn't figure into things, even if he's stupendous in the sack—which you sure as certain haven't proved."

She kept challenging him, and damn it, he kept rising to

the challenge, in more ways than one. He hoped like hell she wouldn't notice his Jones pushing against the stiff fabric of his jeans.

She went on, thankfully keeping her narrowed eyes on his face. "Between college and work and an uncle who wants me out of his life, I don't have time for distractions, at least, not a distraction that takes more than a night or two."

She reached the door and put her hand on the doorknob, looking at him expectantly. Axel stared back. Oh no, he wasn't about to leave. Not yet.

"A night or two?" he questioned.

"That's right." She shrugged. "I'm twenty-one. Since Mom died six years ago, I've spent every available minute working toward independence. You might see me as a naïve babe, but let me tell you, doc, there's nothing naïve about a fifteen-year-old girl left homeless."

Fifteen. Damn. Overwhelming sympathy damn near choked him up. He wanted to hold her. He wanted to hug her and console her six years too late. "I am so sorry—"

"Don't you dare." She raised an imperious hand. "The last thing I want from you is pity. I don't need it. My uncle eventually took me in so I had a roof over my head and food to eat."

Eventually? What the hell did that mean? And she mentioned the basics, but had she been given love? Had she gotten all the things a young girl needed from her parents? Axel didn't know, and looking at her set face didn't tell him a damn thing.

Regaining his attention, she said, "But understand something here, doc."

"Call me Axel."

She did a double take. "That's your name?"

He half grinned. "Afraid so."

She ignored that to continue on her tirade. "Right. So anyway, Axel, I worked my tush off and graduated high school when I was seventeen. Thanks to my GPA, I earned several grants and scholarships, but not enough to pay for a four-year program to get my BSN. Because my uncle wanted me to feel financially responsible for good grades, he insisted that I pay half of my remaining college expenses."

"You're working your way through?"

"In a way. I took a year off before starting college and took any job I could find. Other than what I paid my uncle for room and board—"

"He charged you?" No way could Axel hide his incredulity. What type of abnormal relative was he anyway?

She rolled her shoulder. "Sure he did. I was still living with him then. But other than what I had to give him, I saved every dime until I made enough to get started. Working part-time has slowed me down a bit, so I have one more year of nursing school before I graduate. But don't think for a single second that I'm going to let you or anyone else get in my way."

She sounded equally proud of herself and defiant. And full of spirit. Axel stared at her in wonder, and burgeoning respect. "I had no idea."

"Yeah, well, you never bothered to ask. But somehow that doesn't surprise me. You seem like the thick-headed sort to run wild with assumptions, especially where women are concerned."

She dished out more insults than any female he'd ever known. It wasn't what he was used to. Ready to get some of his own back, he said, "I realize name-calling is a sure sign of adolescence, but do you think we could stick to the point?"

Temper snapped her spine straight and brought her storming away from the door and back to him. She appeared so livid that Axel braced himself, thinking she might slug him. Instead she went nose to nose with him and snarled, "The point is that I might be young, doc, but I prefer that to being old and set in my ways."

"Damn it, call me Axel." He scowled. "And I am not *old*."

"Forty is old."

"Forty! But I'm only—" He caught sight of the satisfaction twinkling in her eyes and knew she'd just gigged him on purpose. "Brat." And to make sure she knew, he added, "I'm thirty-five as of a few months ago."

"Downright ancient." She snickered. "You old people are so easy to provoke."

In soft warning, Axel said, "You're just begging for it, aren't you?"

"No way, buster." She crossed her arms under her breasts again. "Not anymore. A few weeks ago, sure, you had me to the begging point. But in case you've forgotten, you went off in a huff and I didn't hear from you—"

"I had no idea how to reach you."

Blue eyes fried him. "Like you would have?"

No way would he admit to anything with her so antagonistic.

She sniffed. "That's what I thought. Not that it matters because now I've got my sights set on *younger* game."

That bugged him worse than anything else she'd said. "Who?"

"I don't know yet." She went to her bed and flopped down onto the corner, curling her bare legs beneath her. "But it can't be that hard to find an agreeable guy, right?" With a coy look, she added, "Someone young and open to new experiences, like virginity."

Feeling protective again—and, damn it, jealous—Axel circled the bed and seated himself on the edge of the mattress beside her. "Your virginity is something special, Libby. Don't throw it away."

"Yeah, it's so special it left you speechless and running off like a scared rabbit."

"I was *not* scared. Have you been listening to anything I've said?"

"Whatever. Holding onto my virginity has lost its appeal." She patted his chest. "Thanks to you and that little taste in the garden, I'm just dying to find out what I've been missing."

Axel's guts cramped with the urge to show her. He covered her hand on his chest to keep it still. "Don't go out with anyone you don't know well."

"Thanks, gramps. But I'm not stupid. I'm not looking to get strangled."

Tamping down his annoyance at her continued jabs on his age, Axel gripped her wrist and urged her closer toward him. "I'm glad to hear it. But don't think birth control pills will cover all the bases. These days you need a—"

"Condom. Rubber. Raincoat. Yeah, I know. STDs and all that." She wrinkled her nose. "It almost makes sex unappealing, huh?"

To his mind, nothing could make sex with her unappealing.

"I guess that's one reason I didn't rush into bed with anyone." She looked at his mouth, and her voice softened a bit. "I have been busy, and the idea of having to get a clean bill of health from any interested males just seems very unromantic."

He could show her appealing. He could show her romantic. Instead he thought of a few questions he wanted to ask. "You don't live with your uncle anymore?"

Her gaze came back to his. "Like I said, he kept me housed and fed when I was underage. But he never had children of his own because he didn't want them—then he got saddled with me. Believe me, he's made no bones about the inconvenience of raising his sister's kid." She lifted a hand and swept it around her. "Hence my apartment. He said he'd prefer to pay rent than have me underfoot, and he figures I'll learn to take care of myself this way. Like I didn't already know how to do that. Believe me, between Mom's crazy lifestyle and my uncle's disinterest, I've been taking care of myself for a long time."

"So your uncle pays the rent for this place?"

She nodded. "Yeah, but I've kept a tally of everything he's spent, and I intend to pay him back as soon as possible."

Scowling, Axel looked around at the miniscule efficiency apartment. It wasn't very close to the local college and it couldn't be all that safe, considering the neighborhood.

He decided her uncle must be a real prick.

"That's why you were working at the party the other night?"

"I still take any odd job that doesn't interfere with my class schedule so I can make headway in paying him back."

Somehow, Axel's free hand had gotten into her braids and he cradled her skull. And even worse, she leaned toward him, her head slightly tipped back, her mouth *that* close.

An admission was torn from him. "Damn it, but I hate the idea of you experimenting with some yahoo who may or may not show you the right way of things."

Taunting, egging him on, she eased closer still. "I don't have much choice . . . now do I?"

He could give her choices. He could give her mind-numbing pleasure . . .

Her small pink tongue came out to lick at her lips. "So . . . you said you'd thought about it, about me?"

Every day, damn near every minute. Not that he'd confess such a thing to her. "It was a memorable event."

She put her other hand on his chest—right over his now thundering heart. "I have too," she admitted. "The last few days, I haven't been able to eat. I haven't even been able to sleep. I've barely been able to study."

Regrettably, he said the first thing that came to his mind. "You're too thin to be skipping meals."

Her provocative expression gave way to blank surprise, then she rolled her eyes and half laughed. "Too thin, huh? Are you sure you're good at this seduction stuff? Because from what I've seen, you're batting a big fat zero."

Axel locked his jaw, feeling guiltier by the second. He didn't want to put her in a funk and have her skipping meals on his account—not if he could ease her. And he sure as hell didn't want to distract her from her studies, not when they were so important to her. "I'm good," he assured her. "And you should already know from our first encounter, thin or not, I have no complaints with your body."

Her fingers curled, stroking his chest, testing his pecs with sensual curiosity. "Same here." She looked down at his mouth again. "Never in my life did I do anything as crazy as I did at that party. I'm usually the most level-headed, circumspect gal around. But that night . . . everything just felt right."

And that described the problem in a nutshell. He wasn't the type of guy that she should feel *right* with.

Axel half turned away, and her hands knotted in his T-shirt, bringing him back around. "For a fling, doc. For an experiment. Not right as in life-altering or earth-shattering or till death do us part." She tried to shake him, smiling, exasperated. "Just . . . right for that moment. Between us."

Axel closed his eyes. "I am not an honorable man, Libby."

"Is that so?"

He drew a breath, and met her gaze. "Outside of my work, which always comes first, I'm a selfish bastard and I know it. Hell, everyone knows it. But even so, I don't want to hurt you."

Libby bit her lip, fighting a laugh. "But don't you see? I don't really give a flip if you're selfish. Be any kind of obnoxious, egotistical chump that you want, it won't matter to me, because other than sexually, I have no interest in you at all." Her nose touched his. "Now, if you're saying you're selfish in bed, then—"

"No." He gave up. Hell, to be honest, he'd given up the moment he saw her in his office and knew he'd be able to find her again. "You'll enjoy yourself, I guarantee it."

Her breath snagged on a sigh, her eyes turned hopeful. "Does that mean . . . ?"

"Yeah." He looked at her crazy braids, her teddy bear shirt, and her purple toenails, and was gripped by the most violent lust he'd ever experienced. He was already hard. His hands were shaking. His stomach knotted.

But he knew it wasn't *just* lust. Lust was a familiar thing, and this was . . . more. Hotter, gentler, explosive and tender. Consuming.

It left him floundering. Lust he understood. The other stuff . . . Too unfamiliar to examine closely. "I want you, Libby. Right now. Right here." He touched her cheek, and was struck by the incredible warmth of her velvety skin. "You okay with that?"

She came up to her knees and her eyes darkened—with uncertainty or excitement? "Yeah, I am."

Axel eyed the short, narrow bed. It didn't look big enough to accommodate two people, but he'd make do. At the moment, he could take her standing up. Hell, he could take her standing on his head.

He just really, really needed to take her.

They stared at each other, Libby waiting for him to make a move, Axel trying to determine what the best move might be for a virgin.

Getting her naked topped his list, so he asked, "Have you seen any nude men?"

Her eyes widened. "Not yet, but don't let that stop you."

His grin came reluctantly. She was a cheeky little thing, quick with a comeback, a delightful mix of shyness and bravado.

Having no modesty to speak of, Axel reached back, grabbed a fistful of his tee and yanked it off over his head. Watching her watch him, he dropped it to the floor and simply stood there. He liked the way she stared at his chest and abdomen, sort of agog, her eyes rounded and her lips slightly parted. Her gaze dipped lower still, visually tracing the bulge in his jeans.

When he didn't move, she said, "Go on."

Axel laughed as he pulled off his boots, then sat on the side of the mattress to peel off his socks. Leaving his jeans on for the moment, he settled back into the corner where she'd been earlier. The back of the love seat served as a headboard of sorts, but with arms. Axel caught her waist and pulled her onto his lap.

She might be tall, but she didn't weigh much, and she was soft in all the right places.

"The braids are cute," he told her, "but how hard would it be to lose them?"

Both her hands were on him, stroking through his chest hair with single-minded absorption. "Not hard."

"Great." He lifted one skinny braid and the cloth-covered band holding it slid off the end. Her hair was so thick and silky, the braid unraveled with no help from him. In minutes, he had all eight braids undone. Her hair looked slightly wavy now, but after stroking his fingers through it, it smoothed out. "I love your hair," he told her, his voice going a little deep with the reality of having her so close, his for the night.

He just had to keep his cool and make it good for her. From what he remembered—how many years ago was it?— virgins were tricky. They needed more care. More time. More finesse.

He could handle it. Maybe. If he thought about other things, like getting the oil changed in his BMW, or facing the chief of staff over a reprimand, or how Booker and Cary would react if they knew the predicament he currently faced.

"Will you kiss me again?"

"Damn right." Axel took her mouth, slow and deep and wet, his fingers tangled in her hair, her fingers on his shoulders, kneading like a cat. She squirmed on his lap, distracting him with the way her bottom moved against his boner. And thinking of her bottom . . . His hands went there without his mind's permission, and damn, she felt good.

The television played in the background, but not loud enough to cover the sounds of their deepened breathing.

Forgetting his own rules about slow and careful, Axel turned and laid her flat beneath him across the bed. One of her slender legs got trapped between his, the other rested alongside his hip. She made a soft sound of surprise, hugging him tighter to her, arching up, provoking him.

"Shhh," he whispered, raising his head to look at her. Her eyes were heavy, her mouth swollen and deep pink from their kisses. "Be still, Libby. Relax."

"No." She pushed up again, her hands spread wide across his lower back. Her eyes closed in pleasure. "You feel *so* good. All hard thick muscle. I like being squashed."

He didn't want to squash her, damn it. "Libby . . ."

"Do you ever think about this with your female patients?"

Appalled, Axel thrust himself away on stiffened arms. "Good God, no!"

"Really?" With him above her, she explored his chest again, dragging her palms over his nipples, sliding one hand down to his abdomen, making him nuts. "I heard that gynecologists see women the same way a mechanic sees a car engine. Is that true then?"

"I really don't want to talk about my work right now." Talking about it gave him the willies, and made him very uncomfortable. The women he saw as patients . . . No, he never thought of them in sexual terms.

Thank God Libby hadn't been a patient.

Her hands opened on his jeans-covered ass, slid into his back pockets, and squeezed. "The thing is," she whispered, suddenly looking shy, "I didn't feel funny about you seeing me naked until I found out what you do."

Oh. Axel relaxed, realizing the source of her questions. He came down to his elbows and pressed a tender kiss to her mouth. She sighed and her warmth drew him again, so he continued kissing her, lingering a little more each time, licking over her lips, then sinking in for a long, leisurely, tongue-twining smooch that left her breathless and grasping at him.

"What I do at the office," he said while working his way

from her lips to her ear then her throat, "has nothing to do with this. I separate my work from any sort of intimacy."

"But . . ."

"No buts, honey. I can't say I see women as engines. I care too much about their well-being to see them as anything other than living, breathing human beings. But I see them with an eye for health, not beauty. There's nothing sexual in that—and everything sexual in *this*." His hand cupped her breast, gently molding, lifting.

Her lashes sank down, hiding her eyes. She gave a small purr of pleasure and pressed into his palm.

Her breasts were firm and soft, her nipples already painfully tight. He wanted to see her. He wanted to suck on her and hear her moan and see her writhing in excitement.

Axel moved to the side of her, ran his hand down to her waist, and traced a teddy bear with his fingertip. "Let's get rid of this, okay?"

She bit her lip, then nodded. "You swear you won't be thinking anything medical?"

"I promise it'll be the furthest thing from my mind." He put his hand on her thigh and slowly dragged the thin cotton nightshirt up, up, up, until he could see her sheer panties and her dark pubic hair beneath. His control slipped.

Pausing, he bent, kissed her flat belly, a hipbone, then pressed his mouth to those glossy dark curls.

Libby drew in a deep, broken breath.

In no hurry, Axel inhaled the spicy scent of her—and growled in response. He couldn't wait to taste all of her, to hear her scream again with a climax, and most of all, to sink into her tight and hot and his alone.

A dangerous thought—but undeniable all the same. She would be his, at least for now. And damn it, he liked that idea.

He liked it a lot.

Five

Libby did her best to hold still as Axel pushed her nightshirt up the rest of the way, dragging his palm over her breast, across her stiffened nipple, until he cupped her shoulder. No matter where he touched, she felt it in other places. Low in her stomach. Between her legs.

A sweet, swirling ache filled her and she wanted to tell him to get on with it, even as she enjoyed his casual lack of haste.

He urged her upright enough that he could remove the sleepwear completely. After tossing it off the other side of the bed, he allowed her to lie back again.

Excited, anxious, and a little uncertain, Libby watched his face to see his reaction to her nudity. He'd said she was thin, but she knew she wasn't skinny. He'd probably seen hundreds, maybe thousands of naked women. Between his sexual freedom and his vocation, naked women were nothing new to him.

Would she measure up?

Given the hot expression in his narrowed eyes, both intense and scrutinizing, he liked what he saw. His mouth tightened, his nostrils flared . . . Libby took a deep breath. He looked so sexy, she could barely wait.

Without diverting his attention from her body, he reached for the snap on his jeans, saying, "Damn, woman, you are irresistible."

Relieved, she gave herself over to the experience of watching a man, in her bed, shuck off his jeans. And Dr. Axel Dean wasn't just any man. Thick with muscle, oozing cocky confidence and blatant sexuality, he was more man than she'd ever met or ever thought to meet.

He eased his zipper down over a rather impressive erection, and in rapid order the jeans came off, along with a pair of snug black boxers. He retrieved his wallet from the back pocket, dug out a condom that he put close at hand, then turned back to her.

Libby got her first up close and personal look at an erect penis.

Truthfully, the whole package was ultra nice. He was firm everywhere, muscular in all the right places, with just enough dark body hair to enhance all his masculinity.

The silky line of hair below his navel to his erection especially intrigued her. It added nice decoration to a rigid abdomen and led the way to that long, solid penis.

"Staring is rude," he told her, smiling a little, balancing himself on his elbow beside her. Biceps flexed with his pose and his heavy, hairy thigh brushed hers, tickling a little. His large dark hand came to rest on her white belly, his fingers idly stroking, as if enthralled with the texture of her skin.

"Is it?" What would an experienced woman say to that? Should she apologize?

"Mmm. But I can maybe hold off for another ten seconds, before I lose it, so for those ten seconds feel free to look all you want."

"What about touching?" She reached out, but he caught her wrist.

"Could be disastrous. Maybe later. After I've had you. Twice."

Still holding her hand, he pressed it up beside her head

while moving over her. "You are so warm," he said, nuzzling her neck at a very sensitive spot, teasing her ear, leaving small damp places on her flesh before taking her mouth with voracious hunger.

Kissing she'd done, but not kissing like this. He had a way of making it seem so suggestive, so sensual. So intimate and hot and thrilling. She could kiss him for hours and not tire of it.

His hands came back to her breasts and she tried to gasp, only his mouth was over hers, taking the sound and filling her with his own responding rumble of pleasure. He caught her nipples, rubbing softly with his thumb, then plucking not so softly until she didn't think she could take it anymore. But again, her cries got muffled into low groans.

His hard thigh pressed between hers, and she found herself lifting into him, moving with his body, until it almost seemed they had their own rhythm.

"That's it," he murmured hotly. And rather than come back to her mouth, he kissed his way down her throat to her chest. While cuddling one breast, he closed his mouth over the other, suckling her nipple gently, his rough tongue rasping over her, his teeth nipping.

A very high-pitched, girly sound of excitement filled the air, and Libby realized she had made that sound. But she couldn't help it. Sensation spread through her in pulsing, sizzling waves. Eyes closed, she pressed her head back, feeling those now familiar, explosive tremors swelling and swelling . . .

Axel made a rough sound of approval and continued to suck and tongue and tease her breast. He insinuated one hand behind the small of her back, then down to her behind, lifting her up so the pressure against her sex became more acute, his whole body stroking, igniting her—and she came.

"Oh God."

His fingers clenched into her bottom, keeping her poised against him, prolonging the orgasm until the very last quiver had left her.

Panting brokenly, her muscles useless, Libby stared at the ceiling and wondered if she was easy or he was just that good.

Struggling to regain her breath, she waited, expecting him to come up to her, maybe hold her, smile at her again.

Instead, she felt his hot, open mouth on her abdomen, his hand now over her behind inside her panties, pushing them down.

She didn't get time to recoup? "Axel . . ." she groaned.

"Say my name again." His tongue dipped into her belly button, then trailed down to the top of her panties. Feeling his mouth there, lightly sucking her skin, tasting her, sent a new rush of sensations crashing over her.

"Oh, uh . . ." Surely he didn't really expect her to be coherent while he did that?

He skimmed her panties down to her knees and she found herself completely naked in front of him. He loomed over her, his palms gliding from her knees up to her thighs and back down again while he stared at her, his expression nearly violent with need, color high on his cheekbones.

Libby held her breath, uncertain, anxious—and suddenly, his fingers dug into her flesh and he pressed her knees apart.

She should have been embarrassed, but the rough, hungry sound he made obliterated rational thought. His fingers moved over her, petting, delving, opening her, and then his mouth was on her *there*, and all she could do was melt.

He slipped off the side of the bed to his knees, moved between her thighs, and pressed them farther apart still, pushing her knees up and back. Oh wow.

His whiskered jaw rasped her inner thigh as he whispered, "You're wet, Libby, and so damn hot." His thumbs opened her, stroked, going deeper and deeper, and then he tasted her, licked, shifted so he could lift her up, giving himself better access, and through it all she panted and twisted and felt another orgasm surging through her tired body.

It was the most unbearable pleasure imaginable. Her hands

gripped the sheets hard, as if to anchor herself. So many sensations bombarded her senses—the stroke of his tongue, over her and in her, his hot breath, the sexy sounds of desire he made, the scratch of his beard on places no other person had seen, much less touched.

"Come for me again, baby," he ordered, his tone harsh with demand, and she did, her thighs tightening, her muscles rippling, everything inside her clasping and undulating.

This time he didn't wait. Her mind still spun with disbelief when she heard the tear of foil, felt Axel fumbling near her, then he moved over her, lifted her knees, and pressed inside her.

With little aftershocks still sparking, Libby felt the broad head of his penis pushing past her virginal opening. He stretched her, but in a good way, and given that she'd had two mind-blowing orgasms, she knew it'd be easier for her to accommodate him.

His mouth was wet from her, rubbing against her jawline as he murmured encouragement and hot phrases of need and pleasure. "So tight," she heard him say, and then, darker and with more feeling, "Fuck, yeah."

He sank deeper, his hands holding her face, turning her toward him for a ravenous, eating kiss, and then he was buried inside her, filling her up. Libby held herself perfectly still, panting, trying to get accustomed to the wonderful, taut feeling, the incredible closeness, the emotional intensity that she hadn't expected but relished all the same.

Tears stung her eyes, because she realized he was right. This was more than mere sex. He was the only man who had ever caught and held her attention, the only man to ever distract her from her goals. She didn't know him well, but something about him called to her, brought out emotions she hadn't known she possessed.

By small degrees she got her limbs to move, twining her arms tight around his broad back, lifting her legs to keep him close, and closer still. The new position tilted her pelvis and sent him deeper. She responded with a catch in her breath, freeing her mouth and inadvertently tightening around his thick erection.

Axel held her face and watched her, keeping her gaze captive as he eased out, then thrust, slow, deep, taking it easy, heat pouring off him and off her, their bodies melded together. It was almost too much, that visual connection combined with the pleasure of having him buried inside her. Libby kissed him, biting at his mouth, sucking at his tongue, and with a growl, Axel lost it. He pumped into her, picking up the pace, going faster and harder until suddenly he stiffened, his head back, his teeth locked. He growled, a feral, dark sound of primal satisfaction, his big body shuddering over hers, muscles tight and delineated.

It was the most wonderful, intimate thing Libby had ever experienced. He looked almost dangerous, and then, for a single moment, vulnerable. As his groans faded, his body relaxed and his muscles unclenched. Libby stroked his sweaty shoulders, speechless, awed. His head dropped forward, his dark hair over his brow, his eyes closed. He still labored for breath, but kept his chest off her with stiffened arms.

Feeling a little silly after all that intensity, Libby whispered, "Wow."

His broken laugh turned into a groan, and he went to his back beside her. The moment he left her, she missed him. Her skin now felt cool, her body empty.

One arm covered his eyes but the other held her thigh with blatant possession. Seconds ticked by, measured by the slow beat of her heart, then he lifted his arm and looked at her, his eyes dark and full of triumph.

"You're too far away," he rasped. "Come here." And she did, turning into his side, his arm going around her, keeping her near to him.

Libby had no idea what to do, but she had no complaints with cuddling. After several minutes had passed, he heaved a great sigh and tucked in his chin to look down at her. She met his dark gaze with uncertainty.

Would he leave now? Was he finished with her?

He looked ultimately relaxed and lazy. "You hungry?"

"Ummm . . ." She hadn't expected that. "No, but I can fix you something."

"Stay put. I'll help myself." He patted her hip, stood, stretched in front of her. "You got a waste can in the bathroom?"

Speechless at his casual attitude, Libby nodded. She watched Axel remove the condom as he headed to her john. His muscled behind was a thing of beauty, especially in motion.

He left the door open, which amazed her, considering a minute later, she heard him flush, then heard him splashing water.

He came out with his face and hair slightly wet, still gloriously naked, and went into her miniscule kitchen. "What movie did you say you rented?" he asked, while rummaging in her fridge.

Well, she didn't have his indifferent attitude toward nudity. She pulled the rumpled sheet up to cover her body and scooted up in the bed, sitting with her legs bent, her arms on her knees. As if the entire day hadn't happened, as if he weren't totally nude, they chatted about food, about the movie, and even about the size of her apartment.

Ten minutes later, Libby found herself snuggled in the dark next to a naked Axel while he fed himself a cheese sandwich with one hand and absently fondled her with the other. The movie she'd missed earlier again played on the VCR.

She paid no more attention to it this time than she had the first.

She hadn't expected this careless camaraderie, but it was . . . nice. More than nice.

Halfway through the flick, Axel hugged her a little and

said, "It's getting late," as if the time were no more than an afterthought.

She'd been in a haze of comfort, enjoying his closeness, half asleep, more than a little lethargic. "Is that a hint that you need to go?" Pride forced the words from her constricting throat. "Because I already told you, I'm not going to cause a scene."

"No." He squeezed her closer still so he could kiss her nose. "It's a hint that I'd like to stay the night, maybe make love to you a few dozen times more before the sun comes up. What do you think?" He took the last bite of his sandwich, chewed and swallowed. "Does a sleepover fit in with your independent plans, or should I get my tired, still horny butt out of here and head home to my lonesome bed?"

Stay, her heart screamed, but she pretended to think about it. She really was wiped out, and still achy, and her stomach wasn't all that settled.

Sex, she found, took a lot out of a person. "Can I nap for a while before we indulge in more extracurricular activity?"

"If you don't mind me wrapped around you."

She wouldn't mind that at all. "All right." His natural body warmth felt good, but it wasn't enough. She dragged the blankets a little higher and got comfortable beside him. "You can finish the movie. I'll just doze off."

"Do you need to be somewhere early tomorrow?"

"No, my uncle is expecting me in the afternoon." She made a face. "I'm to serve at another meeting, this one for high tea."

"Pompous ass." Axel shifted in the bed and let her use his chest for a pillow. Aiming the remote, he turned the television volume low. "I'm free for the weekend, so we'll work around your plans."

Did that mean he intended to spend the whole weekend with her? Having sex and doing . . . this? Cuddling and chatting and just being together?

"You sleep," he told her. "I'm going to finish the movie, but I'll wake you up if anything exciting happens."

"Exciting, like . . . ?"

"Like this." He cupped her breast, put several damp, skin-tingling kisses on her neck, and then pulled back with a smile. He smoothed her hair, pressed one last kiss to her forehead, and gave his attention back to the television.

He was the oddest, boldest—and the most wonderful—man she'd ever met. Libby chuckled and, giving into her fatigue, dozed off.

She slept like the dead, like having a man in bed with her was no big deal. On the one hand, Axel supposed he might have worn her out with her first full-fledged sexually satisfying experience. That wasn't an entirely repugnant thought.

On the other hand, he wanted her awake and as turned on as him.

Since it was well past midnight, he'd let her nap for a few hours. She was curled against him, hot as a Bunsen burner, making him sweat. Time to have more fun.

He slid his arm out from under her so that she lay flat in the bed. Utterly limp, she didn't so much as flicker an eyelash. For a few moments he just looked at her, at her thick dark lashes, her small nose and stubborn chin, and that super sexy, glossy black hair all tumbled.

Normally her skin was very fair, but at the moment, a deep rose chafed her cheeks. Using only his fingertips, Axel smoothed the hair off her forehead and spread it out around her.

She wasn't beautiful, but something about her drew him in and turned him on and made him want to touch her in a hundred different ways—not all of them sexual.

Pushing the sheet down to her knees, then kicking it the rest of the way off her legs, he looked at her nude body. In total relaxation, she appeared very young indeed. Innocent and fresh. Sweet. And undeniably sexy.

Her belly was so pale and soft, her dark, glossy pubic curls a striking and sensual contrast.

Her nipples were now smooth, a deep pink, and very appealing. Unwilling to wait, Axel leaned forward and drew her right nipple into his mouth, sucking gently.

She moaned, her legs shifting a bit, and Axel rested a hand on her flat belly. Another moan, but it didn't sound carnal at all. More like . . . discomfort.

He frowned, lifting his head in alarm. "Libby?" She didn't stir. "Come on, baby, wake up."

She mumbled something in her sleep and turned her head away from him.

A niggling fear skittered through him and Axel put his palm to her forehead.

Scorching heat.

"Shit." Sitting up, he caught her shoulders and gently shook her. "Libby?"

Her eyebrows twitched, her lashes fluttered then opened. Her eyes were bloodshot, unfocused. Her lips looked dry. In a froggy voice, she rasped, "I don't feel good. You should go." And she tried to turn away from him.

Well, hell. "You have a fever, honey. Where's your thermometer?"

She gazed at him in confusion, her eyes vague, her chest laboring painfully. "My what?" She started to shiver and groped blindly for the blankets.

Unbelievable. Axel helped her, pulling the sheet and single blanket back up for her. "I need to take your temperature, sweetheart. You're sick."

Damn it, he should have realized it earlier. She'd felt warm, too warm, each time he'd touched her. Idiot.

He'd thought she was hot for him.

Axel silently cursed himself and pushed out of the bed.

Rather than reply to him, Libby curled onto her side and snuggled tight into the blankets. "Oh God, Axel, I'm freezing."

"I know, baby." A hundred and one problems crowded into his brain. "Do you have anything for fever?"

In strained accusation, her teeth chattering, she groaned, "I never get sick."

"Well, you're sick now." He stalked into her bathroom and looked in the medicine cabinet. It overflowed with female junk, but nothing that would help her. "Where the hell do you keep your medicine?"

When she didn't answer, he went back to her. She looked to be asleep again, but shivers racked her slender body, the blankets up around her ears, her knees curled up to her chest in the fetal position. Sitting beside her, Axel again touched her forehead, then flinched. "Does anything else hurt?"

She frowned, still without opening her eyes. "My chest, a little. I had a stupid cold, but . . ."

Afraid that her cold had developed into pneumonia, Axel pulled her upright and into his arms, cradling her close to his heart. "Listen to me, Libby. I think I should take you to the hospital."

"Oh no." She sounded raw. And very upset at the idea.

Axel cupped her burning cheek. Jesus, she was hot. And she'd said she'd had trouble eating, sleeping. "Listen to me, young lady—"

She pressed against him, trying to lie back down, trying to pull the blankets closer around herself. "Just go away, doc. I'm not your problem, not your patient."

"Don't get stubborn on me now." He held her shoulders, refusing to let her pull away. "You're sick, and from what I can tell, you have nothing here in the way of medicine. You're burning up, but it's too late to call your family physician."

Looking very small and vulnerable, she whispered, "You can't take me to the hospital, Axel."

"Of course I can. They know me there. They'll give you first-rate treatment, I promise."

Eyes closing, she swallowed painfully. "If you do, Uncle Elwood will find out about you."

Elwood.

A rush of blood pounded into Axel's ears. Alarms went off in his head. His throat damn near closed up on him. "Elwood . . . ?"

"Peterson." She peeked up at him, small, frail, the epitome of misery. "He's . . . my uncle."

Oh. Dear. God. Barely squeezing the words out between his clenched teeth, Axel barked, "Your uncle is the *chief of staff?*"

She flinched. "Yes."

Young, a virgin, and now this. Three strikes, and he was out.

Numb, Axel pushed to his feet and stood looking down at her. He couldn't be that unlucky. But to be sure . . . "You're a twenty-one-year-old virgin—whose uncle just happens to be the chief of staff?"

She looked away. "Yes."

"Un-fucking-believable."

Libby jumped at the fury in his tone, took in his appalled expression, and moaned. "Here we go again."

Six

Never in her life had she felt more miserable. She hurt everywhere, in every bone and joint, and it felt like an elephant sat on her chest. It took enormous effort just to move, just to breathe. But she forced herself into a mostly sitting position and even managed a half-baked smile. Shivering, her teeth clattering together and tears stinging her eyes, Libby rasped, "It's been swell, doc, but I can see the party's over."

Instead of being relieved that she'd let him off the hook, fury darkened his face. "Don't push me, Libby."

Why was he mad? And at the moment, did she even care? She was so damn cold, deep down inside herself, that she couldn't stop shaking. "I know how to treat illness. Remember, I'm a nursing student, soon to graduate. Go with a clear conscience. I'll be fine."

Axel closed his eyes, looked to be counting to ten, then opened them again. Composed, he said, "I'm not leaving you, so forget that."

"You already told me what a self-centered ass you are, remember? It's all right to leave."

"I said no."

She couldn't stay upright a second more. Collapsing back on the bed, freezing, she said, "Bastard."

"Hush." He moved with sudden purpose. "I know what I'll do. I call Cary. He'll come over and take care of you."

The very idea of imposing on someone else left her speechless. Why couldn't he just leave her in peace?

Knowing she had to move whether she wanted to or not, she hugged the blankets and started to slide her legs off the side of the bed.

Her feet never touched the floor. In one swoop, Axel pulled her into his arms and held her like a child. That stung. As if her weight were negligible, he strode to the other side of the bed and snagged his jeans.

"Why are you doing this?" He was so wonderfully warm and comfortable that she wanted to crawl inside him. Exhaustion pulled at her, and she laid her head on his hard shoulder.

"You just be quiet." He sat on the side of the bed, holding her, rocking her a little, and used his thumb to press one number on his cell phone.

A second later, some unfortunate soul actually answered.

Axel wasted no time. "Damn Cary, I'm sorry to bug you — what? No, I'm okay. It's Libby. She's . . . If you'll shut up, I'll tell you who she is. She's . . . a woman I'm seeing."

Libby hid her face in his neck. God, this only got worse and worse.

"Damn it, I know you don't know her. But I'm with her now and her uncle is the damn chief of staff . . . Yeah, *Elwood.*" Axel paused, rolled his eyes. "No, I'm not crazy, but for the record I didn't know her uncle was chief of staff. Cary, do *not* laugh, damn you."

Libby realized by the way Axel said Elwood's name that he didn't exactly like him. At least she wasn't alone in that.

"She's sick, maybe pneumonia given her temperature and how fast it came on her. No, she doesn't want to go to the hospital but she's burning up and . . . Yeah, could you? Thanks." He gave her address to his friend, said, "I owe ya," and hung up.

Pressing a kiss to her forehead, he said, "Cary'll be right over. He's a fine doctor, a family practitioner, and he'll know what to do."

"You're a doctor, too," Libby reminded him.

"Wrong kind." He stood again, carrying her as if she weighed no more than a pillow. He entered her tiny bathroom, got a towel off the rack, and using only one hand, doused it in tepid water. "I'm going to wipe you down to try to get your fever under control before Cary gets here."

"No." Libby gripped him with all her puny strength. Logically, she knew it was the fever making her cold, but the idea of anything wet touching her body made her shake that much more.

"Sorry," he said, and went back to the bed where he laid her down, unwrapped her against her protestations, and used the corner of the towel to bathe her face, throat, chest, and arms.

"Oh God." Again, the stupid tears stung her eyes, and she hated herself for it, which made her hate him.

Axel looked as agonized as she felt. "I'm sorry, honey." He kissed her forehead, and continued pressing that cool cloth to her burning body. After a few minutes, it did help, but not enough.

Teeth chattering, Libby said, "I didn't think doctors made house calls anymore."

"Like I said, Cary's a friend."

Axel covered her again, then got dressed and went to put on coffee. Feeling a little more comfortable, Libby half dozed.

A few minutes later, Axel bent near her ear. "I'll be right back."

She stirred enough to ask, "Where are you going?"

"I brought your paperwork with me from my office. Cary might like to see it. Don't move."

No, she wouldn't move. She heard the front door open, and when Axel returned he had someone with him. Libby pulled the covers up over her head. Good grief, she was naked, and couldn't do a thing about it.

"That lump on the bed is her," she heard Axel say. "Libby, Dr. Rupert. Cary, meet Libby Preston."

The bed dipped, and a second later the blanket was pulled from her face. She stared up at a man with rumpled brown hair and tired green eyes and a gentle, kind smile.

"Hello," he said. "I'm Dr. Rupert." Then he stuck a thermometer in her ear, waited all of two seconds and said, "A hundred and two."

Behind him, Axel fretted. "Pneumonia?"

"Can I tell that from her ear, Axel? No, I can't. Why don't you go sit down somewhere and stop pacing behind me?"

Libby felt just put out enough to say, "Old people tend to fret."

Dr. Rupert's mouth twitched, but he didn't say anything.

Axel wasn't quite so restrained. In low warning, he said, "I'll get even with you for that crack, little girl—but not until you're in full fighting form again."

Libby glared at Axel and clutched the sheet when Dr. Rupert tried to lower it. Utilizing great bedside manner, he said, "Miss Preston, Axel tells me you're to be a nurse, so I'm sure you already know this, but I need to listen to your lungs."

She glared at Axel again. "Turn around."

His eyes widened. "For the love of . . . I've already seen you naked, Libby."

She wanted to kill him. "Not. Like. This."

He threw up his hands. "Fine." Giving her his back, he groused, "Damn fickle women."

Dr. Rupert ignored them both. He lowered the sheet just enough to slip his stethoscope inside. He listened, frowned, moved it, listened again, and frowned some more.

When he finished, he pulled the sheet back up to her chin. "Where's her medical history?"

Axel turned back around and handed it to him. The good doctor asked some questions, nodded in that doctorly fashion typical of his vocation, and finally said, "Well, I'm certain you have pneumonia, but we need X-rays, of course. Axel, you can bring her to my office first thing tomorrow for that. Say eight o'clock, before my regular schedule begins. Given how fast this came on her, I'd say it's likely bacterial, so I'm going to go ahead and give her a shot of antibiotic tonight. Are you allergic to anything, Miss Preston?"

"Call me Libby, and no." She didn't want a shot. She wanted to sleep.

"All right, Libby. And you can call me Cary. If you're going to be seeing Axel, I suppose we should all be friends."

"I'm not seeing him."

"No?"

Axel sounded like a bear when he growled, "She'll be seeing me."

Cary hid a smile. "You'll need plenty of bed rest, at least until your temperature returns to normal. Lots of fluids. At least six to eight glasses a day." He turned to Axel. "You'll see to it?"

"Yeah."

Libby's mouth fell open, which caused her to start coughing. Dr. Rupert helped to elevate her until she could catch her breath. Wheezing, she said, "I don't need his help."

Axel folded his arms over his chest. "Yes, you do."

"No—"

"Be gracious, Libby," Cary told her, and then went on before she could argue further. "Acetaminophen or ibuprofen to help control pain and fever. And use a cool mist humidifier or vaporizer to increase air moisture. It'll make it easier for you to breathe. Cool mist, Libby, not steam, understand?"

She bit her lower lip. "I don't have a cool mist humidifier and I don't have any medicine—"

"I'll run out," Axel told her. "The department store is open all night."

It wasn't to be borne. "You said you're a selfish bastard! Why don't you just leave?"

Cary drew back. "You told her?"

"Ha ha," Axel said. And as Libby groaned, drained from her outburst and hacking again, he said, "You got anything you can give her now for the fever? I hate for her to have to wait for me to shop."

Despite his concern for her, Cary seemed to be thoroughly enjoying himself. "Sure." He dug in his magical bag and produced two white pills. Axel hustled to get a glass of water, then lifted her with an arm behind her back and supported her while she drank.

He eased her back down. "Give her the shot, and I'll walk out with you."

Cary was already preparing the injection. He gave her an apologetic look. "In the hip, Libby. Can you turn to your side for me?"

She looked at Axel, who rolled his eyes. "Right, I know. Turn my back so your delicate sensibilities won't be lacerated."

Cary waited while she adjusted the sheet the best she could, trying to show the least amount of skin. "This will sting," he told her, but truthfully she barely felt it above the rest of her miseries.

She thanked him for his help, and he patted her shoulder. "I'll see you tomorrow."

As the men prepared to leave, she curled in on herself and wallowed in self-pity. Why did she have to get sick now? She'd only just met Axel, and odds were after seeing what a fun date she could be, he'd never return. And she had graduation in a few weeks. The timing couldn't have been worse.

She didn't realize Axel was close until he brushed his knuckles across her cheek. "I'll be back within an hour. I took your keys off the kitchen counter, so I'll let myself in. Just try to sleep, okay?"

He'd taken her keys? How presumptuous. Eyes narrowed, she whispered, "Axel?"

His smile was very warm and tender. "Hmm?"

Libby gave up. "Thank you."

He searched her face, nodded, and finally took himself off. Sometime later, Libby became aware of him beside her in the bed. He tilted a glass to her lips and she drank it all, but declined when he offered to help her to the bathroom. She only wanted to sleep.

He lay down with her, once again naked, and spooned against her back. His lips touched her ear. "The vaporizer is on. I'm going to wake you in a few hours to take more medicine. Let me know if you need anything else."

Libby nodded, but one thought filled her mind: for a self-proclaimed selfish pig, he was more giving and caring than anyone she'd ever met.

She was the most pig-headed, obstinate woman he'd ever met. "You are *not* going to work, Libby. Jesus, you still have a fever. You can't take two steps without looking ready to collapse. I figured you to be a smart girl, so why are you talking so dumb?"

She sat huddled on the passenger side of his car on their return ride from Cary's office, where her pneumonia had been confirmed—not that there'd been any doubts.

Her hair was lank, her face ashen, her lips shivering. Wearing baggy sweats and a blanket, she looked like a drowning victim barely hanging onto life.

"My uncle will be furious if I don't show up."

For most of the previous night, Axel had wondered how he would keep his involvement with Libby—and he *was* involved—private from her pain-in-the-ass, all-too-important relative. But at that moment, he decided he didn't give a damn. "Let him be mad. I'll call him. I'll tell him you're ill. If he doesn't like it, tough shit."

With an expression of death, she peered at him. "Don't be an idiot. You can't call Uncle Elwood. He'll want to know what you have to do with anything."

Axel pulled into the parking lot. He needed to get her back in bed. "So I'll tell him."

"Tell him what?"

"That his niece is the sexiest piece of ass I've had in ages."

Libby almost slid to the floor of the car with a hard, cough-inducing gasp. "You *can't*—"

"Just kidding." He put the car in park and circled around to her side to open her door. "But it's true." As he scooped her up, she put her face in his neck. "You are a seriously sexy piece of work." He smiled.

She moaned. "Yeah, sweaty, hacking broads with chronic coughs really turn you on."

"*You* turn me on." And it didn't seem to matter that at the moment, sex was the farthest thing from his mind. He carried her up to her dinky apartment, enjoying the opportunity to show off his strength and play the gallant. He kicked the door shut. "Are you hungry?"

"No."

"How about soup anyway?"

"How about a nap?"

"After the soup."

And so it went. Everything he suggested, she argued about. She was the worst patient he'd ever had. And still, for some unfathomable reason, he enjoyed being with her.

After he force-fed her half a bowl of chicken noodle broth and she looked more asleep than awake, he broke the news. "I'm going to call Elwood now."

Her eyes snapped open. "Don't do this to me, Axel."

"To you? I'm the one who'll probably be kicked out of the hospital."

"You just don't know."

Such a desolate voice. He sat beside her and took her hands. "So tell me." Weariness etched her face, and he wanted to hold her again. But first things first. "Come on, Libby. Spill it. What awful things could Elwood possibly do to you? Will he have you blackballed from the hospital? Make you relocate to Alaska to find work? What?"

She turned her face away and her voice went flat. "He can tell me, again, that I'm just like my mother."

Keeping his tone gentle, Axle prompted, "How's that?"

"I look like her, and I suppose in a lot of ways I have her outlook on life."

"I take it she was a hard-working, independent, stubborn woman, too?" Axel teased.

She actually laughed, relaxing a little. "I don't remember much about her being stubborn, but yeah, she was independent. Elwood was her much older brother and they used to be close. But when he didn't accept or support her choices, she ignored him. See, Elwood is all seriousness and ambition, and my mother just enjoyed life. She didn't need fancy cars or jewelry or a big house. She used to tell me all she needed to be happy was me."

"A smart woman."

Libby looked at him, and a half smile curled her pale lips. "Elwood hated it that Mom got pregnant by a car mechanic who took off the moment he knew I was on the way. Sometimes I think he hated me. But Mom told me it was just that he had to work long hours and didn't have time to visit very often."

Her eyes, her smile, were very soft when speaking of her mother. It was easy to see she'd been well loved, and had given a lot of love in return.

"Doctors are always on call," Axel told her, for the first time wondering what a woman would think of his own hectic schedule. "How do you feel about that?"

She gave it serious thought. "When someone's health, maybe even a life, hangs in the balance, of course doctors have to help when they can. But Elwood doesn't really care about people. He only cares about his reputation and the respect he gets."

Axel didn't want to insult her uncle again, so he let that go. "Not all doctors are like that."

She covered a yawn before saying, "I know that. I wouldn't want to be a nurse if I didn't respect the medical profession."

Leaving her apartment for the X rays had really worn her out. Axel knew he should let her sleep, but first . . . "How did your mother die?"

Sadness clouded her eyes and she withdrew from him. "I wanted to swim, but Elwood wouldn't let us use his pool. So Mom took me to the river. She was out too far, flirting with some guys . . . and a boat went out of control." She shook her head and began to cough. "She drowned."

Axel pulled her upright and held her against his shoulder, rubbing her back, wishing he hadn't brought it up. "I'm sorry." He kissed her ear, her cheek. "Shhh. Here, take a small drink."

When she'd regained her breath, she gave him a level, too serious look. "So you see, you can't let my uncle know that I was with you."

Insult mixed with exasperation. "Libby, no offense intended, but I'm not a mechanic. Elwood blusters a lot, but he respects me. Twenty years ago, when he was still my age, he was in the same position as me. It doesn't matter what my personal reputation might be."

"You mean your reputation as a 'me first' male slut?" She shook her head. "Forget it, Axel. I'm not buying that anymore, not with the way you enjoy playing nursemaid." And she tacked on, almost absently, "Not since my mother's death has anyone pampered me. Selfish, egotistic people don't do that."

Axel paid no attention to her, unsure whether she was complaining or complimenting. "Even sick, you're good company. But what I mean is that my professional reputation is rock solid."

"I never doubted it."

"Good. Then you should realize that Elwood would probably be pleased to know—"

Her raspy laugh interrupted his diatribe, and didn't sound

the least bit nice. "What? That you're having a brief, purely sexual fling with his niece? Yeah, that'd thrill him."

It definitely wasn't just sexual, not on his part, and Axel wasn't sure he wanted it to be so damn brief either. After only one night—which usually was enough to satisfy him— he couldn't even begin to think of walking away from her. He'd meant what he said: she was good company. She didn't complain, she didn't simper or put on airs. She was herself at all times, friendly, funny, independent, serious, sexy, and giving. He liked her. A lot.

He maybe even more than liked her.

But he could hardly start declaring himself yet. "What we do sexually is none of Elwood's business. You're a grown woman, or so you keep insisting."

"Start up on my age again," she warned, "and sick or not, I'll get up and kick your butt."

Axel grinned, knowing she'd try, and knowing he'd enjoy her efforts if she wasn't sick. "No need to tax yourself. Believe me, I know you're a woman." He propped his hands on his hips, attempting to look stern. "But woman or not, you're still too ill to go to work."

She rolled to her side and groaned. "I know. I feel like crap." She held out a hand. "Could you give me my phone?"

He didn't want to. The urge to protect her was almost worse than the urge to hold her. And the urge to make love to her. "All right." He held it out of her reach. "But don't grovel. Don't apologize. Give him the facts and let him deal with them any way he wants."

She snatched the phone away from him and made the call. Axel kept close, deliberately listening in, frowning when she repeated, for the third time, that she was just plain too sick to work.

When she finally hung up, he said, "I take it he wasn't pleased?"

"He threatened to drop in on me, to make sure I'm okay."

That made her shudder. "A first for Uncle Elwood. Then again, I've never called in sick before." With a long sigh, she sank into her pillow. "Now go home so I can sleep."

Axel had no intention of leaving just yet. He took her dirty dishes to the kitchen, refilled the humidifier, checked in with his answering service, and then made a few necessary calls. Basically, he bided his time till she woke again. Then he helped her bathe—a distinct pleasure—made her eat again, and even napped with her.

Given his history and usual preferences, it made no sense how even the mundane with her seemed special. Napping? He snorted to himself. If anyone found out, he'd never live it down. But being beside her, feeling her body snuggled in with his, filled him with contentment.

By the following day, thanks to the antibiotics and his excellent care, she felt much more human. He helped her do some studying, then rented several movies and sat with her in the bed, sharing meals, laughing a little, and just plain enjoying a woman's company.

It was weird. It was relaxing. Axel thought it might not bode well for his bachelor status. But finally, by Sunday, he accepted the inevitable.

He knew he'd been caught—hook, line, and sinker. Only problem was, did she feel the same?

Seven

After the strangest weekend of her life, Monday should have been comforting, a return to the familiar. Once again Libby had her space to herself. There was no naked man to bump into, no one hovering over her or monitoring her every move. No one fretting, no one holding her, kissing her nose and forehead and ear. No one making her wish she was well so she could take advantage of the proximity of that hulking, muscular, totally male bod.

But instead, it felt odd to have the place to herself, and worse than that, she felt . . . empty. How had she gotten used to him so quickly?

And how would she handle it if she never got to see him again?

Pining over her circumstances was just plain dumb. Axel was still a doctor, which meant he had patients to see, women who depended on him for a lot more than she did.

And against his wishes, she had classes she couldn't miss. Graduation was just around the bend, with plenty of exams to take between now and then.

She told herself it'd be wise to relegate the weekend as an aberration, an event never to occur again. If Axel called, and that was doubtful given what a pill she'd been, she'd be blasé about it. She'd resort to their original agreement of a fling. And flings did not include exclusivity or duty calls.

By the time she got home from school, she was again as limp as a used dishcloth, ready to nap, and determined on her course.

She checked the answering machine first thing. No messages. So . . . he hadn't called.

Deflated, despite the lecture she'd given herself again and again throughout the long day, Libby pulled off her jacket, kicked off her shoes, and flopped down on the bed to stare up at the ceiling. She should eat something. Take her medicine. Maybe do some studying.

But she was still there, half asleep and in the same position where she'd landed, when a knock sounded on her door.

Startled, she sat up, and ridiculous girlish hope swelled her heart. Before she could leave the bed, a key scraped in the lock and Axel pushed the door open. Libby blinked at him in mute surprise.

"Hey." He smiled at her, shut the door. "How do you feel?"

"Uh . . ."

He approached her with wary indifference, tossed a suit coat onto the back of the loveseat, and loosened his tie. "Have you eaten?"

Even for Axel, keeping her key to come and go as he pleased was outrageous. She tried to think of some way to berate him, but he looked really, really good in a tie and five o'clock shadow, and that distracted her. "No."

"Got plans for the evening?"

She shook her head, unsure of his intent, still ripe with hopefulness. "Studying to do. That's all." She noticed that he dropped the key back into his pants pocket. "You planning to keep that?"

He met her gaze with a searing challenge. "Did you want it back?"

She tried to answer, but she couldn't come up with anything intelligent. She should say yes, but her heart said, *Keep it, visit whenever you want, stay a while.*

Deciding to get things out in the open, Libby sighed. "I just . . . I don't know what we're doing here."

Another smile, this one full of sensual promise, gave her half an answer. "You agreed to a torrid sex affair, remember?"

She remembered. "What does that have to do with my key?"

"You don't want anyone to know we're seeing each other, so coming here is safer than using my place." He cocked a brow. "I figure sooner or later you'll be recovered enough to appease my lust—"

She opened her mouth to agree, and he said, "But not today." He gave her a quick once-over, then tsked. "You look wiped out."

With him opening the top button on his dress shirt and rolling up his sleeves, her recovery seemed to be happening at an alarming rate. "It was a long day."

"You should still be in bed." As if by rote, he went to her kitchen and got her a tall glass of iced tea and her medicine. He carried it to her. "How about we shower, order a pizza, and then just relax?"

Shower with Axel? Now that had promise.

"You don't have anything more important to do?"

Her question made him defensive. "I can be as lazy and self-indulgent here with you as I can at my own place."

"You aren't . . . seeing anyone else who would be more fun?"

A new seriousness entered his gaze. "One woman at a time, Libby. And right now, I'm anticipating what we'll do once you've recouped."

Wow, he made that sound so promising. "Being sick sucks." She washed down her antibiotic and two aspirin with one long gulp.

"I can make you feel better."

He was *such* a temptation, and she hated disappointing him. "Sorry, Axel. The soul is willing, anxious even, but the energy level is just kaput."

Axel caught both her hands and pulled her to her feet. "Come on. You'll be more comfortable after a shower."

She groaned.

"I'll do all the work." He began backing toward her bathroom, tugging her along. "You can just stand under the spray and let me soap you." His voice dropped. "And rinse you."

Libby felt a wave of heat that had nothing to do with illness and everything to do with Dr. Axel Dean. "This is so unfair."

Smiling at her flushed cheeks, he whispered, "And dry you."

Disgruntled, she stood docile while he undressed her. "I was supposed to get a turn touching you."

His fingers froze on the snap to her slacks. "Yeah, well, we'll save that for when you're one hundred percent again. Today is just my time to play."

Going to one knee, he pulled down her pants and kissed her belly. "You'll enjoy yourself, I promise. And then you can nap while I get food together."

Libby stroked her fingers through his dark hair. "For a selfish bastard, you're pretty good at giving."

Putting both hands into the back of her panties and sliding them down, he said, "In this instance, giving is also taking. Now hush."

After he had her naked, he stepped back and eyed her from head to toe. With one trembling hand, he cupped her right breast. "The things you do to me, woman." He shook his head, then turned to start the shower. Libby leaned against the wall, eyes closed, legs weak.

When Axel slipped his arm around her waist, she opened her eyes again to be greeted with his now familiar nudity. "You realize this is the equivalent of tormenting a diabetic with a basketful of sweet treats?"

His smile quirked. "I'm salty, not sweet." He pressed a warm, gentle kiss to her mouth and lifted her into the shower with him. "Now just relax."

"I already know this is going to be torture."

"For me, sweetheart. Never for you."

Libby didn't understand what he meant by that, and a few minutes later, after Axel's slick, soapy hands had been all over her body, she no longer cared.

"Axel?" she moaned, leaning into him while his fingers slipped over and around her nipples, teasing, driving her crazy.

"Let me rinse you," he whispered, and he turned her to face the spray, bracing her with his body at her back. The warm water washed over her, and still his hands were on her, over her breasts, her belly, and down between her legs.

"No," she whimpered, so weak she wasn't sure she could stay on her feet. "No more."

"Shhh. Trust me." He held her upright with one arm around her rib cage, just beneath her breasts. With the other, he parted her sex, stroking, delving.

Libby pressed her head back against his shoulder. Her breath stuttered, her muscles tightened.

Two thick fingers pressed into her, making her cry out with the wonderful sensation.

"You see?" he murmured in satisfaction, and then his thumb was on her clitoris, moving back and forth while his fingers pressed, retreated, pressed again. His open mouth moved along her throat and shoulder, the water cascaded over her breasts, and she felt the orgasm building, stronger and stronger.

She cried out again, her fingers clamping down on his hard thighs, her legs stiffening.

He supported her, held her, pushed her completely over the edge, and when she went limp, he eased his fingers out of her and turned her into his body. "Damn, you are so beautiful."

Libby felt herself fading away. She'd been mush before the orgasm, but now her legs actually felt numb and staying awake seemed more trouble than it was worth. "Sorry," she mumbled, letting the fatigue take her.

"Sleep, baby. I've got you."

He turned the water off and Libby was only vaguely aware of being wrapped in a towel and carried to the bed.

Over an hour later, she awoke to find Axel sitting in a chair near the bed, fully dressed, eating pizza and watching her. Her hair was still damp, spread out around her, and she sluggishly pushed up to one elbow.

As if he hadn't been sitting there staring at her, watching her sleep, he got up and fetched a slice of pizza and a cola. He handed them to her. "Hungry?"

"Humiliated," she replied, moving to sit up so she could eat. "I keep passing out on you."

With an odd sort of affection that had nothing to do with sex, he ruffled her hair. "You need your rest."

After a big bite of cold pizza, Libby eyed him. She didn't understand him and the things he did. "And what do you need?"

"Nothing that can't wait." He winked and picked up his suit coat. "I have rounds at the hospital early tomorrow, so I'm going to head out and get some sleep. When you finish eating, take your meds again, okay?"

"And here you told me that you didn't see me as a patient."

"I don't." He bent, stroked her bottom lip with his thumb, and kissed her. "I see you as a woman I want, and I can't have you till you're well. So help me out here and do what you can to recover good health, okay?"

Put that way . . . "I promise to follow doctor's order to the letter."

"That's the spirit."

She caught his hand before he could leave her. "Axel?"

He raised a brow.

"You do realize that you're ruining your reputation as a bad boy bent on his own pleasure, right?"

He cupped her face and kissed her again. "Maybe it's time I got a new reputation."

He left before Libby could question him on that.

Axel thought he'd figured out a very nice plan of attack. For the fourth day in a row, he'd taken care of her, tending her health, her body, and her sexual needs.

He'd confused her, no doubt about that. But his goal was to get her addicted to him, so slowly that she might not even notice.

He'd enjoyed himself, but he didn't think he could take too much more. She was so cute when she felt helpless, so surly in her struggle for complete independence—and so sensually honest in her physical satisfaction.

He liked everything about her, even her purple toenails and her tendency to insult him. He especially liked the way she came, how she made those sexy, carnal sounds deep in her throat and how she clutched at him—as if she never wanted to let him go.

The weekend was fast approaching again and he wanted to spend it in bed, making love to Libby. She no longer had any fever, and other than the dragging fatigue typical of pneumonia, she seemed her old self again.

Not that he really knew her old self since each and every day he learned something new about her. Eventually, he wanted to know all her secrets.

"Daydreaming again?" Cary asked.

Axel looked up from his desk. He'd finished his paperwork an hour ago. "You here for Nora?"

"Actually, Nora left a while ago. She's going shopping with Frances."

Frances was his sister-in-law, the woman who'd made his brother Booker a very happy man. "I didn't hear her leave."

"I know. Like I said, you were daydreaming." Cary folded

his arms and leaned in the doorway. Since his office was in the same building complex as Axel's, they often met up after work. "Want to have a drink or something?"

Axel glanced at his watch and pushed back his chair. "If we make it quick. Libby should be getting home in about an hour."

"Home?"

"Her place." Axel removed his white coat and hung it on the peg behind him. "Can't take her to my place because she still doesn't want anyone to know she's seeing me."

They walked out together, pausing for Axel to lock up.

"Now there's a twist," Cary remarked. "Usually you're the one dodging things, trying to make certain it doesn't get too serious."

"She's not dodging." God, he hoped she wasn't. Axel hated to think he'd be falling for a woman who didn't want him. "It's her uncle. He gives her a hard time over everything."

"So you're . . . what? Just keeping it quiet until it—whatever *it* is—runs its course?"

"No." Axel frowned. "I'm . . . I don't know yet. Things got out of whack with her being sick and everything. I'm sort of feeling my way right now."

"But it will run its course, right?"

Axel snorted. "What's with the it talk?"

"Okay." Cary stopped as they reached their cars. "You name it."

Axel stared at him, blank-brained. "Why does it need a name, damn it? We're involved. End of story."

"*Secretly* involved."

"So?"

Cary held up both hands. "So nothing. It's just unusual for you to get involved, secretly or otherwise."

Axel had the awful suspicion that it was more unusual for Libby. "She's different."

"I know. Everything you claimed not to want."

Was Cary deliberately baiting him? Axel slanted him an evil look. "What the hell is that supposed to mean?"

"Young?" Cary held up one finger after another. "Sweet. Serious. Not really all that . . . stacked."

"Get your hand out of my face." Axel unlocked his BMW and opened the door. Behind him, he could practically feel Cary snickering. "She's young, no denying that. But she's also mature. And if you think she's sweet, then you haven't heard her insulting me with inexhaustible energy."

"She insults you, huh? Well then, that's another for the list."

"And yeah," Axel said, taking an aggressive stance. "She's serious, but she's also damn funny. And just because she's not top heavy doesn't mean I can't be attracted to her."

Again, Cary held up his hands in the universal sign of surrender. "Hey, I think she's really cute. And she has great legs."

Axel's hair damn near stood on end with that jibe. "Just when in the hell were you were looking at her legs?"

This time, Cary laughed outright. He took in Axel's deadly frown and laughed some more. Slapping him on the back, he said, "Damn Axel, you've got it bad. I remember a time—not that long ago, mind you—when you'd have been listing the attributes of any conquest. But this time, I'm not supposed to notice that the girl has legs? Whipped. That's what you are. Totally whipped."

Axel took a mean step toward him, but Cary defused his temper with a smile. "Go home to the girl. Profess undying love. But do me a favor, okay? Try not to hurt her. Whether she insults you or not, she's still sweet and I'd hate to think of her ever crying over you."

Feeling lost at sea, Axel watched as his best friend strode away whistling, a married man without a care. Maybe marriage did that for you, put everything in perspective because, really, if you had the right woman waiting for you, what else mattered?

It was a question Axel had asked himself a few times since his brother and his best friend had both hitched up. But never before had he wondered in such a personal way, as if his own happiness hinged on the answer.

No, he would never make Libby cry, and he'd punch out any guy who did, maybe even including her uncle. He was jealous. And possessive. And making love to her was the most exciting thing he'd ever experienced, but he also enjoyed just plain being with her.

He considered the ramifications of his situation all the way to her apartment. Unfortunately for her, he'd worked himself into quite a state by the time he arrived, and she was there in the kitchen making dinner.

For the two of them.

Like they were some happily married couple or something.

Axel stormed in, took one look at her, and wanted her with a need so violent, he shook. She didn't look overly tired, her fever was long gone, and she actually smiled.

"Dinner will be ready in a minute," she said, oblivious to his mood.

Axel shrugged out of his suit coat and let it drop.

Libby didn't look up as she closed the oven door. "Pork chops, baked potatoes, and salad. I hope that's okay."

Axel yanked his tie free, unbuttoned his dress shirt. It, too, got dropped.

"I even picked up a lemon meringue pie for dessert."

He kicked off his shoes, unbuckled his belt—and Libby glanced up.

Her eyes widened. "What are you doing?"

"Take your clothes off," he ordered. He stepped up close to her, reached around her, and turned off the oven.

Libby glanced sideways at the oven dial. "I suppose the food will keep."

Axel shoved his pants down, taking his boxers and socks off at the same time. "You'll like it hard and fast, babe. I promise." He fished a condom from his wallet and tore it open with his teeth.

Lips parting, eyes going heavy, Libby whispered, "Okay."

She wasn't going fast enough to suit him, so he whisked her long-sleeved tee off over her head and with one hand opened the front clasp on her bra.

Catching her under the arms, he lifted her and fastened his mouth on one tender nipple.

Stiffening at the shock of it, then softening in immediate acceptance, Libby moaned and tangled her fingers in his hair. "Axel."

Still holding her like that, he walked them both to the bed and tumbled her onto it. He straightened, opened her pants, and stripped them off her. "Sorry. I know you've only just recovered, but I've wanted you too much for too long to be patient."

She opened her arms and her legs to him. "I want you, too."

Damn. Axel rolled on the condom and came down over her, kissing her hard, taking her mouth with demand while letting his hands roam everywhere. He caressed her, stroked, sought out all the hot, humid places on her body, and less than a minute later, with two fingers pressed deep inside her and her anxious, panting breaths on his shoulder, he knew she was ready enough.

Slowly, he pulled his fingers out, trailing them up and over her turgid clitoris. She groaned out loud, her whole body clenching in reaction. Unwilling to wait a second more, Axel slipped his arms under her thighs, caught her knees in the crook of his elbows, and spread her wide. His gaze holding hers, he told her, "It's deeper this way," and he pushed the broad head of his penis into her with a long, low groan.

She was tight, but wet, making the way easy.

Lost in her pleasure, her slender legs strained against his hold, but Axel had a hundred pounds on her and easily controlled her. By small degrees, he sank in, pulled back, sank in again, each time giving her another inch, each time relishing her aching moans and gasping breaths and the bite of her sharp nails on his shoulders.

Her back arched, inadvertently giving him better access.

Axel felt her clamping tight around his cock, felt the soft, slick giving of her body, felt himself touching against her womb, and he almost lost it.

He looked at her face, twisted with exquisite need, her teeth sunk into her bottom lip, and he had to lock his jaw to hold back. But more than his own release, he wanted hers, he wanted to see her come, to know she belonged to him.

As he leaned into her, thrusting harder, faster, her thighs pressed into her breasts and she went wild, crying out, struggling to match his rhythm, and then she was coming, her movements suspended, her breath held for a beat before she exhaled on a long, shuddering, high-pitched moan of surrender.

Axel never once closed his eyes because looking at her, seeing her beneath him, made it that much better.

When she was spent, he carefully freed her legs and rested atop her, enjoying the beat of her heart against his.

She stroked his back with an idle hand. "You didn't . . . ?"

"No, I didn't."

"Why?"

Because he didn't want it to end. Ever. "I want it to last a while longer."

"Oh." Then she whispered, "You were wrong."

His own lust unappeased, Axel could barely breathe, much less think. "About?"

"Liking it hard."

"I felt you come, Libby."

"Mmmm." She gave him a brief hug. "But I don't just like it. I *love* it fast and hard."

He turned his face in and kissed her throat, before lifting to his elbows to look at her. "What else do you love?"

She nuzzled him, inhaling, breathing him in. "The way you smell after sex, all hot and male."

His big hand slid into her silky hair. "Anything else?"

"I especially love feeling you on top of me."

Axel stared into her blue eyes with his heart full and his body taut. Slowly, he pulled back, then just as slowly, he sank in again. "Do you love this?"

Her chest expanded on a breath. "Yes."

"And this?" He slid one hand beneath her bottom, arching her pelvis up to accept his next thrust.

"That . . . ah, that, too."

Maintaining a leisurely pace, he kissed his way from her lips to her throat to her breast. "This?" And he suckled on a ripe nipple, tonguing her, leaving her wet and tight and hot.

"*Yessss.*"

Suddenly he clamped down, sucking hard, thrusting harder. "Tell me," he said, briefly lifting his head, his fingers digging into her tender flesh. "Tell me you love this, too."

"*Axel.*"

The way she called his name set him off, and he started coming. Too soon, he thought, but he couldn't pull back, couldn't measure his strokes or his intensity, couldn't make it last any longer. As the release rolled through him, his tension ebbed, draining him, stealing his strength. He slumped onto her.

"Oh God," she groaned, then laughed softly. "That was . . . amazing."

Heart still thundering, as if it wanted to break free of his chest, Axel asked, "You loved it?"

"I did."

He swallowed hard, squeezed in closer to her. "Do you love me?"

Eight

Libby froze, her hands flat on his back, her legs around him.

Axel rose up enough to see the fear in her eyes, the paleness of her cheeks. It didn't matter. He just plain didn't give a damn.

"Because I love you." He was still inside her, a part of her, and never before had that carried so much meaning. What if she was as cavalier about sex as he'd always been? What if she didn't feel the special closeness now, closeness so precious that it choked him up and put him in knots?

He struggled to find the words. "I love making love to you, and sleeping with you." He pushed her hair back from her face with both hands. "I love talking to you and just being with you."

Time passed, and with each second of heavy silence, Axel grew more rigid.

"Maybe . . ." She cleared her throat, looking trapped. "Maybe you just think you do because things have been weird."

"Weird how?" He wouldn't move until he got the answer he wanted.

"I've been sick and you've felt responsible for me."

"No, I took responsibility because, sick or not, I wanted to be with you."

"You're used to lots of sex."

He shrugged. He couldn't deny liking sex, and true, he seldom had to go for long without. "With you, it's different."

"You get what you want from a woman," she accused, "and then you get over her and move on. But you haven't been able to get what you want from me . . ."

"Of course not. Because I want everything from you."

She started breathing too fast. "You want sex. You said so yourself."

"I'm not an idiot, Libby. I know the difference between what I feel now and what I've felt with other women. If you don't love me, I'll work on you. I'll somehow get you to change your mind. But don't think I'm an idiot."

"I wouldn't!" She smacked his shoulder. "I don't. You're the most . . . well, remarkable man I've ever met."

It was a start. "Remarkable, huh? But you don't love me?"

"I don't know."

The words cut deep, but he still smiled. "You don't have to worry that I'll interfere with your plans or make your life difficult. I know you have priorities, and right now graduating is top of the list." She started to say something and Axel hushed her. "It's okay."

He moved up and away from her, going into the bathroom to remove the condom, to splash cold water on his face and get his thoughts in order. Talk about getting off track. He could hardly sneak his way into her life if he went around blurting out frigging love sonnets. Jesus.

By the time he left the bathroom, Libby was sitting on the side of the bed, the sheet around her.

"Here's what we'll do." Axel pulled her upright and removed the sheet. "First, don't ever hide from me. Whether we're in agreement or not, modesty between us is ridiculous."

Her chin went up. "I wasn't hiding."

"Good." Damn, she was cute when riled. "You feel fully recovered?"

"Yes."

He knew she still suffered some fatigue, but he wouldn't debate it with her. "So there's no reason I can't get my fill of you now, is there?"

Suspicion, maybe a little worry, edged into her expression. "I suppose not."

Axel bent and kissed her. "Then let's see how long that takes. If by the time you graduate we're both still interested, we'll tell your uncle about us. Agreed?"

Her brows shot up and she laughed nervously. "Believe me, Axel, Elwood won't like the idea any more in two weeks than he will right now."

Axel stared her straight in her beautiful blue eyes and said, "If I tell him we're getting married, he won't object."

Libby's mouth opened. Her lips moved, but nothing came out.

Not even an objection.

Grinning, knowing he had her, Axel said, "Now, did you say pork chops? My favorite. And I think I've worked up an appetite, so let's eat."

With Axel at her side, his hand on her waist, Libby stared at her uncle in complete stupefaction. "Come again?"

Elwood harrumphed and blustered. Libby knew he wanted a private word with her, and she knew he didn't understand why Dr. Axel Dean loomed so close. But it seemed he had something more important to discuss with her first. And besides, Axel looked as stubborn as a mule, glued to the floor, unwilling to budge a single inch.

She was used to that, though. Since that day he'd declared himself, he'd shown her in a hundred different ways that he cared. Being with her now, during her graduation, was only expected.

Having Uncle Elwood approach was not.

"I said I'm proud of you."

Axel's frown eased away and he nodded. "About time."

Elwood glared at him. Usually a glare from the chief of staff sent doctors scurrying. Axel just pulled Libby closer as if to dare Elwood to question him.

Since her return to good health, Axel had been glutting himself.

He was such a sexual man, he probably defied the record books, being ready day, night, and sometimes in between, when their schedules allowed. It seemed the more they made love, the more he wanted to make love.

And variety . . . Lord have mercy, the man loved variety. He'd taken her in the shower, in the kitchen, on the bed, beside the bed . . . Libby sighed. Before they left for her graduation service, just to make his point, he'd hoisted up her long gown and made love to her against the wall with a tenderness that had her floating through the ceremony.

But it went beyond the sex. Axel talked with her, watched movies with her, slept beside her and held her close and touched her for no apparent reason other than that he enjoyed the feel of her hair, her skin, her palm to his, her heartbeat mingling with his own.

After years of planning and, more recently, weeks of study, she'd completed her education. It should have been a monumental moment. But truthfully, her priorities had changed since meeting one very sexy doctor. Her education and independence were still important to her, but they weren't nearly as important as Axel. He'd become so enmeshed in her life, she couldn't imagine the days without him. She wanted to marry him and be with him forever. She wanted him to tell her again that he loved her.

But she didn't want him coerced. And if he kept acting so familiar with her, her uncle would catch on and then he'd be making demands and issuing insults, and Axel's career could be threatened.

Axel had to know it, too, but he didn't seem the least concerned.

"I know I haven't been very supportive." Elwood rubbed the back of his neck, showing an uncommon uneasiness that almost made Libby feel sympathetic. "I've told you many times that you're like your mother. And in so many ways, you are."

Axel's hand tightened on her waist. "I hope you mean smart, beautiful, and ambitious."

Elwood nodded, but spoke directly to Libby. "Not only do you look like her, but you're as vivacious, as outspoken and witty and strong as she ever was. I loved your mother, Libby, and it destroyed me that she didn't show better judgment with men. She let herself be used, and in the end it—"

"That's enough." No matter what, Libby wouldn't let him insult her mother.

Elwood stiffened. "I'm sorry. I know you feel defensive of her. What I'm trying to say is that you have all your mother's better qualities, with none of her weaknesses."

Libby wasn't in the least complimented. "Enjoying life isn't a weakness, Uncle Elwood."

"It is when you allow it to damage your future and your reputation."

Axel heaved a sigh. "I think you two are at cross purposes here. Elwood, why don't you just spit it out?"

Libby said, "Be quiet, Axel," and that seemed to stun her uncle. Especially when Axel just gave her a smart salute. But she'd already learned that Axel didn't get insulted easily. Oh, if he thought he was in the right he'd argue her into the ground, but he had the good sense to know when to back off.

And sometimes he had the good sense to divert her with a kiss. Or a touch.

He always supported her. And God, she loved him for it.

Bringing her mind back to her uncle, Libby curled her lip. "I know my illegitimacy is a tough pill for an esteemed man like yourself to swallow."

"That's not what I mean at all." Appearing more flustered by the moment, Elwood clasped his hands behind his back and cast a nervous glance at Axel. "You were a gift to your mother, and I had hoped the responsibility of a child would make her settle down. But until the day she died, she showed no moderation with men. It was flirting with strangers that got her killed that day on the river, and I've blamed myself forever."

Libby felt her jaw drop. "Why in the world would you blame yourself?"

"If I'd let you both come to my pool that day . . ."

Incredibly, Libby softened. "It's old news, Uncle Elwood." She even touched his arm, offering the only consolation she could. "Like you said, Mom enjoyed male company. You can't blame yourself for her actions. But please don't judge me by them either. I've never chased after men, or made them a priority in my life."

Axel cleared his throat. "I can vouch for that. No chasing from Libby."

Elwood gave him another dirty look before facing Libby again. "I know that. You've been extremely levelheaded." He reached into his suit coat and pulled out a thick envelope. "From the moment you came to live with me, I was determined that you'd be different from her. I wanted you to be more responsible. I wanted you to live a long, full life."

Libby could only shake her head. So he'd only done what he thought was best for her—by alienating her? By making her feel unloved?

Elwood straightened his shoulders. "I could have easily given you everything, but I wanted you to earn what you got in the hopes that it would mean more to you."

Axel stepped forward. "What about love, Elwood? How hard was she supposed to work for that?"

Libby couldn't believe Axel would go toe to toe with the chief of staff on her behalf.

Affronted, Elwood scowled darkly. "Just what do you have to do with any of this, Dean?"

Oh no, Libby thought, please don't tell him what you have to do with it! But one look at Axel's face and she knew the bomb was about to blow. "Axel," she said in warning, but it was too late.

"I love her." That statement landed with all the subtlety of a tsunami.

Hearing him say it again made Libby almost melt. Sure, he'd said it a few weeks ago, but after her protestations, he'd kept his feelings to himself. He'd shared everything else, his hands, his mouth, his affection and camaraderie, his time and attention, but he hadn't spoken words of love again.

"Axel?"

His fingers brushed her cheek. "What? You thought I'd changed my mind? Silly girl." And then to Elwood: "If I can talk her into it, I'm going to marry her."

Oh geez. Despite the many people milling around her, despite her uncle's bristling confusion, Libby focused only on Axel. "You still want to marry me?"

Now Axel scowled. "Of course I do. Elwood can blunder around all he wants trying to find the right words. But I already know them. You, Libby Preston, are a very special woman. Beautiful inside and out, strong but soft, determined but giving. I think I fell in love with you that very first night, at Elwood's party."

Elwood went rigid in indignation. "You've known her since then?"

Rolling his eyes, Axel said, "Oh, lighten up, Elwood. I just told you I love her, so what does it matter how long we've been associated?"

"It matters." Elwood turned a stony glare on Libby. "Do you love him?"

Talk about being put in the spotlight. Libby's cheeks warmed and her heart swelled. She hated spilling her guts in front of her uncle, but Axel looked very vulnerable as he waited to hear what she'd say, and she didn't have it in her to keep him in suspense. "Almost from that first moment I saw him."

A grin burst over Axel's face. "Damn, I'm glad to hear that."

Elwood went so far as to smile. "Then I suppose I'll need to come up with a wedding gift, as well." He handed her the envelope. "But this is for your graduation, for making me so very proud of you."

Libby took the envelope hesitantly. "What is it?"

"Every dime you've ever given me. The room and board, the college loans, everything. I've saved it all, from that very first summer job you got, and I've added a few thousand in."

"Oh no." Libby tried to hand it back to him. "I don't want this."

"Please." He folded his hands around hers, closing the envelope in her grasp. "For once, let me do what's right. I always intended to give the money back to you, you know. I took it in the first place as a way to teach you a lesson. I thought I'd be returning it with regrets. I thought I'd have a lecture to share on the weight of the world and the trials you'd face." He shook his head, saddened. "Now I realize that I've been your biggest trial. But you're strong enough, capable enough, to handle anything life brings you. You certainly don't need the money, but this is my way of trying to help you make a good start with your new career."

Numb, Libby kept the envelope and stared at her uncle.

"So," Axel said, "you won't object to us marrying? Not that I care, you understand, but I won't have you hurting Libby."

Libby rolled her eyes. "I can take care of myself."

Together, Axel and Elwood said, "Don't I know it."

With the exact words between them, they looked at each other in startled surprise, then laughed out loud.

When his chuckles had died down, Elwood wiped his eyes

and said, "No objections at all. Just see that you treat her right." And he added, "Treat her better than I did."

"You can count on it."

After Elwood left, Axel pulled her close and kissed her. "Now, that went better than I thought."

Libby shook her head. "I suppose my uncle does respect you, because he didn't faint." She laid her palm on his chest and said, "Thank heavens I've graduated. That means I can put my mind to wedding plans."

With a devilish twinkle in his eyes, Axel said, "I thought Elwood's gardens might make the perfect place for the ceremony."

Libby choked. "The gardens!"

Axel pulled her close, kissed her nose, and whispered, "They have special meaning to me. And when I get you there this time, believe me, I'll say all the right things."

"Like?"

He cupped her face, all teasing gone. "Through sickness and in health, till death do us part."

"Oh." Grinning, Libby put her arms around him. "In that case, I agree, the gardens will be perfect."

LADY OF THE LAKE

Erin McCarthy

One

Violet Caruthers had known that Frank wasn't the most attentive of boyfriends. But if she had been asked, she would have thought that even *he* would have noticed that his girlfriend had fallen off the back of his fishing boat.

She would have been wrong.

Violet coughed as the shock of cool lake water splashed over her face, and she flailed her arms in panic to keep herself afloat. "Frank!" she screamed at the back of the retreating boat.

The churning motor, the spraying surf, and the obnoxious laughter of the fool she was having sex with drowned out her cry.

She hated dating.

Hated flirting, and posturing, and all the awkward accompaniments of sharing an intimate relationship with a man. She was painfully shy, always had been, and if it wasn't for one deep, driving urge, she wouldn't be forcing herself to do it at all.

Except she wanted a baby.

"Frank!" she shrieked again as the enormity of the situation smacked her like the rocking wave from the boat's wake. "Oh, this is bad, this is really, really bad."

Frank was too busy chatting with his buddies, boasting over his walleye-catching prowess to even notice that she had lost her grip walking to the cooler for a bottled water. Before she could even blink, she'd fallen right off the side of the boat like some lackwit in a Steve Martin movie.

She wasn't athletic, but she'd never thought of herself as a klutz before. But that was neither here nor there because she was covered in briny lake water, her glasses dripping from the spray, and she was in the middle of bleepity-bleep nowhere.

Surely he would notice. Seriously. In just a second or two. Any minute now. After all, she was his girlfriend. They had been dating for four months, having sex for weeks and weeks now. They were in a committed relationship. All because she had thought he was just quite possibly nice enough, intelligent enough, and egotistical enough to agree to her plan to have him father a child.

If he was a little geeky, unaware of fashion, and a bit preoccupied with his computer software and fishing hobby, she had been prepared to overlook it. She was no prize herself— leaning towards geeky, unaware of fashion, and a bit preoccupied with her job as a kindergarten teacher. The important thing was he was a good person, with a kind heart. And Frank had seemed like the type that she could lay her plan out to in all its logic. She would appeal to his biological need to reproduce his high IQ in a child, and assure him she expected nothing of him in return. No money, no involvement with the child or her, no nothing.

It had all made complete sense. Before she'd found herself floating in Lake Erie like refuse fallen off the back of a garbage truck and kicked into the water.

The whine of the motor was receding and the boat was going bye-bye and she was going to drown. In a bikini, of all things. She'd never worn a bikini in her life and she'd let her friend Ashley, and the force of her desire to be a mother, talk her into one. That had an American flag pattern with a star right over her nipple. All because she'd thought it might attract Frank's attention, focus his eyes squarely on her, and inspire unmitigated lust, which would be used to her advantage when she suggested forgoing the condom.

Too bad she had been painfully uncomfortable in the micro-bathing suit, wrapping her arms over her not-so-small chest. Bent over at the waist, she had held a hardback book spread open in front of her so neither Frank, nor his two pals Jay and Shack, would notice that she was virtually naked. She'd spent her entire post-puberty life de-emphasizing her big breasts, and she couldn't get over that in an afternoon.

Violet treaded water, her legs already straining.

Bikinis were not her.

And now she was going to die in one.

Dylan Diaz smoothed out his sail and pondered that he was such an ungrateful bastard.

Here he had a life some guys would kill for—major baseball career, money, chicks throwing themselves at him—and he wasn't happy. Tipping back his water bottle, he took a swallow and shook his head at himself in amusement.

What did he want? A flippin' parade? A street named after him? Endorsements?

Hell, now that he thought about it, he already had those. He didn't need them, didn't care about them.

Focusing on a funny spot bobbing in the water, Dylan felt the frustration and discontent roiling inside him. The problem was that he was lonely. The money, the minor fame, none of it mattered when he was surrounded by fakes, hangers-ons, and plastic people.

He missed his family, most of whom were in Miami, while he spent the season both on the road and in Cleveland in a furnished apartment. He missed feeling comfortable around people, trusting they liked him for himself, not for his status or for his money. He'd been a goofball of a kid, loud and mischievous, always having fun. He wanted that back—being just Dylan, instead of Diaz, number twelve, .299 batting average.

"Yeah, they'd be standing in line to feel sorry for me, wouldn't they?" He scoffed at himself and leaned forward a little.

What was that brown speck? It was kind of big to be a bird. A flip of the tiller and he headed a bit upwind in that direction. He wasn't going anywhere in particular anyway. He was just sailing around trying to clear his head before he left on a four-game series in New York, yet the only thing he was clearing was his nostrils.

He could never quite get used to the smell of Lake Erie. It was cold, stark, and fishy compared to the saltiness of the Atlantic Ocean.

Six o'clock on a Friday night and he was ready to pack it in for the night. Grab some wings and eat them in front of the TV. Alone. Nice way to spend his twenty-seventh birthday.

"Lame-ass. Whiner. Douche bag." Insulting himself didn't make him feel any better, and he narrowed his eyes as he scanned the horizon.

If he didn't know better, he'd think that brown spot was a *head* in the water.

He tilted his head, narrowed his eyes. It was a head. With hair. Bobbing.

Ah mi Dios. Oh my God, he'd found a dead person.

With a grimace, he put his water down in the cup holder.

Well, nothing like a floating corpse to make him feel even worse for griping. Ungrateful was an understatement. Here he had life by the balls—he was young, strong, healthy, loaded with cash. This person was *dead*. It couldn't get much rougher than that.

Unless the dead guy's eyes had been pecked out, too. He shuddered. There was a nasty thought.

He'd been hoping for a little excitement, something different for his birthday. This wasn't what he'd had in mind.

Dylan reached for his radio to call his find into the coast guard when the head lifted.

It was wearing glasses.

He scrambled back a foot before letting out a "Yaahhh!" like a kid in a haunted house. *Shit*, it was alive.

Then his momentary shock gave way to relief. Alive was good. Better than dead. Unless the person was injured, which was not so good. "Are you okay? Damn, hang in there! I'll help you out of the water."

He stood straight up, rocking the boat, and leaned over, reaching out. "Lift your arms, I'll pull you up."

The head was actually a woman, with chattering teeth and long hair trailing in the water like seaweed as she stared up at him through waterlogged glasses. He couldn't see her eyes, but he thought she was in shock. She didn't move, didn't speak, and Dylan pawed through the water, locking his grip on both of her wrists.

He pulled hard, and she ripped out of the water towards his boat. But in his eagerness to get her to safety, he misjudged the distance. There wasn't enough room for clearance and her lower half collided with the hull.

A soft moan carried to him as he winced. Then he pulled again, this time sort of scraping her up the side of the boat before she cleared it. His shoe slipped, he went down on his ass, and she fell right on top of him since he was still holding onto her wrists.

There was pain in his shoulder, a whole lot of wet hair slapping him across the chin, and dead weight landing on his lower half. Well, not dead, but damn close, as heavy and limp as she was.

All that exhausted female fell right smack on him, her elbow nailing him in the nuts, but he took the blow like the man that he was. By swearing. "Fuckin' A."

Damn, once a goofball, always a goofball, apparently. Somehow he was managing to turn a rescue into a slapstick comedy act.

With a grimace, Dylan glanced down at the closed eyes, as the wetness of her hair and clammy skin soaked through his shorts. She wasn't moving. At all. Jesus, maybe she really was dead. He was no MD. Of course, she had moaned, but what the hell did he know? It could have been her last breath.

"Are you okay, lady? Please say something." He was afraid to move, afraid to exacerbate any injuries she might have, afraid that he was starting to panic a little and that for all he was a macho ballplayer, he was freaking out here.

"Just give me a second," she whispered in a husky voice.

All right then. Alive, thank God. "But are you hurt? I need to call for help. Let me scoot out from under you." If she was injured, he needed to get assistance, and he was a good thirty minutes from shore. He had his cell phone in his pocket, and he was close enough that he might be able to get a signal. If not, he'd use his radio.

But when he started to shift, she moaned into his pelvis. "I'm fine. Just let me be still for a minute."

Dylan stopped moving. She sounded pretty intact, just tired, which had him staring up at the sky in some serious relief. "Nothing's broken? You're not bleeding, or delirious, or paralyzed?"

"No."

Good, because he was working on an erection, and he was a sick motherfucker if she was hurt and he was getting off on her face being plastered down in his crotch.

But that facial proximity below his waist, coupled with her chest . . . holy hooters, she had a nice rack. It was all pressed against his hips and between his legs, and his body was automatically responding to the position. He didn't mean to, knew that there was a church confessional with his name on it for this one, but damn, her breasts were so soft and *big*.

There was no way those were fake. They felt pliable and bouncy, sort of wrapping around him in a titty hug.

Dylan looked up at the sky and did a practice Hail Mary. He'd be doing twenty of them after this. Might as well make sure he remembered the words.

She turned her head a little, so that her lips pressed right over his fly, her nose burying into his crotch, only covered by thin swim trunks.

The gates of hell swung wide open in welcome for him.

Because he was hard, getting harder by the minute.

"How long have you been in the water? What happened to you?" he asked, followed by, "Hail Mary, full of grace . . ."

Man, he was blanking out after that. His mother would beat him with her rosary if she found out. Second confession needed—forgetting prayers as well as lusting after unknown, helpless woman.

"Are you praying?" the woman asked, her voice sounding a little incredulous.

"Yes. I'm praying that you're okay."

Oh my God, he had just lied. Shit. And taken the name of the Lord in vain.

How many commandments could he break in one day? He was probably coveting his neighbor's wife right this very second.

The problem was, he hadn't had sex in an entire year. His body clearly missed it, given its let's-do-it reaction to a half-drowned woman.

"I'm fine," she said. "I'm just tired. Thank you for the pillow."

"Uh . . ." Dylan tried very hard not to move. She had to be delirious. She had fallen right onto him two minutes ago, not a pillow in sight. His semi-erection was right alongside her ear, and while he wasn't going to brag, he was big enough that she should notice its *existence*. And it damn well wasn't soft. "You're welcome."

But his voice must have given him away—he never could lie well because of his Catholic guilt. Her eyes popped open and she looked up. Wiped her glasses with a finger. Looked down. Looked left to right, then sat up with a scream.

Which gave him a glorious view of her breasts, covered by tiny triangles in a stars and stripes pattern.

Dylan was pretty sure he was saluting the flag.

Two

Violet screamed. She didn't mean to, but when she opened her eyes and realized she was lying on a strange man's crotch, and it was all her fault for being stupid enough to think she could charm Frank into getting her pregnant, well, it was the last straw.

She clapped her hands over her mouth to stifle the volume of her horror. The man had saved her life. She should show a little gratitude.

After all, she had been drifting for what felt like twenty minutes, getting weaker and more worried, resorting to drown-proofing techniques to save her strength.

"I'm sorry, I didn't mean to scream . . . lie on you . . . cause you any trouble." Violet winced. She hated meeting new people. It was so awkward and she never knew what to say. And this was awkward in spades.

He pushed himself up onto his elbows and raised an eye-brow. The position brought him squarely into her space. She blushed. Because he was too close to her, because she had stupidly thought his lap was a pillow, and because she was suddenly aware of the fact that he was really, really attractive.

Like Wow attractive. Like Put Naked Pictures of him on

the Internet attractive. He was muscular and dark-haired, with deep black eyes. He was *Hispanic*, for crying out loud.

"Look, you've obviously had some kind of accident. Why were you floating in the middle of the lake?"

"I . . . fell overboard." Violet scooted backwards, the floor squeaking as she swung her legs around in front of her. She peeled her glasses off and looked around for something to wipe them off on. She'd feel better if she wasn't viewing the world through water droplets, but she was in a wet bikini. No help there.

"Where's your sailboat?" He looked puzzled as he sat up, drawing his knees to his chest. Despite her nearsightedness, she could tell it was a very masculine chest. A rippling sort of chest, with fine black hair and a cross tattooed right in the center.

She bit her lip, stuck her glasses back on, and tried to be vague. The truth was just too embarrassing. "It's a motor boat."

He was quiet for a second. Then, "Did it drive itself away?"

"No."

"Then who did?"

"A person."

"What person?"

"My boyfriend." He was making this really difficult.

His mouth twisted into a frown. "Was he trying to hurt you, kill you? Did you have an argument? We need to call the cops."

Oh geez. Violet shook her head. "No, don't do that! It was an accident. I just fell over when I leaned into the cooler to get a water."

His hand reached out and pushed her wet hair back off her face. Violet jerked away from his touch, startled.

"So . . . why didn't he just turn around and fish you out of the water? You could have drowned out there!"

"He, well . . . He, you see . . . Well, it's just that . . ." Violet did some fishing of her own for words that wouldn't reveal the true breadth of her humiliation.

"Yes?"

Darn it, there was no hope for it. Her mind wasn't devious enough to formulate a reasonable lie on quick notice. She shivered in her wet bikini as a light breeze moved over her skin. She sighed. "He didn't notice I fell over."

"He didn't notice?" His head tilted. His voice was incredulous. "He didn't notice. His girlfriend fell off of his boat, he drove away and never even noticed? That's what you're telling me?"

It sounded even more pathetic by the minute. "He was talking to his friends several feet away from me." Still angry herself, Violet wasn't defending Frank so much as herself. Could she look any stupider? "And you have to understand, Frank has a genius level IQ. He gets distracted, and isn't always aware of his surroundings."

"That's asinine." He leaned across the boat and grabbed his T-shirt.

Thank God he was going to cover that chest up. She was extremely distracted by it. In all her twenty-eight years, she'd never seen that much muscle that close up. All her boyfriends had been pencil thin. All three of them, that is.

"You don't just *not* notice your girlfriend falling overboard!"

Violet winced. "Frank does, apparently."

He muttered something in Spanish, which would have been sexy except she suspected he was calling her a dumb broad.

Which she was. Her pregnancy plan had been ill-fated from the beginning, obviously.

There was no way she was going to let Frank anywhere near her ovulating self ever again. She could forgive him for not noticing that she'd fallen overboard. But it was a good, solid twenty minutes later and there had been no sign of him.

If he hadn't noticed she was gone by now, he would probably bring the boat in, dock, head off with Jay and Shack for dinner, and never even once think of her.

He'd probably already forgotten she'd even been with them in the first place.

It was damn depressing.

"Take your bikini top off," he said.

"*What?*" Oh Lord, it just figured. Why did things like this happen to her? She was a good girl. She was nice to her neighbors. She taught small children. She paid her bills on time. She led perhaps the most boring life in all of humanity outside of a penitentiary prisoner, and yet she had managed to fall off a boat and get rescued by a pervert. "No!"

"You're shivering, you have goose bumps." He pointed to her bump-covered arms. "And you've been in the water for who knows how long. Take your wet top off and put on my dry T-shirt." He held it out to her.

"Oh." He didn't want to see her breasts. He didn't care about her breasts, any more than Frank did. Violet wondered why she'd spent so much time camouflaging her overgrown chest if it faded into the wallpaper just like the rest of her. Not that she should care. She should be glad that he wasn't looking at her breasts. Somehow that message wasn't quite making its way to her brain, though, because she felt mildly offended.

"Thank you." She took the T-shirt and dried her glasses off on it. The clarity of her vision when she popped them back on her nose made her wish she'd lost them altogether. Oh, my he was *hot*.

"Your boyfriend is an asshole," he said.

"Well, he doesn't mean to be," Violet assured him.

He scoffed. "You shouldn't let him treat you like that."

"It was an accident." And why was she defending Frank? She'd already decided she wasn't going to see him again. Sperm wasn't worth this level of humiliation.

"I would notice if you fell overboard. He should have, too."

Yeah, sure he would have noticed. Please. Violet knew the kind of woman she was. She was the kind of woman whom men only saw when they sat down across from her for their child's kindergarten conference. Then she was Miss Caruthers, their child's starchy, sweet teacher. Other than that, she was invisible to men of all ages.

Completely and utterly invisible. She was a spider web. You never saw it until you walked into it.

But still, she knew that Frank should have noticed. She deserved that much.

"You're right."

He nodded firmly. "I know I am. I'm Dylan Diaz, by the way. What's your name?"

"Violet." Why did his name sound familiar? Violet was sure she'd heard it somewhere before, but at the same time she was positive she'd never met a gorgeous, buff Latino. She was so distracted trying to place his name, she forgot to be shy. "It's odd, but I feel like I've heard your name before."

Dylan tugged at the T-shirt she was holding in her hand. "Don't forget to put this on. You'll feel better when you're warmer."

"Thank you." Not that she had any intention of taking her bikini top off. Not until she got home and she could stuff it in her garbage disposal and flick the ON switch.

Violet pulled the sun-warmed shirt over her head and almost choked as the masculine smell of sport deodorant filled her nostrils. She was blushing it, damn it, she was blushing. But at least her breasts were covered, and in another ten minutes or so she might actually be able to look him in the eye again. Maybe.

"I'm sorry to be so much trouble. You can just . . . pull over and I'll swim to shore."

When she chanced a look at him, he was staring at her, dark eyebrows lifted. "Are you crazy? I'm not going to do that." Then he swirled his finger in a circle. "Turn around."

"Why?" But she did it anyway, because turning was better

than looking at him. Because he was gorgeous and she was a nun trapped inside a stripper's body, with a chess club president's head.

It was the prim part of her that squawked in horror when his fingers jerked the ties of her bikini top loose at her neck, then deftly slid under the T-shirt and made fast work of the bottom strings, warm fingers brushing over her clammy skin. He harvested the whole dang thing with one last yank, and Violet swallowed hard.

"I'll just lay it on the deck in the sun to dry." He did just that, and then grinned at her when she turned back around. "You gave me a heart attack, you know. I thought you were a dead body. Scared five years off my life when you lifted your head up."

"I'm sorry," she said sincerely, hunkering her shoulders over so that her tight nipples wouldn't jut out like twin thimbles. Despite the fact that it was July the water was still cold, causing her to shiver, and well, *pucker.*

"I'm sorry for interrupting your night. Like I said, if you just take me to the nearest dock or whatever, I'll get out of your hair. Thank you for . . . rescuing me."

He was laughing. Why was he laughing? Embarrassed, Violet stopped talking. Glancing down to avoid his eyes, she saw the T-shirt had plastered to her breasts in two round wet spots, nipples centered like pornographic bull's eyes.

She almost wished she had drowned.

Dylan wasn't sure why he was laughing, but it was better than drooling, which was what he really wanted to do.

Violet wasn't anything like any woman he'd ever met. She wasn't screaming or ranting or squawking or crying over what had happened to her. She wasn't pissed off.

She was *apologizing* for inconveniencing him.

And she was self-conscious about the T-shirt plastered to her chest. His shirt. Clinging to that beautiful chest. Dylan had had so many ta-tas flashed at him over the years, he was damn near immune to the sight. But Violet had him hard, simply because her breasts were naturally beautiful, and because she was shy about a stranger seeing them.

He'd had so many women and their body parts just shoved right smack into his face, that he liked the allure of knowing there was something gorgeous under there that he wasn't allowed to see. When she'd been on top of him, he'd felt her flesh, but again it had been just a hint, just a tease, enough to make him want to explore her slowly and thoroughly.

Which he wouldn't, because he wasn't a total pig, and she had a boyfriend, no matter how much of an ass he was.

"You're welcome, Vi. But you don't need to feel bad. It's not your fault." He shouldn't say it, but he couldn't help it. Any man who didn't notice his girlfriend was missing was a first-class jerk-off. "It's your boyfriend's fault."

She shook her head. "I'm the one who tripped. And I'm sure he noticed after a minute or two. He's probably looking for me right now."

Violet squeezed the water out of her long hair while Dylan groped in his pocket for his cell phone. She wasn't exactly gorgeous, but more like pretty. Soft. With pale skin and pink cheeks, a pert nose, and a pair of rosebud lips.

Jesus, he was attracted to her. It completely amused him. Maybe he was just feeling protective of her because he'd rescued her.

She licked her lips and tossed her hair over her shoulder, causing her breasts to thrust forward before she realized it and sucked them back in.

Schwing. He could practically hear his dick popping up. Nope, it wasn't a misplaced hero thing. He was really, really attracted to her.

"Why don't you call him and put his mind at ease then?" He handed her the phone.

There was only a slight hesitation, then she took the phone from him, dialed a number, and turned a little away from him.

"Frank? This is Violet."

Dylan rolled his eyes in the opposite direction and reached for his bottle of water.

"Oh, I know, I'm sorry, it was an accident. But someone found me and picked me up." Her voice dropped lower. "No, no, you don't have to stop fishing. I'll just get to shore and call Kindra to pick me up."

Asshole. Dylan sucked down half his water and fought the urge to grab the phone from Violet and tell Frank to go fuck himself.

Two bright red spots of color were in her cheeks now, and behind her glasses her eyes looked sharp and angry, despite the mild tone to her voice. "No, don't come over tonight. I'm not in the mood. But you can stop over tomorrow and we'll talk."

After saying good-bye she pushed the end button and just clutched the telephone for a minute, her breathing a little quick.

It was none of his business, but he didn't suppose that had ever stopped him before. "You're going to ditch him, aren't you? Please tell me you're through with him."

She gave a little sigh. "Yeah, I guess so."

"No guessing. You deserve better than that, Violet. He doesn't appreciate you and you need to stand up for yourself here."

And since when had he become an inspirational speaker?

"It's not Frank, it's . . . something else." She pushed her glasses up. "It's complicated. There's something I want and I can't have, unless I do something I really don't want to do because it seems a little risky and unnatural to me."

She'd lost him with that sentence. "We've got a bit of a boat ride ahead of us. You can tell me all about it, Violet. We're an hour from Sandusky and an hour from Cleveland. Which way do you live?"

"Cleveland. I live in Westlake."

"I'm east of that." The thought of spending another hour on the boat with her was very appealing. And they were really only forty minutes away, but if he held the sail in a little, it would slow them down. Plus, he would have to keep her with him until someone came to pick her up. Maybe his birthday would shake out better than he'd thought it would.

"I live in an apartment right by Burke Airport, with a dock for my boat."

"Those apartments right on the water there?" Her eyes had widened.

He nodded.

"I know where I've heard your name before." She put her hand on her throat and tugged at the neck of his shirt. "You play for the Indians, don't you?"

He gave another nod. "Catcher."

Her breath caught and she looked like she was in pain. "Oh, Lord."

Usually this was the part where women gushed or flashed him. Instead of giggling or asking him how much money he made, Violet closed her eyes.

And kept them closed.

Damn, she was cute. Dylan reached for another bottle of water from his cooler. "Do you want some water?" He put the cold bottle against the skin of her cheek. "You look flushed."

She jerked back and opened her eyes. "I don't want any water."

"What do you want?" Dylan gave her a slow, lazy smile, and let his eyes linger over her lips. They looked so kissable, so smooth and shiny.

"I want you to push me back into the water and let me drown."

Dylan laughed. She had a quirky little sense of humor.

He liked that about her. So far, he'd have to say he liked a lot about her, and it had only been ten minutes since he'd fished her out of the water.

Just think what he could like in the next thirty.

Three

Violet didn't have a sense of humor. It was yet another thing that separated her from the masses and made her feel like a misfit. The first was that she didn't really like sex, and stood around puzzled a lot of times when her friends talked about it, their eyes rolling back in their heads.

If her eyes were rolling back, chances were she was having a seizure and 911 should be called.

She felt capable of a convulsion right now, because she, Violet Caruthers, kindergarten teacher and the epitome of the social wallflower, was trapped on a sailboat with a gorgeous professional baseball player.

It would have been smarter to die wearing the bikini.

"What do you do, Vi?"

No one called her Vi. It made her sound like a fifties film star, which wasn't a good fit. She wouldn't know sassy and sultry if it bit her on the butt.

She chanced a look at Dylan. She wasn't a rabid baseball fan, but she went to several games a season and caught a few on TV. She remembered seeing him at bat, noticing him precisely because he was so good-looking. It wasn't a stretch to picture him wearing a tight uniform and dropping down into that catcher squat, his face confident and serious.

This couldn't possibly be happening to her. "I'm a kindergarten teacher."

He untwisted the top of the water bottle and handed it to her. "Really? Now, that's a worthwhile profession. I bet you're great at it."

"I enjoy my job." She took a sip of the water because it seemed rude not to, and she was really hot. The sun was heating her skin from the inside out. Which didn't make sense, because five minutes ago she'd been shivering.

"I like my job, too." He studied the horizon.

"Then I guess we're both lucky."

The easy grin covered his face again. "Yeah, I guess so. Though I don't think luck has a whole lot to do with it. People make choices."

"That's true." She had made a choice to have a baby, without a husband, because she wanted a child that desperately. And she was practical enough to know that when you went on a date every three years, the probability of meeting Mr. Right was very small.

The sperm bank hadn't appealed to her because of the element of the unknown, but after this fiasco with Frank, she was starting to think that might be her only option.

She searched for something to say. "So, how long have you been with the Indians?"

"Three years. It's a good club." Dylan tipped his bottle back and forth, back and forth. "So how many kids are in your class? Do you have an apple with your name on it?"

Violet gave a nervous laugh. What a geek she must seem like to a pro athlete. "No apple. Lots of 'Best Teacher' mugs, though. And I have twenty students each year."

"How have you been spending your summer break?"

Conceiving a baby. "Relaxing. Reading. Working in my garden."

Which suddenly sounded very lame and tame.

Dylan tilted his head. "Sounds nice. Normal. Does Frank live with you?"

"No." Violet picked at the T-shirt and sighed. "If I can borrow your phone again, I'll call my friends and see if someone can come meet me at the dock." So she didn't have to spend one more second than was necessary with Dylan Diaz, catcher for the Cleveland Indians. Her company must be close to putting him in a coma.

He hesitated, but then handed the phone to her. "There's no hurry, you know."

Yes, there was.

In rapid succession, Violet got the voice mail for Kindra, Ashley, and Trish. Damn it. None of them were home, and she couldn't remember any of their cell phone numbers. She had those programmed into her own phone, which was sitting in her purse on Frank's fishing boat. She didn't know what she could possibly say in a message so she just hung up.

"No one home?" Dylan asked.

She shook her head. Her friends all had social lives, darn them. They should all be losers like her.

"No big deal. I can take you home."

Ye-ah. Like he had nothing better to do. Geez, how humiliating. "Oh, that's okay. I can call a taxi or take the bus or something." She had no idea how to take the bus from downtown to Westlake. Not a clue. But she'd rather walk than force a gorgeous millionaire to baby-sit her.

Dylan let go of the whatever sailors hold and moved towards her. "I'm not letting you take the bus home. First of all, my mother would fly up from Miami and beat the hell out of me. Second, I want to spend more time with you."

"Why?" she asked stupidly, thinking she must have flooded some brain cells during her soak in the lake. What he was saying didn't make sense.

"Because I want to get to know you better."

"Why?" To underscore how truly thrilling his life was compared to hers?

But he just picked at the paper label on his water bottle. "It's my birthday today, you know."

"It is?"

He nodded. "Twenty-seven today."

"Well, happy birthday, then. I'm so, so sorry I ruined your birthday by almost drowning." Could she be any more mortified? Maybe she could vomit on him while she was at it.

But Dylan laughed. "You weren't interrupting anything. I was just out sailing by myself."

Now that he mentioned it, he was alone. "Are you having a party later with your friends? I'll definitely take a cab then."

"No party. My family all called me this morning. That's the extent of the celebrating."

He didn't sound happy and that made Violet forget that he was a baseball player, that he was gorgeous, that she was a geek. She moved just a little closer to him. "Don't you like birthdays?"

"Sure. But I don't have anyone to spend it with this year. It's a little tough to make friends when you're on the road all the time."

"And then I landed in your lap." Literally. "Not exactly what you wished for, I'm sure."

He set his water down and locked eyes with her. He was smiling, a smile she didn't really understand. "Actually, I think you're the best thing that's happened to me today."

"That's not saying much for your day."

"I was having a very unexciting day until you floated along." Dylan touched the tip of her nose with his finger. "But I'm thinking you're a damn good birthday surprise."

"But . . ."

"I'm attracted to you, can't you tell?"

Violet was tempted to glance around the boat to make sure she hadn't missed a gorgeous blonde hiding behind a sail. "I hadn't noticed that, no."

His eyes narrowed, got darker. Hotter. "Do you find me at all attractive?"

She could only stare. Was he absolutely joking? Of course she did. A woman in her nineties with cataracts would find him attractive. She was so amazed, she didn't hesitate to answer. "Well, sure, but that doesn't matter."

"Why not?"

"Because . . ." Because it was like staring through the window at a two-thousand-dollar dress. You could want it, but it could never be yours. Maybe he did find her mildly attractive because she was sitting right in front of him and he liked women, in whatever form they took. Maybe he saw her as just another easy conquest, a little Friday night fun. A staid boring woman, easy to manipulate. And maybe she was all of those things.

Maybe he was drunk.

But somehow she didn't believe any of that was true. Dylan seemed, well, almost lonely. But none of that was important because she wasn't the kind of woman men sought out when they wanted company. "Because it just doesn't matter. So . . . your family is in Miami?"

That wolfish smile was still in place, but he leaned back from her, resting on his elbows. "Yep. Mom, Dad, three sisters, all married, and five nieces, two nephews last count."

"Do you have a house there?" One that hopefully he would be going to in, oh, an hour or so. So she would never have to see him again.

Not that she would. They'd dock this boat and she'd scurry away like the mouse that she was.

And the one chance for a little excitement in her life would be gone.

The thought made her sit up straighter. She had never *desired* excitement. She liked her life. She did. She was happy and well-adjusted. And come Monday, she was going to shop the sperm bank and have a child.

But wouldn't it be fun, just once, to think that she, Violet Caruthers, had been desired by a hottie?

Even if that hottie had baked his brains in the sun too long to want *her* when he could have half the women in the 216 area code.

Maybe he'd already had half the women in town and now he was moving to the bottom dregs. Maybe she shouldn't care why he was interested, but she should just enjoy it. Keep her head square on her shoulders and just take pleasure in his company, attention, flirtation.

"No, I stay with my parents when I'm down there. I got them a really nice six-bedroom house. And I have the apartment here, but the furniture came with the place. It's like living in a hotel. I was actually thinking I should buy my own place in Miami, but it always seems like such a waste for a single guy who's only there half the year."

He looked a little wistful when he spoke, and Violet realized the downside to his career. He must feel uprooted all the time, living on the road out of a suitcase. "Have you ever been married?"

Not that it was any of her damn business, but the sun must have baked her brains, too. She actually liked him. He seemed, well, normal. Needy. Like one of her students who just needed a hug. Of course, Dylan was also phenomenally gorgeous and wealthy, but she wouldn't think about that or she'd scare herself again.

"Nope. How about you, Vi? You look like the marrying kind." He winked.

That didn't sound like a compliment. "No, I've never been married. But Frank would get married if I wanted to." He would. He was a genius, after all. He knew a good deal when he saw one, and she was Frank's dream wife. She was quiet, did his laundry, didn't nag him about his friends or hobbies or the late hours he kept, and would never cheat on him. So they didn't burn up the bedroom together. Frank still got what he needed.

Violet sighed. She must be hopelessly romantic, because

she really just couldn't bring herself to commit to a lifetime with Frank or to a similar arrangement with another man.

Dylan sat back up and scoffed, all amusement gone from his face. "You wouldn't marry that guy, would you? He'd probably forget to pick you up for the wedding."

For some reason, she laughed. It shouldn't have been funny, yet it was. The image of herself standing in white satin outside her front door for two, three hours while Frank lost himself in some computer software was so heinous it was amusing. Frank would be up to his eyeballs in dirty ashtrays and empty soft drink cans, that strange gleam in his eye when he was working. He would never turn that obsessive focus onto her, and she would always be an afterthought.

Not that it mattered.

"I don't want to marry Frank. I never did. But he's a nice guy, decent company, and . . . I had something I wanted from him. I'm not as innocent as I sound here. In a way, I've been using Frank." Shameful, but true. She'd had her eye on the prize since the first time she'd had dinner with him.

"Well, that sounds devious. I'm seeing a whole new side of you, Vi. What were you using him for?"

The breeze ruffled her still wet hair, and she turned her face to catch the full effect of it. It felt a little like she'd fallen off the face of the earth. They couldn't see the shore, just a hazy line in the distance, and in the other direction was a vague promise of Canada somewhere beyond the horizon. The rock of the boat was soothing, the water calm, the sun warm as it made its way towards the west.

It felt like none of what was happening was real and that she could say anything. She could tell this stranger what she wasn't even willing to admit to her girlfriends. That she wasn't all good and sweet and considerate. Her actions with Frank had been manipulative, and falling into the water was really no more than she deserved. "Is there something you want in life so bad you can taste it? Have you ever felt that sort of desperate urgency?"

"I felt that way about baseball."

"So are you content, then? Have everything you want now?"

Violet turned in time to see his head moving slowly back and forth. "No, I'm good, but something is missing . . . and I can't figure out what it is. I feel restless. I feel like everyone I meet wants something from me."

"They probably do."

He gave a snort. "Thanks for the pep talk."

She felt her cheeks heat. "Well, it's probably true. You must be in demand."

"The problem is, people want to use me. No one wants *me*. That's why I don't date anymore. I can't trust that a woman wants me for me, as corny as that is."

Violet nodded. For all his money and fame, Dylan was lonely. Isolated. It almost made sense, then, why he would find her attractive. It had been a while since he'd dated, and she was not the aggressive, pursuing type. The discomfort she'd been feeling, the nervousness, dissipated. "And if you don't trust someone, there really can't be a relationship, can there?"

"Nope. I do have my game, which I love to play. But I can't help thinking that there are more important things in life. What do you want, Violet? Or do you already have it?"

Her want was definitely unfulfilled. It even hurt to say it out loud, so deeply did she want to be a mother. "The thing I want is a baby."

Dylan wasn't sure what he'd thought she was going to say, but she had looked so fervent that he'd been getting a little nervous. But hell, a baby? That seemed damn innocent after some of the wild scenarios that had run through his head.

"So . . . you wanted to have a baby with Frank?" Dylan couldn't stop his eyes from roaming over her body. She had her feet tucked under her legs and the shirt pulled down to her knees, but he knew there were some luscious curves under there. He could picture her pregnant, no problemo, and the thought had him uncomfortable in his shorts again.

He'd never looked at a pregnant woman and felt the urge to do her, but it was running through his mind with Violet. Apparently he wanted to do her any old way he could—front, back, clothes, naked, standing up, lying down, right here on this boat. He really was a sick bastard. She was talking about serious stuff, and he was thinking up ways to get her out of that T-shirt. He almost expected his mother's hand to pop out of thin air and cuff the back of his head.

But he liked the way Violet spoke, and the way she looked at him. Like he was . . . sweet. It had been high school since a girl had just looked at him and liked him.

"I wanted Frank to get me pregnant. Then leave, while I raised the child by myself."

"Whoa." He squinted a little as the sun broke through the clouds and hit him in the eyes. "So, did Frank know about this? He was cool with it?" Personally, he couldn't imagine getting a woman pregnant and walking away. But then again, if a woman he cared about, who would make a great mother, asked him for a little, uh, donation, would he be able to say no?

The whole idea of leaving a woman to raise a child alone just didn't seem right to him, even if that's what she wanted. And the only women he was close to were his sisters anyway, and he'd share a lot with them—money, a kidney—but he wasn't going to go there with sperm. Of course, if they had a surrogate mother and wanted to use his DNA to keep it in the family . . . What the hell was he thinking? His sisters had seven kids between them. Fertility had not been an issue up to this point.

"I was going to talk to Frank about it tonight, but his friends came along—uninvited."

Was that relief he felt? "Why not a sperm bank? It could get messy if Frank changed his mind after the fact."

She smiled. "He wouldn't change his mind. Trust me, he has nothing against children but he has no desire to raise any.

And I didn't want a sperm bank because I was afraid that it was risky. You don't really know what you're getting." Then she shrugged. "But while I was out there treading water, it occurred to me that when you adopt a child, you usually don't know a whole lot of anything, and I haven't heard any adoptive parents complain. And sometimes, even when a couple is married, they don't really know everything about the other person. A reputable sperm bank is quite safe. They screen sociopaths and other mental impairments, so I won't be getting a serial killer's sperm. It will be fine, and I'll finally get what I want—a baby."

It all seemed logical to Dylan. But something about it still bothered him. This woman having a total stranger's baby rubbed him wrong. "How old are you? How do you know you won't get married in a few years?"

"I'm twenty-eight. If I got pregnant today I'd be twenty-nine when the baby is born. I know that's not old at all, but what if I have fertility problems? A miscarriage? What if I want a second child? I don't want to wait too long and find out it's too late. I want to be a mother." She looked at him, serious and soft-spoken. "More than anything."

"Well . . ." Christ, what was he supposed to say? "Good luck." Brilliant, Diaz, just brilliant.

Violet gave a small laugh, one that did all kinds of things to his guts. He felt like he did after he ran hard laps on a really hot day—sort of light-headed and sick to his stomach.

Because for a single, stupid second there, he had thought about offering himself in place of the anonymous test tube turkey baster daddy.

Which was insane.

God, he'd lost his mind.

He wanted to have sex with her, not a child.

Good thing he'd kept his mouth zipped. And to prevent further possibility of blurting dumb-ass things out loud, maybe he should distract himself.

By kissing her.

Four

Dylan's mouth was close enough to feel Violet's hot breath when her hand rammed into his nose and pushed him back.

"Ow," he said, thinking that was an all-time first. He'd never once had a woman ram her palm up his nostrils. He wrinkled his damaged nose, sniffled a little, irritated with the interruption.

"Sorry," she said. "But what do you think you're doing?"

He'd thought it was obvious. "I was going to kiss you. And I'd like to try again if you promise not to hit me."

"I don't want you to kiss me."

Violet looked serious. She didn't look like this was a really funny joke and she'd start laughing any second now.

Dylan wanted to whimper. It had been a whole year, and he'd been fine, damn it, just hanging in there, and now he wanted her so badly he was itching in his own skin, and she was saying no.

But he had to ask. "Why not?" Why exactly the hell not? He was decent-looking. He made a lot of money. He just wanted a kiss. Just a very small one. Maybe with a little tongue tossed in. And a grope over her unrestricted breasts.

That was it, though. He could stop there.

"Because you probably make out with women every

weekend. You've probably had sex with hundreds of women, and trust me, after all of that, I'm going to disappoint you."

Hundreds. Wow. He'd made a decent impression on her after all.

But it wasn't true.

"I have not slept with hundreds of women. Not even twenty." He wasn't going to get any more specific than that. If he said nineteen, she'd think he was a pig. If he said two, she'd think he was a loser. *Just keep it vague.* "And I told you it's been a year since I've dated anyone."

"That doesn't mean it's been a whole year since you kissed a woman. Or had sex, for that matter."

"Yes, it does, actually."

The shock that crossed her face made him laugh, even as he found himself struggling with how much to tell her. But there was something about Violet, about the way she was so different, the way she didn't want anything from him. The way she looked at him, like she saw the real man and not just the jersey.

Her glasses had slipped again, so he pushed them up with the tip of his index finger. "You look surprised. But the thing is, I told you people use me . . . and well, that can leave you feeling empty."

Dylan dropped his hand. "There was a woman about a year ago that I met in a club. I was living it up, you know, partying most nights because I thought if things were loud enough, busy enough, maybe I wouldn't notice that I wasn't having as great of a time as I thought I would be at this point in my life. Like I said, I love playing ball, but I was starting to feel like there had to be more than dropping two hundred bucks in a night on drinks for people who didn't give a shit about me. Anyway, so this girl . . . I took her home, because she was persistent."

The memory made him squirm. "She just kind of led me into sex and I let her. And it was so . . . nothing. You know what I mean? It was just two people screwing and I realized that's not what I want. That's not who I am. She wanted a reason to brag to her friends and I gave it to her, and that's all it was. Bodies slapping. The next day, I was just disgusted with myself."

He couldn't believe he was telling her about that night, about that woman whose name he couldn't even remember. But Violet just nodded, and her small, cool hand lay over his.

"I know exactly what you mean, I'm sorry to say. Sex should not be about what you can get from it and then walk away from. I was using Frank the way that woman was using you, and I'm ashamed of myself."

Somehow he didn't think it was the same thing at all. "Yeah, but you were dating Frank. And you want to have a baby. That's a little more noble than wanting bragging rights."

"The end doesn't always justify the means. It was selfish of me."

"I can't imagine that you're the least bit selfish, Vi."

"I try to be a good person, a good friend, a great teacher. But we all make mistakes."

He was probably about to do just that. But he couldn't resist. "Do me a favor, then."

"What's that?"

She nibbled on her bottom lip and Dylan's thoughts shifted below the belt.

"Give me a birthday kiss."

Oh, geez, he was on that again.

And she wasn't sure she could say no this time. She fiddled with her hair and watched him. "You really want one?"

"Yes. Really, really."

"And it's been a year since you've . . . done that?"

"An entire year. Don't you feel bad for me?"

Well . . . if it had been that long, Dylan probably wouldn't notice that she wasn't the most exciting or experienced kisser ever created. She did sort of owe him a thank you for fishing her out of the water. And she did really want to kiss him.

She wanted to know what it would feel like to have those muscular arms around her. To touch that rock solid chest and to see if a man like Dylan could teach her how to get her eyes to roll back in her head.

"I feel terribly bad for you. I've crashed your birthday and you rescued me, gave me your shirt, your water. I guess the least I could do is let you kiss me."

"The very least," he agreed. "But I don't want you to let me kiss you. I want you to kiss me."

"Oh. Well." She wasn't quite sure she knew how to be the aggressor, but maybe it was time to try. Violet took a deep breath and scooted next to Dylan. If her heart didn't explode in her chest, she could do this.

He bent over, just a little.

Violet could smell him, a masculine blend of deodorant and sweat from the sun beating down on his bare chest. His hair was short, his eyebrows thick, his chin showing a few whiskers this close up. His shoulders were broad, his tattoo detailed and extravagant, making her want to wince at the pain he must have gone through to get it.

Leaning, leaning, she stuck her lips on his, missing the center a little but coming close enough to make it work.

He didn't really move his mouth because she didn't give him time. She just approached, pressed, pulled back.

It was a wimpy kiss, a geeky kiss. The kiss of a woman who hasn't got a single clue how to please a man.

No wonder Frank didn't notice she was missing for fifteen minutes.

She could be kissing a man and he could forget her existence. Doze off for a minute or two.

Dylan took her hand, pulled her closer when she would have darted to the opposite side of the boat. "That's one."

Violet stopped trying to wiggle away from him. "One what?"

"One kiss. I get one for each year. I'm twenty-seven, plus one to grow on, so you owe me twenty-seven more."

He looked serious, but he was cracked if he thought she was going to repeat that humiliation two dozen more times. "That's for pinches, not kisses."

"Not in Puerto Rico."

Having worked with kindergartners for five years, Violet knew a fib when she heard one. This one fell in the same category as "I didn't get a cookie" and "He pushed me first."

"Really?"

"Really." He gave her a smile that was meant to be innocent and instead was just sinfully sexy.

And she decided that if he wanted another one, maybe the first hadn't been as pathetic as she'd thought. Maybe she could even improve on it.

"All right."

"Really?"

He looked so pleased, she almost laughed. "Really."

This time, she let her eyes drift half closed as she tilted her head and moved in. She landed in just the right spot and put more pressure into it. His lips were warm, firm, and she found herself relaxing just a little, enjoying it just a bit.

"That's two." Dylan's fingers went into her hair and he shifted his body, bringing him closer to her.

Somehow she'd wound up between his thighs, and it wasn't difficult to reach out and kiss him yet again, opening her mouth, sighing when he kissed her back and the moment stretched on and on. Their lips moved together and Violet gave in to the urge to rest her hands on his chest.

Desire was stirring, kicking up like a pile of leaves hit with a strong wind. She wasn't a sexual person, she knew that, accepted that, but this feeling was familiar. This new, mild, momentary arousal.

It would fade if they went any further, just like it always did. But for the moment, it felt promising and pleasurable, Dylan's hands shifting lower.

"That's three," he said when he broke the kiss to breathe.

"I think that was more like seven or eight." Their mouths had been together for more than a minute, with lots of shifting and turning and pressing.

"No, sorry. From point of contact to final pull back, it only counts as one. It's in the rule book."

"The Puerto Rican rule book?" she asked wryly.

Dylan laughed and pulled her up onto his thigh. Her wet bikini bottoms pressed down into his swim trunks. "Yes. Now come here and give me number four."

Violet went in to this kiss eager, hungry, and felt a kick of heat between her legs when Dylan's tongue caressed along her mouth. She shuddered as he sucked her lip between his and then gave a light nip. That twinge of want flared up into a throb, and she gave a gasp.

Okay, no one had ever bitten her before. It felt a little wild, a little out of control, a little not-what-nice-girls-do. "Do that again," she said when he panted in front of her, but didn't touch her.

"Kiss you? I never actually did. We're still on number four." He leaned over and around her, reaching for something.

Violet's butt wobbled on his thigh and she grabbed his shoulder for support. "What are you doing?"

"Adjusting the sail. We're about three feet from hitting the break wall."

Violet snapped her head up and took in their surroundings. They were bearing down on a stone wall.

And there were at least a half dozen people milling around the marina in clear view.

"Oh, my gosh."

"Don't worry, we won't hit the wall."

That was the least of Violet's concerns. "People are watching us. People *saw* us."

She didn't even like the man she was kissing to be aware they were kissing. She sure in heck didn't want an audience of strangers.

"That's why we're going to dock the boat and go on up to my place."

"We are?" The apartment complex loomed behind the marina, an imposing structure, once a warehouse, now converted into luxury suites.

"Yep. I want to have my cake. And eat it, too."

Five

Dylan hustled Violet down the dock and up the wooden stairs to the elevator. He said a prayer for it to hurry as he pressed the button, then wondered if it was morally wrong to pray for speed in getting a woman naked.

Probably.

But he did it anyway.

"This is a nice building," Violet said, standing very close to him, arms crossed over her chest.

"It's not bad. It's got a good view and it's quiet. It's kind of sterile, though. No personal touches." He took her hand and pulled her into the elevator.

Violet dragged her bare feet a little. "Are you sure you want to do this? Maybe you should just take me home."

Willingly take a strike-out? No way. "Do you have a key to get into your apartment?"

"No. It's in my purse. My friend Trish has the spare."

"And Trish didn't answer her phone?"

Violet shook her head, her lips pursing. "No."

"Then have dinner with me. Relax. Enjoy the night."

The front of his T-shirt had dried on her, but her hair was still damp, curling at the tips and fuzzing on top. She ran her fingers over the back of it, and looked over his shoulder, her cheeks pink. "Just so you understand, I'm not having sex with you."

Way to burst his birthday bubble. He had a tree trunk size boner, she was half naked and wet already, and she was shooting him down?

But he wasn't going to rush her. She had just dumped her boyfriend, after all.

"Okay, then. We can just have dinner and fool around. We'll have sex on our second date. Wednesday, when I get back from New York." With a grin, he rubbed the small of her back with his thumb and tried to think pure thoughts.

"This wasn't a date. This was an accident, where I was dumb enough to fall in the water and you were nice enough to pull me out."

"So why did you kiss me, then?"

"Because you wanted me to." She cleared her throat and pushed her glasses up with a frown.

"Then you can have sex with me, because I want that, too." He grinned down at her, knowing she was embarrassed, wanting to put her at ease.

Wanting her, plain and simple. But he would wait. As long as it took.

"Uh . . ."

He had her trapped by her words, and she knew it. She'd wanted those kisses just as much as he had.

"But I don't like sex."

The elevator door opened right as she spoke, and they turned to find his neighbor, Mrs. Martin, standing there with her terrier. "You're not the only one, sweetie. Most women don't like sex. They just fake it for the man's benefit."

Violet sighed.

Dylan knew he should just walk on by. But he couldn't stop himself. He was trying to get laid here and Mrs. Martin wasn't helping. So he said, "No woman has ever faked it with me."

It was supposed to shut her up, but Mrs. Martin stopped

and stared at him in amazement as they exited the elevator, and she got on. "Oh, Dylan, honey, baby. I would guess *every* woman has faked it with you at one point or another. Along with a lot of other things. They don't date a baseball player for his sexual skill or his conversation."

The door rolled shut and Dylan just stood there. The old broad had kneed him in the nuts with that one.

Violet touched his arm. "That was cruel."

"But probably true."

"Of course it's not true. There's a lot to like about you. Much more than money or a baseball uniform. You're funny, you're considerate, you care about your family." She smiled, while her hand patted his forearm in a gesture that was strangely comforting. "And lots of women like sex, so I'm sure they weren't faking with you. My friends all seem to really like it. I'm the weird one who can just take it or leave it, and I didn't want you to be disappointed. And I couldn't fake it if my life depended on it. I can't . . . make noises."

She finished that startling pronouncement with a blush.

He knew then what he wanted to do. How he wanted to be unselfish, completely generous in the way she seemed to think him capable of. How for once in his life he wanted to do something that really mattered, to give back a little something for all the many blessings he had in his life.

He opened his apartment door, stepped in with her, closed it. And touched her cheek. "There's a lot to like about you, too. Let me give you what you want, Vi. Let me give you a baby."

"What?" All the pink flush leeched from her cheeks.

Dylan rushed on, making his case. "My family is very fertile. No history of heart disease, diabetes, or cancer, and while we don't fall in the genius range, we're all average intelligence. Reasonably good-looking if you like dark hair and dark eyes. Athletic. All of my sisters can sing and my mom can cook." Maybe he wasn't what she was looking for in a donor, but he had to make the offer. She was an amazing woman, and maybe he had lost his goddamn mind, but this was right. It was just deep down in his gut right.

She'd make a beautiful mother and he wanted to make her happy.

Violet looked very serious, her eyes wide behind the lenses of her glasses. "You realize what you're offering? That my child would be your child? But that I wouldn't want any money or any contact with you?"

Hell, he knew she didn't want money. In five minutes, he had figured out that wasn't what Violet was about. She didn't work that way. "I know that. And I also know you'll be a wonderful mother. You've got that mom vibe through and through. A kid would be lucky to have you for a mom."

And why the hell had he brought this up in the hallway? Jesus, could he learn a little tact?

Violet sniffled. He cupped her cheek. "I haven't done a lot of great things in my life. I haven't been a bad person, but I've had it easy. I've been into my own happiness. Maybe it sounds crazy, maybe it's me feeling like a loser on my birthday, but I want to give you this, if you'll let me. If my sperm is good enough for you."

She gave a watery laugh. "It's more than good enough." And she burst into tears.

Oh shit. "I'm sorry, I'm sorry . . . what's the matter?" Crying was no good. He always equated crying with trouble. His sisters bawled and he got yelled at for making them cry. He hadn't meant to make Violet cry. Dylan hauled her down the hall into his living room. "I didn't mean to upset you."

He pushed her down onto the couch and looked around the room. There had to be tissues around here somewhere. Maybe in the bathroom. He sprinted down the hall to the half bath and skidded to a halt in front of the sink. There was a box of tissues plunked down on the counter and he knew he owed the maid a thank-you. Violet's sobbing was getting louder by the second.

Wine. Maybe some wine would help, too. He grabbed a

bottle on the way past the wine rack and set it on the coffee table. She took the tissue he gave her and wiped her eyes with it.

"I'm sorry. I'm not upset . . . honestly."

Could have fooled him.

"I'm just . . . just really touched . . . that you would do this for me." She choked out her words and Dylan's heart clenched. "It's the nicest thing anyone has ever offered to do for me."

Now he just felt ridiculous. Overexposed. Dylan stood up. "It's not that big of a deal." He fished around in a kitchen drawer for a corkscrew. Then he pulled two glasses down out of the cabinet. He really wanted a beer or a shot of tequila, but he'd settle for the wine. Alcohol in any form was better than none at all right at the moment.

Had he just actually offered to father Violet's baby? And was he really starting to think there might be something to that whole love at first sight crap?

He turned, the glasses in his hand, and stopped cold, wine sloshing over the rims and onto his arm. Violet was just beautiful. She had taken off her glasses and was sitting with her legs tucked under her, hair flowing down over her chest covered in his white T-shirt. Tears streaked her pale cheeks and her green eyes glistened with moisture.

Maybe he did believe in that love at first sight crap.

And he really did want to give her a baby. Like, if he did one important thing in his life, this was it.

"It is a big deal," she said. "And I don't know how to say thank you. Or if I should even accept."

Dylan handed her a wineglass, and drained the other one. "What, you'll take Forgetful Frank's sperm, but not mine?" And he had thought Mrs. Martin had taken a pot shot.

"Well . . ." She sipped the wine. "I'm not sure I really would have. And it was different. I was trying to talk Frank into it. I might have felt guilty if he had offered. Not that that makes any sense."

"You don't have to feel guilty. I'm a big boy. I know what

I'm doing. I want to do this." She was going to use his sperm, damn it, or no one's at all.

Violet stared at him, squinting a little without her glasses. Then she took his hand and squeezed. Moved in a little closer. Brought her mouth very, very close to his.

"Then I'm just going to say thank you, Dylan Diaz. This means the world to me."

"You're welcome." He had a lump in his throat. A big-ass kneecap-size lump. Maybe he was hungry. "Should we order some dinner? And I can throw your bathing suit in the dryer." Since he was hoping to get her out of her clothes immediately anyway.

"In a minute." Violet pressed her hands to his chest, her breasts brushing along his arm. "First I'm going to wish you a very happy birthday," she whispered. "And finish giving you your birthday kisses."

Maybe she was merely acting out of gratitude, but Dylan couldn't bring himself to give a shit. "Sounds good to me."

The words were barely out of his mouth before Violet covered him with her lips, her movements not exactly smooth, but enthusiastic. Mmm, she was doing a little tongue thing, flicking it back and forth.

Then she bit him.

Holy crap, he felt the force of that through every inch of his horny body. His cock jerked in his bathing suit and he gave a moan of approval. Her tongue tentatively dipped into his mouth and Dylan lowered his hands, further, further until he was cupping her ass in the still damp bikini.

She had an incredible body, which brushed against him soft and lush, sparking desperate lust in him with every touch. Her breathing quickened. His hands gripped harder, bumping her against his thigh. Her lips were sweet from the wine and her skin cool, and he was hotter than hell.

After a long seductive minute, she broke the kiss off, much to his profound disappointment.

Dylan sucked in a breath and ran his thumb over her ass.

"That was nice, baby, real nice. And that was number four, remember. You've got to go all the way to twenty-eight."

She licked her lips. "That could take a while."

Amen to that.

"Uh-huh. No rush. We've got all night." And he was going to just ignore that bullshit about her not liking sex. She sure in the hell reacted to him like she enjoyed sex. And he'd be willing to bet his left nut Frank sucked in the sack.

They might need some practice before they tried the whole conception thing. A couple of weeks to learn each other's bodies before they went for the gold. Though the idea of dragging it out for months and months held some appeal, Dylan thought better of it. He didn't want her to be worrying the whole time. Better to hit a home run right off the first pitch.

"Are you busy tomorrow?" she asked, moving away from him to set her neatly folded glasses down on the coffee table.

"I have a plane to catch in the afternoon. Four-game series against the Yankees. But I'm free in the morning." They could stay up all night practicing their conception technique, then sleep in late.

"I'm asking because, well, I'm actually ovulating right now." Violet's back was to him, but he could practically hear her blush. "So I thought, maybe . . ."

Hot damn. That was all he needed to hear.

Dylan shucked his shorts off and patted his lap. "Let's go then."

Six

Violet turned around and nearly fainted. Dear God in heaven, he was *naked*.

"What are you doing?" she shrieked, clamping her eyes shut. The sight was so distracting, she couldn't think. "Why aren't you wearing any clothes?"

"It kind of works better that way." He sounded amused. "Now come over here."

Violet opened one eye. Holy cow. She'd never seen a man that gorgeous in person before. Her experience with male nudity was limited to skinny, quiet types, and the naked hottie e-mails Trish sent her. Dylan qualified as a naked hottie. He was hard and big. Everywhere.

"What works better that way?" And he was crazy if he thought she was getting anywhere near him. That thing looked like a lethal weapon.

Switching eyes, she spotted another tattoo on his hip, but couldn't tell what it was without her glasses. There was suddenly spittle in the corner of her mouth. Oh, shoot, she was drooling.

And she didn't think it was lake water that had her bottom damp.

"Making a baby. It's easier without clothes on. So let's

take yours off, too." He stood up and took a step towards her.

Violet opened both eyes in shock. "You mean make a baby by having *sex*?" Where the heck had he gotten that idea from?

He stopped walking. "Is there another way?"

"Yeah! I was thinking we could stop by my fertility doctor's office tomorrow and they could withdraw a sample from you." Violet chanced a glance at his impressive penis. Artificial insemination was much simpler, though maybe not as interesting.

"Withdraw a sample?" Dylan's jaw dropped. As did something else. "In the doctor's office? How do they do that?"

"I think they sort of . . . electrically stimulate you and it comes out." *Come* was probably a bad choice of words, but she didn't think he heard anything past electrical.

Dylan stuck his hands on his head and rubbed his hair. "What? I don't think so! Jesus, that sounds like torture."

"It's modern science. It's the civilized way to handle this so there aren't any entanglements. I told you I don't like sex."

"But we were making out! You liked that, didn't you?" Now his hands were on his hips, feet apart, emphasizing just how broad he was. His catcher's thighs were like steel beams and she was flustered, aroused, confused.

"Well, yeah, but . . ."

"But what? Listen, if we're going to make a baby, we're going to do this the way nature intended. I am not getting my dick zapped."

That suddenly struck Violet as funny. She clamped her hand over her mouth, but a giggle came out. If it were her, she guessed she wouldn't want to get electrically jolted either.

"That's not funny. It's a horror film, Vi. What if they move it a little too far in one direction or the other? They could do some serious damage. No, I'm sorry." He shook his head. "I really want to do this for you, but no can do on the clinic, *senorita*."

She laughed louder.

"Stop laughing." But he was already grinning. "Well, this is a hell of a misunderstanding, isn't it?"

Violet rubbed her fingers over her lips and smiled back. "I can't believe you're standing there naked."

"Hey, never say I didn't rise to the occasion."

"That you did."

Dylan's apartment was filled with lots of low, modular furniture in contemporary black, with sage green sofas. Violet skirted a cube end table and moved towards him. "I'm sorry," she said, trying to remember where she'd set her glasses down. Things were a touch fuzzy, and since he was naked, she'd prefer total clarity. "It's my fault."

"No, it's not. It was just a misunderstanding."

He was standing in front of the floor-to-ceiling window that boasted a view of the lake. Violet glanced left and right out the window. "Can't people see you standing there naked?"

"What people? There's nothing but water down there."

"People on boats." Violet tried to move away from the window, but Dylan took her arm and stopped her.

"Who cares?"

He was really close to her and really naked. Violet took a deep breath and concentrated on his face. "Obviously not you. But I would."

"So we'll move into the bedroom before we get you naked." He kissed her neck, sliding his tongue up towards her ear.

"Dylan . . ." Violet shivered. That felt awfully good. She was torn between wanting to fling herself on the bed and let Dylan get her pregnant in the traditional, sweaty, skin-on-skin way, and fear that when it came to the big moment, she wouldn't enjoy herself.

It would mortify her to be naked with Dylan Diaz, accepting such an enormous gift from him, and be unable to please him. Or herself.

"Do you really hate sex, Vi? Did someone hurt you? Were

you forced or something?" His hands were gentle on her back, his voice soft in her ear.

"No! Not at all. And I don't hate it. It's more like I'm just there for the ride."

He chuckled softly. "Funny choice of words."

She couldn't bring herself to laugh. "I don't want to ruin it. I don't want to take this understanding between us and ruin it."

"Okay." He put his forehead on hers. "Here's what we'll do. We'll order some dinner from the marina restaurant. We'll drink some more wine. We'll talk. Take a shower to warm you up and get that lake water off you. And whatever feels right, we'll do. If it doesn't, we won't."

"Okay." Violet kissed Dylan, cupping his cheeks with her hands. He was a most amazing man, she had to say. "Thank you."

"But I'm not putting my clothes back on."

She reared back, having forgotten that he was naked.

"Just kidding." He grinned. "Why don't you hop in the shower while I order something to eat?"

"Great. I like anything without mushrooms." Violet took off in the direction he pointed and closed the bathroom door behind her.

With trembling hands, she turned on the shower. His bathroom was large, with chrome fixtures and a black and white checked tile floor. Big, white, fluffy towels were stacked on three shelves next to the shower. Violet grabbed one and shook it open, then stripped off the T-shirt and bikini bottoms.

Wrapping the towel around her, she checked the water temperature and adjusted it. There was shampoo and shower gel already in the shower. Two minutes later she was under the stream of hot water, sighing and rolling her shoulders. It felt good to be warm, good to get her fuzzy, half damp hair off her face, good to wash the slimy sensation of lake water off her skin.

The bathroom door opened. Violet jumped, but then reassured herself that there was a shower curtain in faux gray suede, not a clear shower door.

"I brought you something to wear," Dylan called.

"Thank you."

"I ordered crab legs and salads. Sound good?"

"Great." Surely he would leave, any second now. She felt just a touch vulnerable.

"What? I can't hear you with the shower on."

Violet pulled the top of the curtain back so she could stick just her face out. Dylan was leaning on the counter, steam rising around him. He had what looked like a hand towel wrapped around his middle. It covered all of about three inches of him, but at least his you-know-what was out of view.

"I said, that's great."

"Oh, okay." He moved towards her so fast, she didn't have time to react.

He was kissing her. Oh, good grief, he was kissing her, with his hands in her wet hair and tongue plunging into her mouth.

She was naked, hot water sluicing down over her backside, her breasts brushing against the shower curtain, and he was kissing her. Everything in her felt hot and tight, moist, a burn stoking in her inner thighs.

Violet sighed when Dylan pulled back. She wanted to be a wild woman. She wanted to just fling back the curtain and leap on him in a soapy, slippery, wet maneuver. But she didn't have the guts, the nerve, to do it. And if she did it, she wouldn't know what to do once she made the leap.

Instead she ducked back into the shower. The bathroom door closed as Dylan left the room, and Violet turned to the little shelf in the shower containing products. There was a disposable razor there. She picked it up and flicked off the lid. She had noticed a row of stubble on her right leg that she had missed. If she did wind up sleeping with Dylan, she didn't want to be hairy on top of stilted and insecure.

She stuck her leg up on the interior edge of the shower and squirted shower gel on it. The position challenged her balance and she wobbled a bit, grabbing wildly at the curtain. "Darn it!"

Stabilized again, she picked up the razor and bent over.

Dylan turned from shutting the bathroom closet and pondered how badly it would frighten Violet if he just stepped into the shower with her. He was in pain, man. Suffering. Agony.

There was a wet, sexy woman three feet away from him. Who wanted him to get her pregnant, yet at the same time didn't want to have sex with him. It made no sense. It was pure torture.

He was sure that he was going to die before the night was over. Might as well call up the last rites and stick on his headstone that he died from unfulfilled lust. His mother would be mortified.

Violet said something from the shower.

"What, Vi?"

The curtain rattled and it sounded like she slammed into the wall. Concerned, Dylan called out again. "Vi?"

She didn't answer him, and he pulled back the curtain, afraid she'd wiped out in his shower and conked her head. She'd had a hell of a day and hadn't eaten and it was possible . . .

Holy shit.

Violet wasn't injured. She had her leg straight out, propped on the bathtub lip, her tight ass sticking up, her breasts falling forward. Her hair hung in thick, dark ropes down her back, and her flesh was pink everywhere from the hot water bouncing all over her.

Dylan almost swallowed his tongue. Instead he must have

made a sound, maybe a gurgling from all the excess saliva, because Violet turned, an orange razor in her hand.

"Dylan!" she said, and put her free hand over her breasts. Like that covered anything.

He was having none of that modesty bullshit. Ripping the towel from his waist, he stepped into the shower behind her, preventing her from leaping away. If it made her nervous to look at him, he'd just stay behind her.

But he was going to touch her.

Violet stood up, and Dylan placed both of his hands on her waist and pulled her back until she was fitted against him, his cock nestled in the smooth slit between her cheeks.

"What are you doing?" she asked breathlessly.

"Joining you in the shower to help you wash yourself. To conserve water. Save on soap. Get my jollies. Take your pick."

Dylan reached up and cupped Violet's full breasts. They both groaned. Her nipples were tight little pebbles when he brushed his fingers across them, and she sucked her breath in hard when he gave a little tweak to each.

She felt gloriously curvy, soft yet firm, her hair clinging to his chest, and her head turning back towards him. Her lips were open, sighs tripping out, and he kissed the corner of her mouth.

"You feel so damn good, Vi. All woman."

"I always thought I had a stripper's body," she said, her little backside wiggling against him like she wanted something. "Which is a total waste on me, since I don't know how to use it."

With a laugh, he slid the palm of his hand over the flatness of her stomach and parted her wet curls. "I don't think it's wasted on you at all. God knows it's making me happy right now. I'm going to go to hell for all the things I want to do with you."

Playing with her curls, he moved his hand around and

around, skirting her clitoris and tugging on the springy hairs, spreading her apart, then letting her fall closed again. He kissed her shoulder, licking her dewy flesh from side to side. Her back started to bow, and her breathing changed from slow and deep to rapid and shallow. He moved over her again and again, never really touching, never really leaving, teasing and plucking them both into arousal.

"I . . ." she gasped.

"Hmm? You what, sweetie?" Dylan stroked his cock between her tight thighs, just once, then twice, clenching his teeth down on the urgent need to thrust and take. He wanted her so fucking bad, but he wanted to draw it out, soak them both in pleasure and wring every last drop out.

When he tapped her clitoris, she shuddered. "I want . . ."

"What, baby? Tell me what you want." Dylan dipped his tongue into her ear, moved it in and out while he cupped her mound with his immobile hand. She jerked forward against his hand.

"I want you to touch me."

"Inside, you mean?" Dylan whispered in a raw, low voice, the palm of his left hand brushing back and forth over her nipple, his right hand still holding her, index finger flicking over her clit.

"Yes. Inside."

He could barely hear her, but the quiet words, the desperate need nearly did him in. He throbbed against her, wanting to give Violet the passion she had never felt before, wanting her to understand how it could be, wanting to remember himself that sex could be intimate, personal, a gift between two people who cared about each other.

"Whatever you want, beautiful." And he moved his finger down between her folds and inside her with a deep push of his middle finger.

Shaking the shower water off his face, he leaned over her shoulder to watch his hand covering her, his finger pull all the way out of her, then plunge deep inside her body again.

"Oh, yeah, Vi, that's perfect." She was creamy wet, swollen, tight around his finger. When he wiggled his finger forward, stroking like he was dipping into frosting, she jerked away with a moan.

Their feet squeaked in the wet tub as they readjusted. "Don't get too far away from me," he teased.

She shook her head, chin tilted up, eyes half closed. "No, no, I don't want to stop you. This feels . . ."

Dylan added a second finger to the first and her words dissolved into a gasp. She was holding the wall with both hands, leaning farther and farther forward, her ass bumping into his cock as she started to move with his thrusts.

"That's it, baby. Damn, that's sexy."

He plucked at her nipple as she squirmed, little mewling sounds leaving her mouth at regular intervals. Dylan was sweating, water racing down his taut body, steam rising between them, and he thought without a little self-control he could come just like this, resting along her backside. She was racing forward, and he was pushing her to the finish line.

Bracing his feet as far apart as the bathtub would permit, he let go of her breast, pulled his fingers completely out of her.

She made a sound of distress, head snapping up.

Dylan slipped his thumb down her clitoris, then twisted right inside her.

Violet came with a loud agonized cry, her fingers clutching at the smooth tile wall, her body shuddering around his thumb.

He stroked in complete triumph, reveling in the abandon of her cry, the tightness of her body, the length of her orgasm, which went on and on.

Dylan kissed the back of her neck as Violet quieted down, her back straightening.

"Oh my," she said.

And she had said she didn't make noise.

Hah. She just hadn't met him yet.

"There's more where that came from." Dylan turned the water off and stepped back, then out of the shower. Violet wobbled a little, so he grabbed her waist and lifted her out of the tub.

Limp, she fell against him, her breasts colliding with his chest. Oh, man they felt even better this way. Dylan couldn't wait to get his mouth on one of those.

He grabbed a towel from the rack and lifted her up, hands under her butt. "I'll dry you off on the bed."

"Dry me off?" she whispered. "I can do that myself. But, well, if you *really* want to."

Dylan dropped her on the bed flat on her back. "I really want to."

Violet clamped her thighs closed, crossed her ankles, and stuck her hands over her chest. She fiddled with the ends of her hair and looked thoroughly aroused, yet completely embarrassed.

Frank the Fuck-up probably only did it in the dark.

"Shouldn't you close the blinds?" she asked, darting a nervous look at the window.

Dylan didn't see anything but the lake, and a couple of aggressive seagulls swooping back and forth. He figured the birds didn't care if she was naked or not, but he wasn't going to argue and delay his pleasure.

He ripped the vertical blinds closed with his bare hands instead of using the cord.

The doorbell rang as Violet unfolded the towel and spread it over the front of her.

"Damn, that's the food." Dylan stripped the towel right off of Violet's body.

"Hey!" she protested.

"I've got to answer the door." He tied it around his waist. "You look better naked anyway."

She thunked a pillow down over her nakedness. "You're going to answer the door in a towel?"

"Yep." He jogged to the door, almost losing the towel at one point. He was going to get rid of the delivery person, throw the food in the kitchen, then get back to his real dinner.

Violet.

Seven

Eyes closed, Violet clutched the thick down pillow to her crotch, listening to the sounds of Dylan chatting with the deliveryman.

He had given her an orgasm. In the shower.

She was shocked down to the tips of her water-shriveled toes.

It had felt so *good*. Easy. She had made sounds, for crying out loud. At one point she had been sure her back was going to snap from straining towards him.

Now she felt a touch embarrassed, a bit sleepy, and a whole lot satisfied. She could go for months on this high.

She was positive she could just slip under his navy duvet and fall asleep. But Dylan expected more. Turnabout was fair play. She owed it to him to let him finish, after the way he had yanked more pleasure out of her in five minutes than Frank had in four months.

So she was mentally prepared to give it to him when he came back into the bedroom, chewing, a cherry tomato in his hand.

"Tomato?" He held it out to her as he tossed the towel to the floor and climbed onto the bed.

"No tha—" Her words were cut off by the tomato being shoved between her lips.

"Eat it. It will tide you over until we get to our dinners."

Violet chewed, the juice running down her throat and making her want to cough. Dylan tugged the pillow out of her hands and flung it so hard it hit the wall before dropping to the floor. She tried to muster up some enthusiasm as she spread her thighs, letting him know she was ready for him.

With a little luck, he'd be quick about it.

He stopped crawling on his knees between her ankles and just looked at her, his eyebrows raised.

"What?" she asked nervously.

"You look like you're calculating how fast I can be in and out. I think you're hoping for sixty seconds or less."

Her cheeks burned. "Why would you think that?" And how was she so transparent?

"The grimace on your face is a dead giveaway."

"I'm sorry. I tried to tell you." Violet tried to roll away, reaching for the towel. Maybe she could strangle herself with it. This had to be the most awkward moment of her life, and to this point, her life had really just been a whole series of awkward moments.

The only time she was comfortable and confident was when she was with her students. Who were all five years old.

But this moment had to surpass all others in pure humiliation.

"Shhh." Dylan put his hand over her mouth. "Don't apologize. You did tell me. And I said we'd only do what feels right. Did it feel right in the shower?"

Violet's body hummed just from the memory. "Yes. Really right."

"So, let's just experiment and see what feels right here on the bed, okay?"

"Okay." She wanted to relax and let it all hang out. She wanted to be able to get down and dirty with Dylan so that he would enjoy himself. "But I need you to tell me what to do, how to please you, Dylan."

His lips brushed across hers. Dark eyes swept over her face. "Just be you. Just that you care enough to want to please me is enough."

It didn't feel like enough. He was willing to give her a baby, the thing that mattered most to her, and she couldn't even give him a good time in return.

"You don't have to do anything, Vi. If you don't want to do this, I'll go to the clinic. I promise you'll get a baby one way or the other."

That made tears well up in her eyes and her heart swell like a balloon. Violet reached up and gently stroked his cheek. "You really have no idea how wonderful you are, do you?"

He shrugged. "Don't make too much of it. For the most part, I'm just an overpaid jock, Vi."

"And I thought I had confidence issues? There's nothing wrong with success, you know. It's the result of your talent and hard work. You should enjoy it." She pulled his mouth down onto hers, kissed him slowly and thoroughly. "Make love to me, Dylan. Please."

He was propped up on his elbows and he pulled back, studied her. "Well, you don't have to ask me twice."

Then before she realized what he was doing, he had dropped down between her legs and kissed her. There. Where she felt it shoot through her insides like an electrical surge.

"Oh!" Well, that was eloquent.

It was instinctive to try and close her thighs, but that only clamped her flesh on either side of Dylan's head and shoved him farther into her crotch. Startled, she dropped them back open. Wide.

Which didn't work either.

Dylan merely reached out, spread her apart with his fingers, and licked her.

At that point, she stopped caring.

Gripping the duvet, she fell back and started speaking in tongues. "Oh, ah, ye-, bu-, geez, he-," all flowed out of her mouth in incoherent babbling as he stroked up and down from the very tip of her clitoris to way down low, lower than it had ever occurred to her you could go.

Just when she thought her heart would actually burst out of her chest like an alien entity, he lifted up. And licked his lips.

"Mmm."

There was a gorgeous professional baseball player between her legs licking his lips like he'd had a good meal. This had to be a wet dream. Or whatever you called them when women had them. She didn't usually, but this had to be a dream, because there was *no way* this could be happening to her.

Dylan bent his head again and did something that made her sit halfway up. Shit, this was real, because she never would have even thought a man could do that. She was pretty sure he was sucking on her, because there were little slurping noises and a tug-pull sensation right at the tip of her . . . Yowsa.

She was point five seconds away from coming when he let go.

Violet lay on the bed and panted.

"Like that?" He crawled up along her, his erection pressing into her thigh, brushing against her curls, and sending another little shock of lust rippling through her.

Holy crap, she actually wanted him inside her. She ached to have him inside her. Now. This was very, very strange and she hoped like heck it would last, because damn, damn, it was good.

Dylan's mouth closed around her nipple and he sucked, good and hard, with the kind of pressure that had her straining on the mattress, arching up to him, digging her feet into the bed, clawing at his shoulders. Then the other one—lick, suck, pull, and back to the first. Then over to the other, and back again, until she was slick everywhere on her chest, her inner thighs were dripping with desire, her cries were loud and urgent, her breasts were tingling with sensation.

There was time for one kiss on her lips, his tongue dipping deep inside, twirling and swirling around hers with the musky taste of her own desire, then he was gone again, descending over her chest, fingers plucking, lips sucking on his way by, before he reached her pussy.

Violet had always hated the "P" word. It reminded her of a randy Tom Jones frolicking with Vegas showgirls, and pubescent boys trying to be dirty as they scrawled it over bathroom walls. But for the first time in her twenty-eight years, she felt like she had something more than a vagina, designed to birth children. She had something just for sex, something for pleasure, not function, and when Dylan thrust with his tongue deep inside her, it went into her pussy, damn it, and it felt really, really sexy.

She figured the sexual liberation of Violet Caruthers was complete when she grabbed onto his hair, rammed his head deeper into her, and yelled, "Oh, Dylan, yes!" at volumes she hadn't even thought she was capable of.

And she wasn't the least bit embarrassed.

So when Dylan jerked back and moved up the length of her, she knew what was coming, and she wanted it. Seriously, big-time wanted it.

His hair was sticking up from where she had yanked, and his eyes were ink black, cloudy with need, his lips shiny and slick.

"Are you sure you want to do this?" Dylan asked, wanting her so bad his arms trembled as he hovered over her. He had her on the edge, he was pretty sure, and he knew he had himself on the edge, but he had to hear her say it was okay. There wasn't a condom in sight, and she couldn't have any doubts.

He was sure. Sure that giving Violet a child was the least he could do after she had renewed his passion and excitement for life. His trust in other people. His belief that he was worth something beyond his batting average.

She wiggled beneath him in a way that tested his resolve. "Dylan, please."

Cock resting at her hot entrance, he swore. "I need to hear you say it. We could get you pregnant and you have to be sure."

Violet stilled. Stroked her fingers down his arms. "I'm sure. I would be honored to have your child. Truly honored."

That did him in.

Dylan pushed inside her in the raw, and almost came on the spot. Christ almighty, he hadn't had sex with a woman without a condom since . . . ever. Everything felt so tight and slick and pulsing, extra aware.

He had also never had sex with Violet, and that in itself made the experience ten times more arousing.

Violet wasn't jaded. Violet wasn't greedy. Violet had claimed not to like sex, and yet here she was, beneath him, clamping her ankles together right on his butt, urging him forward.

But he needed a second to just savor, wait. Throb. Try not to come.

He bent his head over her glorious breasts and ran his lips over her nipple.

Using a word Dylan wouldn't have thought Violet would know, she lifted her hips and spread her legs wider, forcing him deep inside her. They both moaned.

"Want it, do you?" Almost as much as him, he'd bet.

She moved her hips again, and met his thrust so that they were as connected as it was possible for them to be. "Yes, I want it. I want it, all of it."

Dylan leaned down and kissed her, bit her lip, giving up the fight to hold back. He pushed into her, harder and harder, the headboard smacking the wall, the force of his thrusts dragging the sheets off the mattress. His stomach connected with hers each time he sank into her, and he could hear the sound of their bodies joining, the slick suction intermingling with their hot desperate breathing and Violet's urgent gasp as he drove air out of her lungs over and over.

Violet strained with him, then suddenly went limp on the bed, her hands falling to his waist. Her eyes locked with his, and she paused before arching up in a silent, graceful orgasm, her body squeezing around his, lips softly parted. Dylan had never seen anything so beautiful in his whole life, the way she took her pleasure and then dropped back down in steps, body relaxing until she was boneless against the mattress.

A feminine smile crossed her lips as she brushed her hair off her face, and that enigmatic expression, that look of complete and total satisfaction had Dylan gripping the headboard with one hand and driving faster into her, the aftershocks of her climax milking his cock and hurtling him into his own orgasm.

He gave a shout as he pulsed, the feeling of his hot come catapulting deep inside her shocking and arousing in its intimacy. It was a new sensation, something he had never done before with any other woman, and he felt a burst of male possessiveness. This woman, his seed.

They were connected forever now.

Eight

Violet stuck a pillow under her butt the minute Dylan pulled out of her.

"*What* are you doing?" he asked, wiping the sweat off his forehead with his arm.

"Keeping it in there." She lifted her hips up and clamped her legs together. She had read this little technique in a book and figured it was worth a shot. It probably looked stupid, but she felt so relaxed, she didn't care.

Even if she didn't get pregnant, Dylan had given her the most incredible sex she had ever had. He had shown her there was nothing wrong with her sexually, that she wasn't some kind of mutant lacking certain hormones needed to get it on.

"Keeping what . . . Oh." He flopped onto his side next to her and kissed her shoulder. "Keeping the ball in the glove, I get it."

She laughed. "Ball in the glove? Could everything in life and sex be described by a baseball metaphor?"

"Probably." His big hand brushed lazily over her stomach as he grinned. "We're hoping to hit a home run here, right?"

"Yes." She licked her dry lips. "And I guess you do have a bat and balls."

Dylan laughed. "And I slid into home plate."

"Eww! That sounds kind of yucky."

"Okay, okay. I scored. Is that better?" He put his hand under her knees and lifted them, further tipping her vagina.

The gesture was casual, but Violet knew it was intentional. He was trying to help ensure a pregnancy.

Like they were a couple planning on having a baby together.

Like they wanted this.

And while that wasn't the case, Violet was truly grateful that she'd been given the next best thing. This wasn't a sterile doctor's office with injection conception. Nor was it Frank giving her the old wham, bam.

This was a happy, pleasant moment, with a man she could fall in love with under different circumstances.

She had to be careful or she just might do that anyway.

"That's better. And this may be out of left field . . ."

He groaned and she giggled.

"But you have the sexiest eyes I've ever seen, Dylan. I just thought you should know." It was a sign of her satiation that she could say that without blushing.

Dylan grinned, his thumb shifting a bit so that he was stroking across her butt, which was pretty much sticking up in the air.

"Thank you. And you should probably know that you have the best pair of t—"

He looked right at her breasts and she smacked his shoulder.

" . . . toes I've ever seen."

"Toes don't come in pairs."

"No? Well, I guess you'd know. You're the teacher." He set her legs back down and sat up.

Violet pulled the pillow back out from under her. It was up to fate and his sperm at this point. They'd done all they could.

Dylan leaned over her, inches from her face. She could feel

the heat of his breath, smell his sweat and deodorant. He had her caged in with his arms and she had to admit she liked that feeling of being feminine next to his extreme masculinity. "Seriously, I want you to know that I think you have the best of everything. You're beautiful both inside and out, Vi."

No man had ever said anything quite that sweet to her before.

It felt natural to reach up and kiss him. Their lips fit together so perfectly, and she felt renewed desire just from that little contact. He felt the same way, if the pressure on her thigh was any indication.

Violet wanted to show him what he had given to her, show him how much he pleased her. And she was curious, very curious, if other aspects of sex with Dylan would be different as well.

She dropped down onto her side and took his erection in her hands and gave a soft squeeze. He groaned in approval, and Violet stroked over him, felt him grow harder in her hold. Even without her glasses, she had a good view of him, of his muscular thighs, dark hair, thick erection.

Giving oral sex to a man had never appealed to her. She had an oversensitive gag reflex and always felt a bit like there was a tree trunk going down her throat. And when you could compare sex acts to forestry it really just wasn't the least bit sexy.

But as she stroked and squeezed and watched, as Dylan got louder and louder in his approval, and a tiny bead of clear fluid appeared, she wanted to taste him. She wanted to take him in her mouth, lick her tongue over his hot flesh and feel the power of pleasing him.

The tip of her tongue reached out and flicked over him. He jerked a little and said, "Yes, do that again."

She did. He jerked again, his hand coming down on her head and holding her against him.

When she took him in her mouth and he swore, Violet gained a whole new appreciation for the experience. This was fun. He tasted delicious, warm and salty, and as he filled her mouth, her inner thighs ached with jealousy.

Darn, she was starting to squirm against the bed herself. This was arousing.

He tried to pull back, but she grabbed the bottom of his shaft and sucked in her cheeks.

Dylan exploded with a primal roar, pulling back so that he came in her hand. "Shit, shit, shit," he said. "That was incredible. What was that for?"

That was for him. That was for her.

A smile on her face, Violet looked up at him. "Happy birthday, Dylan."

Nine

"I'll let you know what the test results are in a few weeks."

Dylan stopped checking out the family pictures on Violet's wall and turned to stare at her. "Excuse me?"

He had driven her home after a nice lazy morning at his place, coffee and eggs and lots of groping. If it wasn't for his game, he wouldn't have taken her home at all, but he had to be at the airport in a few hours. She was wearing a pair of his sweat shorts, having pulled the drawstring so tight the shorts overlapped at the waist in a pleat. She'd put her bikini top on like a bra, then one of his smaller T-shirts. He liked seeing her standing there in his clothes, but he didn't like the look on her face.

She seemed distracted as she glanced over at her answering machine. "Shoot. I was hoping Frank had called. I need to get my purse from him."

"I can take you over to his place." Dylan swung his keys around on his finger. "Now let's go back to what you said before. Test results?"

He had a sickening feeling in his gut. One that told him his plans to have Violet on the road with him for the rest of the summer weren't the same plans she was making.

"It will be two weeks before I'm supposed to start my period. If I'm late, I'll take a test and let you know."

No, no, no. He was not going to play along with this. "I was planning on seeing you before then."

"Why?" She blinked up at him through her glasses, her arms up in her hair, twisting it around and around. She pulled a rubber band out of her kitchen drawer, and wrapped it around the bun she'd made from her thick hair.

He couldn't believe what he was hearing. "Because I want to! Because last night we started something and it's not finished yet. I want us to be together."

She bit her lip, crossed her ankles. "That wasn't something we even talked about."

"So let's talk about it now. I want to date. I want to see where this can go." Man, this was ridiculous. He finally found the one woman he thought he could fall in love with and want to spend an entire lifetime with, and she was playing word games with him.

"I'm not so sure that's a good idea. It could get complicated if I am pregnant and things don't work out between us."

"Then we'd be like a million other couples who aren't together but have kids." He put his hand in his hair in frustration. She was leaping way ahead on this one. He just wanted to take it one day at a time.

"Exactly." She nodded. "Which is not what I want. This child is supposed to be mine and mine alone. No money, no interference. That's what we talked about, that's what we agreed on. If we date, and it ends in disaster, I don't want to be dealing with custody issues and conflict when I should be concentrating on raising a child."

Dylan felt floored. Slapped. Used. "So I really was just a sperm donor? Even after everything we . . ."

Shit. That hurt. That hurt bad.

Her eyes got moist, damn her. Like she was the one hurting. She put her arms around her middle and hugged herself.

"I care about you, Dylan, I really do. In a way I can't quite believe after just one night. But I don't fit in your world, and you don't fit in mine, and if there is a baby, it's my sole concern right now. So yes, you were a sperm donor. And I should remind you that you offered, by the way."

Because he was an idiot, apparently.

But God, he wanted her so much. He wanted this woman to be his, totally and completely, to want him the way he wanted her, to have a child together with him.

"Don't . . . don't do this, Vi. Please. We'll just take things slow. I'm a reasonable person."

Violet hesitated, than shook her head. "I can't. Please understand."

So that was it. Angry, hurt, confused, he scoffed. "I understand this is total bullshit." He threw his hands up. "Goodbye, Violet. Have a nice life."

The slamming of her door should have made him feel better, but it only made him grimace.

Well, that sucked. He'd just been dumped.

Ten

Three weeks later Violet sat on Ashley's sofa and tapped her thumb on her knee.

"Who's keeping time?" Ashley asked, her hands in her blond curly hair.

"I am. I told you that three freaking times," Trish said, eyes on her watch.

Kindra sat down next to Violet and put her hand on her shoulder. "It's okay, sweetie, no matter what the test says, it's going to be okay. We're here for you."

Violet felt a pit in her stomach that wasn't a baby. It was guilt. She hadn't told her friends about Dylan, wanting to wait to see the results of their night together, if there were any. If there was no baby she wasn't sure she could ever bring herself to talk about him.

It had just about cracked her heart in half when he had left her apartment that morning, his face hurt and angry.

She had thought she'd done the right thing at the time. Now, she wasn't sure about anything.

It had been a hellish three weeks, her thoughts straying to Dylan over and over again. Wondering if she should call him. Wondering if somehow or other they could work it out.

Alternating between desperate desire that they had made a

baby, to the almost shameful wish that they hadn't so she could find him and fix things between them.

"Thanks, Kindra. I'm going to be fine. Either way." She said it to convince herself. She had a feeling that if she wasn't pregnant—despite having sex during ovulation and being five days late for her period—she was going to be absolutely devastated.

After what she had shared with Dylan, she knew she absolutely could not go to the sperm bank and grab any old DNA. She would have to hold out for Mr. Right. Who she suspected she had already sent packing.

If she was pregnant, she was going to be equal parts thrilled and sad, that she had denied her child a father when he had been willing to give it a go.

Her brain hurt. Her heart hurt. Her stomach was doing flips.

"I want to have a baby, you know. That's all I've ever wanted."

"Good thing," Trish said, carrying the test out from the bathroom. "Because it's positive. You're pregnant."

The room sort of swung around in a disco ball splash of color and light. Violet grabbed the arm of the couch. "Oh, my. I'm going to have a baby. I'm going to have a baby." She started to cry, tears of joy and relief. Excitement. A twinge of fear.

Her friends crowded around her, giving her hugs and murmuring words of reassurance. "I'm happy, I am. I'm really, really happy."

Suddenly there were footsteps on the interior stairs that came up to Ashley's apartment. Violet sat up straighter and wiped her face. Geez, it was Lucas and Mack, her friends' significant others.

"Ashley has a bigger TV than I do," Lucas was saying. "We can watch the game up here."

"Go away, you guys," Trish said succinctly. "I'm serious."

Violet sniffled and hid her face behind her hair as the guys stopped and took in the situation.

"What's the matter?" Mack asked, shoving his hands into the pockets of his jeans. Kindra's fiance frowned at Trish.

"Mack, just give us five minutes," Kindra said with a quelling lift of her eyebrows.

When neither guy moved, Ashley made a sound of exasperation. "We're having a girl moment here, okay? We just found out we're pregnant!"

Lucas's jaw dropped, his face turning chalk white. "You're pregnant? Oh, shit, Ash. I told you those glow in the dark condoms don't work!"

There was a moment of stunned silence while they all processed this, then Trish burst out laughing.

"I'm not pregnant," Ashley said with a grin, smacking his arm. "And thanks for sharing our sexual habits with all our friends."

Lucas put his hand over his heart. "Whew. Damn, you scared me half to death. I mean . . . having a baby isn't a bad thing, if you're ready." With an enormous sigh of relief, Lucas turned to Mack and clapped him on the shoulder. "Congratulations, Dad."

Kindra gave a squawk. "Hold on, there! I'm not pregnant, either. Though it wouldn't be a crisis if I were, since Mack and I have been together for almost a year. Though it would screw up our October wedding . . . my God, I'd never fit in my dress." She shook her head vehemently. "But no, it's not me."

"Trish?" Lucas eyed her dubiously. Given that she was the least maternal of the four of them and wasn't even dating anyone, Violet wasn't surprised at his expression. Yet it made her wonder why he'd pass right over her and had concluded Trish.

"Then who the hell is it?" Mack asked, putting his hand on his hips. "Oh no, it's the dog, isn't it? See, I knew that nasty bulldog was sniffing around Bitsy again. Damn, we're going to have mutant puppies on our hands. Poodles can't breed with bulldogs, it's going to be just ugly."

Violet clapped her hand over her mouth, the urge to laugh mingling with the need to cry hysterically.

"Your precious poodle isn't having puppies." Kindra stood up. "*Violet* is pregnant."

"Violet?" Mack's eyes bugged out.

"Yes, Violet."

"Well . . ."

"Uh . . ."

Really, just excuse her. They didn't have to look so damn stunned.

Violet found her voice. "Why do you both look so surprised?"

They shuffled. Looked at each other. She wasn't feeling up to mercy. They had insulted her with their assumptions that she couldn't be the one knocked up.

"Because I didn't think you were all that serious with Frank," Lucas said, tossing his hair out of his eyes. "We haven't even seen him in weeks."

"Besides, I didn't figure Frank had sperm," Mack said.

Kindra gasped. "Mack!"

With a sigh, Violet folded her feet under her on the couch. It might be her imagination, but her denim shorts were jabbing her in the gut. "Frank didn't get me pregnant." Might as well come clean with them all at once.

They all stared at her.

"Then who the hell did?" Trish demanded.

Ashley grabbed her hand, horror on her face. "Oh dear God, you were raped? Sweetie, why didn't you tell us?"

"No! I had a one-night stand, okay?" Even saying that seemed wrong, though it was true. Yet it had been something much more than bodies slapping, as Dylan had said. "I slept with the guy who picked me up out of the water the night I fell off Frank's boat. His name is Dylan Diaz and we're not dating or anything."

Which was her fault.

"That's funny," Mack said, breaking the stunned silence. "The catcher for the Indians is named Dylan Diaz." He reached for the remote control and flicked Ashley's TV on. "What a coincidence."

Yeah. A huge one. Violet gave a sigh and braved a glance at the TV. Mack had found the Indians game and was pointing. "See? He's behind the plate right now. Dylan Diaz. Wow. Weird. And he's having a great season. He's been pounding them out of the park the last few weeks."

"I know, it's amazing," Lucas said. "His average is through the roof all of a sudden."

"Violet?" Kindra was looking at her strangely. "Is *he* the father?"

Violet couldn't pry her eyes off the screen. There he was. Dylan was down in the catcher's squat, and he jumped up, ball in his glove, and threw it back to the pitcher. She couldn't see his face particularly well because of the mask, but she recognized his movements, the shape of his body, the muscles of his thighs.

Oh, geez Louise, she missed him. "Yes, he's the father."

"Whoa," Lucas said.

"That's cool," was Mack's opinion. "The kid will be a ball player."

"That's not cool!" Trish yelled. "Think of the legalities here. Custody, child support, it's a paternity suit waiting to happen."

"I don't want anything from him." The room was starting to spin and whirl again and Violet clutched the couch. Undid the snap on her shorts. Sucked in some deep breaths.

"Then we need to get him to surrender parental rights so he can't request custody down the road."

Violet knew Trish was a lawyer, and she was only trying

to protect her rights, but Violet just couldn't think about this right now. "I think I'm going to faint."

Ashley pushed her head down between her knees. "Just take slow breaths, sweetie."

Violet stared at the hardwood floor, the grain of the wood undulating bigger and smaller, the black spots shifting.

She didn't know why she was so hot and light-headed all of a sudden. She'd gotten exactly what she had wanted.

Except she was very much afraid she'd been wrong.

Dylan was drinking a Coke as he headed down the hall from the locker room, his gym bag on his shoulder.

"Hey, Diaz."

He turned to see one of the assistant coaches coming up behind him. "Hey, what's up?"

"I've been looking all over the damn building for you. They got a certified letter in the front office for you. They overheaded you, then asked me to play errand boy if I saw you."

"I was in the shower." He couldn't imagine what he would have gotten in the mail, and he didn't really give a shit. "But thanks, I'll take care of it."

Nothing seemed to mean a whole lot of anything for the past month, except for cracking his bat against the ball hard enough to force all the ugly, painful feelings right out of him.

So far it wasn't working, but it was good for his career.

At first he wasn't even sure why he was so hurt, so upset, but now he realized it was because Violet had showed him a glimpse of something that he wanted. A home, family, love. A wife. Who loved him just as he was, with or without the ball career.

She had shown him a glimpse of that and then taken it all away.

He wanted to love Violet. He wanted to be with her, and every day he spent missing her.

The secretary thrust an envelope in his hand the second he

walked into the front office. "Legal's down the hall if you're getting sued," she said, smoothing her hair back from her plump face.

"Gee, thanks." Dylan ripped the envelope open and pulled out a greeting card. It had a flower on the front and on the inside it read:

> Dear Dylan,
> Thank you. You hit a home run.
> With love,
> Violet

Well. Dylan dropped his Coke can in the wastebasket and stared at the words again. Violet was pregnant. He had gotten her pregnant. And she was thanking him. With love.

Shock gave way to pleasure. Elation raced through him. A baby. They were going to have a baby.

He grinned at the secretary. He couldn't help but be a little bit proud that he'd only needed one time up to bat. Not every guy could claim that kind of average.

"Good news?" she asked.

"Yeah." Dylan handed her the envelope. "Can you throw this away for me, Kathy? I need to go see someone." He needed to go to Violet, tell her how happy he was for her. Beg her for a chance to take things slow, to date and really get to know each other before their child was born.

She had said she didn't want that, but Dylan just couldn't accept that. He wanted a future with Violet.

"There's something still in this envelope, Dylan." Kathy pulled out a sheaf of papers stapled together.

"What is it? Read it to me real quick." His leg was jiggling and he dug his keys out of his gym bag. He could be at Violet's in twenty minutes.

"'Dear Dylan'," she read. "'Please sign and notarize the following relinquishment of parental rights . . .' Uh-oh."

Kathy shoved the packet of papers into his hand.

Shocked, Dylan stared at it, the words blurring in front of him. It was a two-page document of legal bullshit, outlining how he would never have contact with his child or that child's mother.

It shouldn't be news. It was everything Violet had asked for, everything he had agreed to. Everything she had reaffirmed that morning when he had dropped her off. But damn, it hurt deep inside, right about where his heart was, that he could want her so much, and she could have so little interest in him.

And it made him angry, that she would shove this at him, like she didn't trust him, and right now, when he was feeling excitement and pride that she was going to have his child.

With a nasty curse, he ripped the papers right in two. Kathy jumped in her office chair.

Stuffing the torn pages and the crumpled card back into the envelope, he strode out of the office.

He had a few things he wanted to say to Violet.

Eleven

Violet glanced at her watch as she checked her tomato vines for ripe vegetables, on her knees on her gardening mat. Dylan should have gotten her letter by now. With a sigh, she picked a tomato and put it in her basket.

She shouldn't have listened to Trish. Her gut had told her not to send him that impersonal document, but Trish had scared the daylights out of her, insisting that without it Dylan could contest her custody at any point in her child's life. So she had sent it, and now she regretted it.

Whatever feelings he had for her had surely been killed by that move.

Which should have made her happy, but only made her profoundly sad.

How downright stupid that the first man to treat her with respect, admiration, and sexual interest was the very man she had intentionally hurt.

She heard footsteps in the grass coming from the driveway, and when she looked up, she only needed to see as far as the ankles to know it was Dylan. She could feel his anger, emotion, before she even looked up and saw the fury racing across his face.

"I'm not signing this." He threw the certified mail envelope down, where it hit her in the knee and landed in the grass, the torn document sliding out.

Violet picked up the pieces and put them back in the envelope, her heart pounding. "I guess not, since you've ripped it in half."

"How could you send that to my work?" He was standing there in jeans and a T-shirt, feet apart in sandals, looking angry and belligerent, yet his voice cracked.

"I didn't know your home address. And my friend, Trish, she's a lawyer. She said we needed to do this or you could contest custody." It sounded cruel, even as she said it. "I'm sorry."

"You could have just talked to me. We could have worked this out between us before we went straight to the lawyers."

He was right, and Violet sighed, setting her basket of tomatoes down. "You're right. I'm sorry. I just feel really scared, Dylan, and unsure what to do."

Looking out over the common green space her condo and two others shared, he shook his head. "What is it that you want, Vi? Just tell me exactly what you want deep down inside. I want to respect that, I do."

She was going to cry. She already felt tears welling up. The tears had been coming pretty much nonstop in the last week since her stick had turned pink. It was time to be honest with herself, honest with him.

"I want what I can't have."

His swung his head to look at her, black eyes boring into her. "What's that?"

"I want . . . you." Now that she'd said it, admitted it out loud, she knew that was absolutely what she wanted. Tears rolling down her cheeks, she added, "I want you and me. I want our baby. Together."

Dylan's jaw moved. He squatted down in front of her. "Well, fuck me, Vi, that's what I want, too."

She choked back a startled laugh.

"So, what's the problem?" His thumb wiped her tears away.

"I don't want you to feel trapped. I don't want to force you into what you're not ready for. And I don't want to regret that you got stuck with me when you could have any woman you want. I'm not the kind of woman a man would feel proud to have on his arm." It hurt to say that, to admit her fears and insecurities, to acknowledge that she wanted him, but understood he had better options.

But after everything she had put him through, she owed him complete honesty.

Dylan stared at Violet and wanted to just laugh. Holy crap, she had put him through five weeks of hell because she was afraid he'd leave her for a bimbo? That was what he was hearing, wasn't it?

"I've had a six-foot-tall, built blonde on my arm before and it leaves a hell of a lot to be desired." Dylan brushed her hair back and stroked her cheek. "You're more attractive to me than any other woman I've ever met. When a guy cares about a woman, she becomes his standard, you see what I'm saying? Now come here."

He pulled her into his arms, breathing in her scent, squeezing her tight to him, sighing with pleasure. God, he had missed her. "I like your hair like this, by the way. I think it's the first time I've ever actually seen it completely dry."

She sniffled against his chest. "Dylan, I really thought I had a logical plan and that it all made sense. I really thought I needed to use my head, not my heart."

"I know. And now we've both agreed that was stupid." With a grin, he rubbed her back and kissed her forehead. "We'll just take it slow, okay?"

She nodded, her eyes shiny, her teeth digging into her bottom lip.

"Now, is everything okay? You're feeling okay? You've been to the doctor?" It was starting to sink in that he had gotten her pregnant. Which meant she was having a baby. His baby. In actuality, not in theory.

"I'm fine, so far. I'm going to the doctor in two weeks for my first appointment." She kissed him softly. "Please come with me if you want."

That nearly did him in. "I'd love to." Then, so he wouldn't embarrass the hell out of himself and bawl, he gave her a smug smile. "And damn, I'm good, aren't I? Home run first time at the plate."

Violet laughed. "I did hear you've been having a great season."

"I'm looking forward to a long career. With you." He touched his lips to hers.

She smiled up at him. "More baseball metaphors?"

"Hell, yeah." He pulled her up and stood next to her. "Now let's go in and I'll practice my swing."

Rubbing her finger across her lip, Violet peered at him from behind the veil of her long, lustrous hair. "I'd like to try batting, too."

Dylan went hard. He wasn't sure what in the hell she meant by that, but it sounded kinky. "Another player has been added to the roster. Violet Caruthers, number sixty-nine."

She clamped her hand over her mouth and flushed a very charming pink. "Oh, Dylan, that's awful. I like it."

He almost groaned. Instead he lifted her up a little, hands on her ass, so he could give her a very open, tongue-filled kiss. "I've never had sex with another player before, but there's always a first."

With a smile, Violet touched his cheek. "I'm very happy."

"Me, too, gorgeous." Instead of a dead body, he'd found a future. A family. Everything he'd been lonely for. Much better than a corpse.

Violet kissed the corner of Dylan's mouth. "I'm so glad I'm a klutz and fell off that boat."

"Let's go inside, you can put that bikini back on, and we'll reenact the whole thing, especially the part where you put your face in my crotch."

Violet was feeling so content, satisfied, and pleased with the way things had turned out, she didn't hesitate. "Sounds fun."

The look on Dylan's face was classic.

And the last thing in the world she felt like was shy when she stepped into her condo and peeled off her T-shirt.

HARDHATS AND SILK STOCKINGS

HelenKay Dimon

To Lori Foster for providing the opportunity.
To James for encouraging me to take it.

One

"Just like a man to show up after all the hard work is done."

Not the warmest welcome Whit Thomas had ever received from a woman, but then this woman had been sending him the big chill for weeks. Her brown eyes, the color of rich caramel, sparked with anger every time he had the nerve to ask her a question.

"I got tied up on another job."

"Whatever." She shrugged her slim shoulders.

A weaker man would have given up, written Hannah Bridges off as frigid, and moved on. Not Whit. Not after that day last week when he caught her peeking over her metal clipboard at his shoulders with barely disguised hunger.

"Good afternoon, Hannah. I'm fine. Thanks for asking."

"Glad to hear it. So, did you want something or did you just stop by to say hello?" She asked the question without lifting her head.

"I need your help." He figured an hour or two between the sheets should do it.

"Lucky me."

Whit had enjoyed his share of women over the years. Success on that front had never been a problem. Until Hannah.

She had a voice as smooth as aged whiskey. And the stinging tongue of a viper.

"Hannah—"

"Look, Thomas, it's been a long day. I'm sure I can pencil in some time for us to argue tomorrow, but not now."

"I never argue. Suggest and help. Cajole, even. Never argue."

"I think you're proving my point."

Her sunny blond hair and soulful brown eyes covered a growl fierce enough to send jaded and scruffy men twice her age scrambling for the nearest exit. The sexy sweetie was all of five-five but wielded a power over burly men who could throw her spinning into the air with one little finger if they were so inclined.

On the job site, she hid her petite frame under some of the ugliest oversized flannel shirts he had ever seen. Today's version was a hideous shade of yellow-brown. Every now and then one of the overly large sleeves slipped down her slim shoulder, revealing a tiny white tank top that hugged her sleek midsection and framed her high round breasts.

He lived for those sightings.

The stubborn woman was so damn hot his insides flamed into a raging inferno every time she swept by him with her perfect button nose pointed in the air. A light fruity scent hovered around her, wrapping around his balls and squeezing tight.

For the first and only time in his life a hardhat turned him on. Watching her move, toting that battered metal clipboard around like a shield, sent blood rushing to his groin and his brain cells packing for vacation. Of course, the object of his lust liked to pretend he didn't exist.

He planned to change all that today.

He pushed away from the doorframe and stepped into the dismantled kitchen of the historically protected house, careful not to trip over an unopened box or one of the pieces of heavy equipment scattered around the refurbishing project. "There's something you need to see."

"Look, Thomas, if you want this job to come in on time, you have to give me some space." She kept her intense gaze centered on the thick wedge of papers clipped together in her hands. She tapped her pencil against her front teeth then perched it behind her ear.

"You can call me Whit. Everyone else does."

"I'll call you Toaster Oven, if you want. The problem's still the same. I don't have time for chitchat today."

Chitchat?

She continued. "Maybe one of your wealthy friends can keep you entertained until I can finish these calculations."

"Ahh, there it is."

Her head snapped up. "What?"

"The subtle 'you're a rich asshole' crap you always pull on me."

She smiled. "I have no idea what you're talking about."

"Right. You just don't like architects, I guess."

"Actually, I like *most* of the architects I work with."

Subtle as usual. Never mind that the National Trust hand-picked him to oversee this job. Never mind the fact she wasn't supposed to lift a hammer without his approval.

Never mind the fact he owned the damn house she was ripping apart and piecing back together again.

The little vixen had worked her way into his brain until all he could think about was working his way into her tiny silk panties. And it was time to do something about it.

"Since this is my property—"

"Your family's property."

He mentally grabbed for his last ounce of patience. "Last time I checked, I was vice president of Thomas Properties, the group that owns this house."

This time she actually snorted, an unattractive sound that only stoked the heat running through his veins.

"As such," he continued over the offensive noise, "I'm in charge. Not you."

That did it.

Those stunning high cheekbones of hers seemed to fall flat. If he was bothering her before, he was clearly pissing her off now. She emphasized her displeasure by dropping her clipboard on the table and letting it land with a loud clank.

He finally had her attention. He wasn't so sure he wanted it anymore.

"Please go on. I'm hanging on every word."

Definitely not good. "Hannah, we have a problem."

"You mean in addition to an ancient electrical system, walls so thin they're peeling off like tissue paper, and a plumbing mess bad enough to warrant consideration of a permanent Porta-Potty off the library, something more than that?"

"Yeah, in addition to all that."

"If that's the case, maybe this should wait until Monday. I'm not sure I can take another setback."

"Sure you can." Whit suspected Hannah could handle almost anything. He was ready to see if she could handle him. "This problem is downstairs."

"Up until now the basement was the only floor of this three-story disaster you call a house that didn't require a major overhaul."

"This isn't a construction problem."

"Really?"

"Yeah, really."

"Is the problem breathing? If so, just kill it. You don't need me for animal control duties. It's Friday. I've sent everyone home and I'd like to get out of here myself."

"As the boss, I'm afraid I'm going to have to insist."

Boss.

A steady pounding knocked against Hannah's temples. The second she had seen one Whitman Goodard Thomas, all wickedly handsome and perfectly groomed, the earth shifted. The usually firm ground beneath her blue-collar feet actually crumbled. No man had ever made the settled landscape move before, especially one from such a hoity-toity background.

She didn't care for the uncomfortable sensation one bit.

Looking at the tiny dimple in his left cheek, Hannah knew one thing for certain: she was in deep trouble. The kind of trouble that led to naked panting bodies rolling across satin sheets and bare toes pointed to the ceiling.

The vision was becoming far too easy to picture. As a rule, Hannah never got involved with any man connected to her work. Right now, a sex life was out of the question. She had a deadline looming. This job was her one opportunity to prove that she had what it took to run the company without the help of some pencil-pushing male.

But Whit made her want to chuck all that responsibility for a few minutes of mind-bending passion. She looked into his piercing green eyes, the color of summer grass, and her usually fierce control took a tumble.

She didn't want minutes alone with him. She needed hours. Long, hot, sweaty hours.

Maybe it was the soft lilt threading through his Georgia-bred voice, the same subtle accent that grew more pronounced the more frustrated he became. Maybe it was the wide expanse of his shoulders or the unruly mop of sandy brown hair framing his near perfect face and square chin. Heck, even those nerdy button-down oxford shirts he wore made her insides grow all dewy.

Whatever caused the unsettling attraction had to end. Maintaining control was essential. Stripping him naked and letting her hands wander over the muscled chest she guessed lurked under those conservative clothes was an idea better left for fantasizing in the dark privacy of her bedroom.

"Show me."

He blinked several times. "Excuse me?"

"You mentioned some huge problem that couldn't wait two more seconds. I give up. You win. Take me to whatever it is."

"Oh, sure. Let's go."

She marched around him and took the lead. The last thing

she needed was a wide-open view of Whit's tight backside. The man filled out a pair of flat-front khakis better than anyone she had ever seen.

"It's in the basement. Right side," he called over her shoulder.

Whatever "it" was. She walked down the stairs and entered the dank cement-lined basement. Piles of junk, boxes, and blankets littered the floor. The only real item of interest was an old coal stove in the back right corner and a new water heater off to its side.

The walls closed in on her. The confined space made her nervous. She tamped down her discomfort.

"Well, what's the big deal?"

"I found something last night. A room that isn't on the house plans filed with the county or on our blueprints." He stepped over a lump of something and headed for a shadowed corner.

Like an idiot, she followed him, her trail taking her around the shapeless mound. Whatever was down here could stay here as far as she was concerned. Forever. Dark, airless rooms were not her thing.

When he stopped, she slammed into him from behind and clenched onto his cotton shirt for balance. For a few seconds, she enjoyed the sculpted feel of his back.

"You okay back there?"

She jerked away and lost her balance, nearly landing on the unidentified heap on the floor. No, she was definitely not okay. Horny and restless, maybe. Not okay.

She inhaled deep and slow, and beat down the temptation to climb on top of him and investigate what he hid under all that silly preppy clothing. She did the practical thing and peered over his broad shoulders.

The faint outline of a partially hidden door sat tucked behind a rickety old bookshelf. Without a sound, or much in the way of visible effort, he pushed the wooden structure to the side, revealing the small but sturdy entrance. Despite his boring conservative outfit, she could visualize his muscles bunching across his wide back and into his biceps.

"See," he said.

Oh, she saw everything. He towered over her, standing somewhere around six feet three inches. Rumor was he had played quarterback for some college football program years ago. From where she stood, glancing over what seemed like miles of endless muscle, the guy still had it.

"Hannah? Are you still with me, honey?" His sly smile was a bit too knowing for her taste. "You're staring. Not that I mind, but I thought you should know."

She wondered if he would be as smug with a fist shoved into those rock-hard abs. "I'm trying to figure out how we're going to fold you up and stuff you in there."

He studied the small opening as if he were considering her question. "You could go in first."

"That's mighty chivalrous of you."

"Just trying to show you my feminist side."

"I'll show you a side," she muttered.

He put a hand behind his ear and leaned in. "Hmmm?"

The gesture brought his body far too close. *Damn.* He even smelled good. All fresh and woodsy like the mountains at the first sign of spring.

"Fine. You want me to lead, boss man? I'll lead."

"That's the spirit. I love a fearless woman." He picked up a moldy piece of wood and swung it in a sweeping arc a few times. The edge of the makeshift bat whizzed by at a safe distance from her head.

"What's that for?"

"Whatever's in there that needs stomping."

"This just gets better and better."

"My thoughts exactly." He winked at her before leaning his shoulder against the solid door. The wood groaned, resisting before swinging open.

Oppressive darkness greeted them. They both stepped to the threshold and glanced inside. One hint of scurrying little feet and she was out of there. She'd run the entire distance from her current location deep in the heart of Virginia horse country to her condo in D.C., all thirty miles, if she had to.

She sniffed, expecting a musty odor. If anything, she smelled the sterile scent of disinfectant.

"Well then, no reason to wait. Let's go in." He shot her a triumphant look over his shoulder. "Unless you're scared."

"Get a clue, Ivy League boy. Nothing about you scares me." She started moving forward, fueled by an overactive ego and little else. Certainly not by common sense.

"Vanderbilt."

She spun around. "What did you say?"

"I graduated from Vanderbilt University. Good school but not Ivy. Third in my class, if you want to know."

He had the nerve to look deadly serious, as if this information really mattered in some way. Little did he know it actually did. Made her feel as insignificant as the dust scattered across the floor.

"I don't. Care, that is," she said.

"I did graduate work at an Ivy League school. Want to know about that?"

They had wandered far enough down memory freaking lane. "Okay, Whit, I get it. You're brilliant."

"Not really. My brother is the smart one."

Having struggled to reach twelfth grade before her head exploded, she knew she was way out of her league with Whit in the intellectual sense. Being reminded of her inability in this area poked at a flaming scar deep inside of her.

She was the only one in her family not to like school. She struggled through every one of her twelve years of education. Could still feel the panic tickling around the edges of her heart at the thought of taking a test. The usual feelings of insecurity and incompetence assailed her, making her even grumpier than usual.

"Are you done with your biographical data?"

He shrugged. "You asked."

"No, I really didn't." She motioned toward the opening. "Go in before I take that stick and smack you with it."

"Yes, ma'am." He ducked his head and turned sideways to fit his broad shoulders through the small doorway.

She watched him disappear. Three seconds later a soft white light flickered on inside the chamber.

"Now this is a room."

The awe in his voice pulled her in. She stepped over the threshold. Straight into an erotic fantasyland.

The air sucked right out of her lungs. Speechless and gulping, her gaze traveled around the ten–by–ten room. Floor-to-ceiling bookshelves packed with thin hardbound volumes lined the far wall. A metal chest sat to her right, covered with an impressive array of what could only be called sex toys. Handcuffs, tubes of heaven knew what, and a bunch of what looked like dildos and other strange-looking objects of differing lengths and widths were scattered around the countertop. She didn't even want to know what was in all those tiny drawers.

And then there was the chair.

A padded chair rested in the dead center of the room. The handcuffs chained to the wall above it certainly were a conversation piece. Although she doubted people used the contraption for talking.

"What the hell is this place?"

She backed up until her shoulders knocked against something hard. She immediately jerked straight again, careful not to touch any surface in the room without a can of disinfectant spray.

He stopped scanning the bookshelves and turned around to face her. A gentle smile broke across his face. The sweetly sensual look sent an unnerving shiver skittering down her spine. He didn't move but she could feel him closing in around her.

The feeling didn't scare her. It made her hot.

"Unless I'm mistaken, we've stumbled into my dearly departed uncle's secret playroom."

"Are you kidding?" she choked out.

"Unfortunately, no."

"But—"

"I have some more news." His smile widened.

"I almost hate to ask."

His eyes gleamed. "Well, when you bumped against the door, you closed it."

Not exactly a news flash. "Uh-huh. So?"

"You locked us inside."

Two

To her credit, Hannah took the news better than he expected. Well, for a heartbeat or two anyway. Then she started ranting and yelling. Two of her least attractive qualities.

She said something about his family being made up of knuckle-dragging crazy people. He let her go on because she wasn't exactly wrong. When he laughed at one of her more colorful streams of profanities, she lost what little remained of her cool.

"This isn't funny."

He tried to look serious. "Of course not."

"I want out of here."

"Hannah, look at the door. There isn't a doorknob or any visible lock that I can see. I checked the only other door in here and it leads to a small bathroom. I'm afraid we're stuck until my brother comes to check on the job."

"That's days from now!" Her voice bounced up an octave.

"The good news is we won't have to wait until Monday. Adam's supposed to meet me here for breakfast Sunday to go over some paperwork."

"We're going to die." A green cast settled over her usually peachy-cream skin.

"There's food in here." If there wasn't, Adam was a dead man. The plan was for him to stock the room with food.

"Get a clue. There is no way I'm going to eat something that's been in this room."

He ignored that. "Good thing Uncle Calvin installed a generator down here or we'd be stumbling around in the dark."

She sat down on the chair then bounced up again as if her butt was on fire. There could only be one use for a chair that titled backward on two spokes and had a leg rest that split open down the middle to resemble a doctor's examination table. From the horrified look on Hannah's face and the red stain on her cheeks, he assumed she had figured out the purpose.

"Good thing your uncle Calvin died of a heart attack or I'd hunt him down and kill him."

"He was always a considerate fellow that way."

"He was a pervert."

A sense of family loyalty sent him rushing to Uncle Calvin's defense. Not rushing, really. More like a slow walk. Pervert was too strong. Sexual voyeur, maybe. Experimenter, definitely. Old dude on the make, he could live with.

"Family folklore says he was faithful to my aunt throughout their marriage. When she died a few years back, he was faithful to his girlfriend. Who also happened to be about fifteen years younger than my aunt, by the way."

"Are you telling me your uncle and aunt used this room for . . . for . . ."

"Pleasure?" He pressed his lips together in a frown. "I'm trying really hard not conjure up an image in my head, but yes. They were said to be a pretty randy twosome. Monogamous but sexually charged."

"Oh my God." Her jaw stayed locked in the down position.

"I was thinking more along the lines of 'yuck', but you've never seen Uncle Calvin and Aunt Theresa, so you can't possibly appreciate how horrifying the thought of them rolling around on a hard floor actually is."

She rubbed her forehead. "Wait a second."

"We have a lot more than a second."

"Are you really saying we're stuck in a sex chamber for the weekend? Together?"

Music to his ears. "To be technically correct, we're here for two nights. Not quite a weekend."

"There has to be a window here somewhere." She flew around the room testing the bookshelves and any other nook that could hide an escape hatch.

If he didn't wander around in a state of perpetual arousal thanks to her, he might have been forced to play hard to get. But he was too busy getting hard to play hard. He could barely think from wanting her so badly.

"You know, there are worse things than being stuck alone with me." At least he hoped that was true.

"I can't think of one."

"You know, some women find me attractive." More than one actually, but now wasn't the time to brag. Not when she was so intent on running like hell.

"Well, go find one and get her to help us out of here." Books crashed to the floor as she threw them off the shelves.

"You're wasting time and a good deal of energy."

He sat down on the chair, careful not to tip the damn thing over. He intended to take the ingenuous piece for a test run very soon and needed it in top condition. From his research, he'd learned that this was a one-of-a-kind item.

"We're getting out of here one way or the other."

"I'll just sit here and watch, if you don't mind. I'm a lot older than you, you know."

"You're thirty-seven, not a hundred." She glanced over her shoulder at him and froze. "Don't sit there!"

"How do you know how old I am?" Her knowing his vital statistics had to be a good sign.

"I read it somewhere."

"Uh-huh. That makes sense. My age is printed just about *everywhere*."

She clapped her hands together. The noise was almost deafening in the tiny room. "Let's focus."

He thought he was. As far as he was concerned she was the one with misplaced priorities.

"Right. Focus."

"Get up."

"Why?"

Her beautiful brown eyes bugged out. "Don't you know what that chair is for?"

Damn right he did. He had fiddled with the thing for three days before he figured out how to make the leg rests open.

"I can take an educated guess."

"Your uncle and aunt—"

"Stop!" He held up a hand. "If you describe the sex act, I'll go blind. Just thinking about all that clumpy white flesh smacking together makes me queasy."

Her blunt fingernails dug into her hips until her knuckles turned white. "So you agree the chair is gross?"

"I agree the idea of two wrinkled relatives slapping skin on it is a bit nasty. But for someone, say, of our age, making love in a chair certainly seems pretty interesting."

"I don't believe this." She touched a hand to her head and knocked her plastic hardhat to the floor. The crash echoed off the chamber walls. She looked so forlorn, he took pity on her.

"Come here, Hannah."

"I have to think."

Wrong. Thinking was the last thing he wanted her doing.

"Plenty of time for that later. Come here."

"Where?"

"With me." He patted his lap.

"I'll sit on the floor." With that, she slid down until that tempting backside thumped against the cement. Her forehead dropped against her upraised knees.

As far as he knew she didn't have a boyfriend. According to his sources, including his friend and Hannah's cousin, Cole Carruthers, Hannah was unattached. Cole also mentioned something about her being prickly, but Whit vowed to prove him wrong on that point.

He knew he still had to ask the question. No matter how much he dreaded the answer. "Did you have special plans for the weekend?"

"Yes."

Her muffled reply hit him like a blow to the stomach. He coughed out the follow-up over a big ball of regret. "Anyone I know?"

She lifted her head and stared at him. Those usually clear eyes clouded with confusion. "What are you talking about?"

"Your date."

"My what?"

Didn't they just cover this? "This weekend."

"Is the lack of oxygen bothering you or something?"

"Um, no."

"I meant work, Whit. In addition to working on your property, I had plans to finish the bid for my next job. It's due Tuesday."

Relief whooshed out of him. Sounded like his leading competition was a calculator, or maybe an erasable pen. He thought he could outlast those two entries.

Her lean fingers clenched and unclenched, gathering fistfuls of faded blue jeans in her hands. Her forehead wrinkled with concern. With his luck, she'd start throwing up any minute.

"Honey?"

"Huh?"

The fact she responded to the endearment without knocking out his teeth had to be a good sign. "You okay?"

"No. Nothing about this situation is okay."

He walked over and plunked down next to her. Instead of scooting away as he expected, she slid closer and balanced her head on his shoulder. The barest touch of her silky hair against his skin made him rock-hard and ready to test the chair. But now wasn't the time.

"Tell me what you're thinking," he said.

"I have trouble with small spaces."

Her voice was so soft and small he barely heard her. When the words registered, he dropped his head back against the hard wall in defeat. His mind battled with his erection to do the right thing. No way was he going to take advantage of a scared woman.

He blamed his mother and all her lessons about treating women with respect. All that stuff about women being equals. About being protective and not taking advantage. He knew those lessons would ruin his fun some day.

She didn't have time for this.

For the panic welling inside her.

For being locked away from her work.

For the kick of interest that slammed into her whenever she got this close to Whit.

"I can't just sit around here for the next few days," she said.

Laughter rumbled against her ear. "Oh, okay then. We could try yelling the door open."

"You don't understand."

"Then fill me in."

He dragged his thumb across her lower lip in slow motion. A shiver pumped through her lungs. She pulled back from the soft contact. If he started touching, she'd start liking it.

"Forget it."

"Ah, I see we're back to the tough-guy routine."

"Right. Because you want to hear all about my deadlines and responsibilities," she said dryly. "In case you forget, you're one of my obligations at the moment, or at the very least your house is. If I complain about work, I'm basically complaining about you."

"Wouldn't be the first time."

She decided to ignore that one. "Not to mention the fact that I'm under contract to the National Trust to complete this job."

"Are you afraid I'll call the National Trust and turn you in?"

"Let's just say I find clients get a little nervous when the contractor starts panicking about missing a deadline."

"Are you that far behind on my job?"

Amazing how he jumped right to the blame game. "The operative word is "we" here. We're in this together, big boy."

He pretended to sniffle. "That's so sweet. You're going to make me cry."

She cracked a smile. Couldn't help it. "You don't seem particularly worried about this job running late."

"I'm not."

Now, how was that possible? Her life ran on a steady schedule. Whit was the most put-together guy she'd ever seen. How could he not care? "I don't believe you."

"Suit yourself."

"The bid on this job included a late charge. If I don't get the work done on time, you get to dock my crew's pay. That doesn't exactly sound like a guy who doesn't care."

He closed his eyes and grinned. "That was Adam. My brother is a master negotiator. There's probably another one or two clauses in there that would make your toes curl if you focused on them."

Or if she were smart enough to pick them out. Which she wasn't. "For once, I'm happy you're the brother assigned to this job."

"Really, Hannah, you have to stop with the flattery. My heart can't take it."

"You're an idiot."

"That's probably true, but the bottom line is that I'd never go head to head with Adam."

"He's a barracuda?"

"If you tell him I admitted that, I'll deny it."

"Whether you care or not about punctuality isn't the point."

"It's not? A second ago I was the client. You know, the one person who mattered."

"I can't be late," she blurted out.

One of his stunning green eyes popped open. "And why is that exactly?"

"Getting on the National Trust's approved list of construction companies wasn't easy. I have no intention of getting bumped off so soon."

"Getting on was tough. Thanks to all the red tape and politics, getting kicked off would be harder. Try again."

This is what came from hanging out with smart guys. She could fool a dumb guy. "It's a long story."

"I've got nothing but time, Hannah. My biggest concern at the moment is that my butt might fall asleep and I won't be able to stand up without your help."

Never one to share her fears and personal life, Hannah toyed with the idea of telling him to mind his own business. But there was something about Whit. About his smooth delivery, his almost nonchalant manner that had her babbling like a fool.

She kissed caution good-bye. If you couldn't trust a man locked in a sex room with you, then who could you trust?

"I have a deadline. I have to bring in three solid jobs, simultaneously, all within eight months, or I lose this company." What she didn't say was that the company was her life. The only thing she had ever been good at in her life. Without it, she was nothing.

"That's a pretty abbreviated version." He bent his leg and hooked an elbow around one knee. "Care to tell me why you have this big deadline and what all this has to do with the National Trust?"

"I'm the family screwup, more or less."

"The light bulb over my head is still out. Maybe a few more facts would help."

She exhaled. "You know that the National Trust only approves certain companies to work on historically protected buildings."

"Sure."

"Well, I studied. Worked my butt off, actually, in order to get the coveted approval. Figured once I got on the list, the sheer number of historical properties in the area would allow me to specialize, and in turn make a good deal of money."

"Sure. Me, too. Architects go through the same process."

"But you own this house."

"All that means is I could get a grant to get some of the work done. You know, pick historically accurate paint and light fixtures and all that. But to work on other people's properties and hold myself out as an expert in this area took a lot more work. So I sympathize with you."

He caught her gaze and held it, his eyes gentle and caring. He was either the master manipulator or he actually wanted to hear what she had to say.

When she hesitated, he groaned. "You can sigh and stall all you want. I'm not going anywhere. Spill it, Hannah."

Fine. If he wanted her life history, he could have it. The chances of them suffocating or killing each other within the next two days had to be pretty good. Might as well go out with a bang, so to speak.

Plus, she knew if they stopped talking, they'd be all over each other. You couldn't put this type of uncontrolled sexual electricity in a confined space and not expect an explosion or two.

"I come from the poor side of the family. My mother disappointed her father by getting pregnant, without the benefit of marriage and before turning twenty, and was pushed out."

"Of her share of the inheritance?"

As if the money ever mattered. "Of everything. No dinners. No holidays. No contact or support, financial or otherwise. It was as if she no longer existed."

"Which made you not exist."

"Yeah, something like that." Or, to be more precise, exactly like that.

"What about your grandmother? Other relatives?"

Asked by a man who had a real family. Hannah could always tell. The sympathetic frown and wide-eyed shock of her story separated those who understood from those who never could.

"Everyone followed my grandfather's lead. Mom and I were out."

"And your dad?"

"Married my mom, but a happy ending wasn't meant to be. He was killed in a car accident when I was ten."

"Jesus, Hannah. I'm sorry."

"Anyway, after my mother died, my grandfather made me a deal. He planned to groom me to be some type of entrepreneur. Not my thing. I didn't want any part of the intellectual, sit-behind-a-desk lifestyle."

"So?"

"Much to his dismay, I opted for one of his less impressive companies. This one. Doubt he even remembered it existed. Probably planned to sell it off in pieces but never got around to it. Apparently, sometime during his business marauding days he had taken over a larger company that owned a small but viable rehab construction company."

"And a new career was born."

"Not quite but the fit was perfect. All I ever wanted was to build things. Use my hands, not my brains, to create."

"Some would say creating takes brains."

If he kept saying cool things like that, she'd be all over him. "Not for Gramps. I'm a disappointment."

"Sounds like he's a—"

"He is but don't say it."

"The man's priorities are a bit confused, if you ask me."

"Yeah, well, Cole is the family star. The good grandchild. I didn't know him when I was younger but I never stop hearing about his virtues."

He swore. "Cole never said a word."

"He was on the right side of the family. Perfect and smart. Everything a grandfather could want in a grandchild."

"Are we talking about the same Cole who almost flunked out of college?"

She couldn't help but smile. Cole acted as a surrogate big brother, trying to set a good example. Hannah long suspected Cole's devilish smile hid a much more interesting history.

"My one shot is this company. If I can prove my competency to my grandfather, the business is mine. For a price, of course."

"Everything has a price. What's his?"

"If I impress him, I get to buy out his interest and he won't sell to a third party as he's threatened to do. But I have to do it his way. Prove my worthiness. If I fail, I go back to the beginning and start all over as someone's employee."

"You do all of this work and the old man still makes you purchase the company. He doesn't just hand the reins over and walk away?"

"That's the deal."

"Your grandfather's not exactly the cuddly type, is he?"

"Hardly." When Whit traced a finger down her thigh, the rest of the grandfather topic lodged in her throat. "What are you doing?"

He squeezed her knee. "What I've wanted to do for weeks. Touch you."

Uh-oh. Time to deflect with joking. "If you really had a burning desire to fondle my leg, you could have told me."

"I think I am."

He clearly didn't understand the purpose of deflecting.

Her head started to spin. She didn't know if the wave of

dizziness came from his touch or her fear over small spaces. Or maybe from her very real concern that getting so close to Whit might mean she'd never be able to break apart from him again.

"Are you making a pass at a vulnerable and claustrophobic woman?"

His finger stopped in its path and breath hissed out from between his teeth. "Not anymore."

Suddenly, that wasn't the answer she wanted to hear.

Three

Whit's brain had just convinced the monster in his pants to give up and find another strategy when he felt the slow slide of Hannah's hand up his thigh. The nerve endings jumped under her light touch and his erection swelled in welcome. Whatever she was doing, he hoped she didn't stop anytime soon.

"Uh, Hannah, I gotta be honest with you. I'm getting mixed signals here."

"I could see where you'd think that."

"Yeah, well, I'm still confused."

"Take my mind off of where we are, Whit." Her husky voice shot from his brain to the soles of his feet.

She was an enigma. One second she cut him short, launching verbal volleys at the speed of sound. The next she turned all gooey, making him desperate to protect her and willing to throw out all of his careful plans. Now, she melted in his arms, making him desperate to have her.

"Is it the space thing? Do you want me to try the door again?"

"No."

Good answer, but he needed a bit more direction before he made his move. "What do you want?"

"A distraction."

Somewhere in the back of his mind a choir started singing. "You sure?"

She glanced up, her eyes shiny and bright. "Absolutely."

That was just about the best news he'd ever heard. No way was he going to fumble this opportunity. Or give her two seconds to change her mind.

"Then let's see what I can do to make you feel more comfortable in this room."

He was willing to try anything to help ease her discomfort. If he couldn't get her mind off the room and on him in two minutes, he'd fake an early rescue. No reason for her to suffer for his lust. Not when he was doing so well suffering all by himself.

He stood up and started unbuttoning his shirt.

Her big brown eyes widened in surprise. "What are you doing?"

"Helping with your education."

"Which education is that exactly?" The green around her mouth faded, leaving her skin bright pink and full of life.

"Your sexual education."

"How kind of you."

"See, there's nothing wrong with this room and everything right with the idea of two consenting grown-ups enjoying each other."

"You sound sure of yourself."

"Let's just say I'm sure of you."

"When I said distract me, I was thinking about some kissing. Maybe a little fondling."

For once, they were on the same track. She was just a lap or two behind. "We'll get to all of that soon enough."

"How about in the next three minutes?"

"I like to think I'm a bit more savvy than that."

"Savvy, maybe. Subtle, no."

That could be his theme song. "I thought you were look-

ing for a distraction. This room calls out for naked distraction."

"You are that."

"Not yet, but I will be."

As each button slipped free from its hole, revealing inch
by glorious inch of fine male chest, Hannah's heart did a little tumble. Whit's green eyes glittered with excitement and
the bulge in his khakis left little to the imagination.

She wondered what about this seductive scene was supposed to make her feel relaxed. She felt the exact opposite of
calm. More like hot and jittery. Like ripping off her clothes
and climbing on top of him. No, not comfortable at all.

She tried one last time to grab onto some common sense.
No need to let a little abject fear rule her interested body. Her
careful plan to keep a safe distance between them hovered on
the verge of vanishing.

"Maybe we should slow down a little. Talk first."

"I think we're done talking for a while. And *this* is inevitable."

Whoa. Hearing him say it made her insides clench. Getting
horizontal with a handsome architect was not on the list of
things to do to get ahead in business.

"Whit, I know I started us down this road but maybe we
should pull back. Just a bit. After all, we don't really even
like each other."

There, she said it. There was no way he could argue with
that kind of logic.

"I like you just fine."

"We fight all the time. You drive me nuts."

"For a smart woman you're being kind of dumb."

He was lucky he said that with a smile. "Are you trying to
woo me with flattery?"

If so, it was working. At this rate, she'd be peeling his
clothes off before the second hand swept around the clock
dial one more time.

"No. I'm saying we've been circling each other for weeks, pretending we don't feel this pull, this thing brewing between us. You've been all business, focusing on work and deadlines and orders, and no touchy," he said.

"Did you say we have a 'thing'?"

"My point is, there's no reason for either of us to deny our attraction."

Now they were up to attraction. At least that sounded better than having a thing.

Her gaze took a little dip, roaming down to his navel and back up to that chiseled jaw again. Attraction, hah! She passed attracted several weeks ago and was down the road of longing.

"That's better," he said.

When did his voice get so damn sexy? "What is?"

His shirt flapped open, revealing his muscled shoulders and chiseled pecs. Whatever this guy did behind his desk to buff that bod was a good thing. A very good thing.

"You focusing on me. I like it."

As if she could think about anything else at the moment. Hell, she was lucky she could still speak since her tongue had swelled up and filled the entire space inside her dry mouth.

"What's the plan here?" she asked. And how soon before he got naked?

"I'm glad you asked. See, we're going to get acquainted with the room using some of the toys at our disposal."

She almost stopped listening when his hands moved to his belt buckle, but his inviting words brought her back. She stilled. "Except the chair."

"No, honey. We'll be using the chair. That's just not lesson number one."

He stepped forward, his muscular body closing in as he encircled her in his strong arms. Her warm and willing body slid into him, each inch fitting like a perfect puzzle piece against his.

In a motion so slow and deliberate her heart flipped over,

he lowered his head toward hers. Small puffs of air brushed against her cheek as he nuzzled first her nose then her waiting mouth with his lips. He cradled her head in his strong hands. His fingers raked through her hair, releasing the silken strands from their loose tie and freeing them to his gentle touch.

His mouth brushed against hers, back and forth, in turn coaxing and igniting. His wet tongue caressed the seam between her lips until her mouth fell open, giving him full access to the hot interior.

When he deepened the kiss, sank into her with his body and eager mouth, sparks exploded behind her eyes. Need churned deep inside her. Her shoulders shook without any signal from her brain. Hell, her boots may have popped off her feet.

Her body grew wet and ready, every inch of her lower body softening and opening for him. The straightlaced anal type had never interested her before. Tidy proper brainiacs left her cold. Not Whit. He made her white hot with need.

He seeped into her mind at work and dominated her sexiest fantasies off the job. With her eyes closed and her mind at rest she saw him. Naked and proud. In bed. On the stairs. Taking her by the kitchen sink. Lowering his body over hers with nothing but bare skin as a blanket. The images clicked by like a homemade movie in her head, lighting her skin on fire.

For once she was going to take what she needed. What she wanted. And for one night, no more than two, forget about the consequences. Forget about her silent internal promise to prove something to her overbearing family.

She inhaled, letting his intoxicating earthy male scent invade her senses, and took the plunge. "I'm ready for my lesson."

His head pulled back. "You're sure."

Since it wasn't a question, she limited her response to a nod.

His hands skimmed against her skin, moving up and down her forearms. "No regrets. No limits."

"I'm all yours."

"Two rules."

Rules? The one thing she didn't want was rules. Let alone two of them. Her time with Whit was about breaking rules, not following them.

"That doesn't sound very sexy, Whit." She tried to kiss him but he moved his mouth away.

"Don't you worry, sweetheart, we'll get to the sexy. Right now we need to be clear with each other."

Would he ever stop talking and kiss her again? "Go ahead."

"I do anything you don't like, you tell me."

Her stomach plummeted to her feet as she kissed her doubts goodbye. The night was for her. He was giving her this gift.

"What if you do something I do like?"

A wide grin spread across his lips. "I'll know, baby. Your body will tell me."

She swallowed, frantically trying to draw saliva into her dry mouth. "And the second rule?"

"This is between you and me. What happens in here stays in here."

Something bubbled up inside of her. Since she wasn't a giggler she decided it must be laughter. "Not the locker room bragging type, are you?"

"Never."

Her snappy comeback died on her lips. He was dead serious. He was going to make love to her. Give her what she wanted, without strings and the fear of career destruction. She leaned back in his arms, prepared to enjoy the show.

"Maybe rule number three should be a little less talking and a lot more action."

"Oh, honey, you'll want me to talk. Believe me." He winked as he stepped back. In two seconds he pulled the ends of his boring shirt out of his pants and dropped the material in a ball on the floor.

She was about to protest his lightning speed. Then she got a good look at him.

Oxygen clogged in her throat, making it impossible for her to breathe. The man was perfect. Not an ounce of fat anywhere on that tight stomach. Just a set of wide shoulders falling in a perfect vee to his slim waist. He was the most gorgeous desk jockey she'd ever seen.

For the weekend, he was hers to do with as she pleased.

"Now the pants," she said.

"On one condition."

Anything. All he had to do was ask. Just ask fast. "What?"

"Take that horrid shirt off."

Hannah glanced down at her offending flannel covering. True, the garment was ugly, but it served a purpose. To ward off any unwanted male attention. Putting a visual wall between her body and the men who worked for her was the only logical choice. The only smart option if she wanted to win their respect. But, for once, she wanted to play dumb. Take a risk.

She wanted Whit's attention.

On her.

All the time.

So she abandoned her checkered shield. She lifted the clunky shirt over her head and threw it to the floor, leaving only a slim-fit ribbed tank top and baggy blue jeans for protection. Despite the warm room, the intimate surroundings and skimpy top made her tremble.

"Much better." His eyes gleamed with appreciation.

"Now it's your turn."

"My shirt is off, honey. You're the one who needs to catch up."

Sure, once she was able to breathe again, she'd get right on that catching up thing.

"You have a good start. I agree." She trailed her fingers

over his bare chest, letting the tips linger over the soft fuzz of hair scattered there. With each brush against his skin, his breathing hitched. When her hands wandered down to his waist, her fingernails scraping against his lightly tanned skin, his sculpted stomach muscles clenched. "But I think we can do better."

He hissed. "I'm all yours, baby."

She believed him. The rush of breath and sly twinkle in his eyes. All of the signs were there. He wanted her. Boring, uneducated Hannah Bridges.

As the intoxicating power filled her head, her defenses weakened. The need to control, to protect her heart from harm, took a backseat to being with Whit in this moment.

"You know, the way I hear it a pupil sometimes learns best with a live demonstration. Sort of a hands-on kind of thing," she whispered.

"I'm always in favor of using hands."

He put his words into action. With his hands on her hips, he treated her to a tiny squeeze. The small touch chased the chill from her body.

"Seems to me we could read about what to do in those dusty books over there or we could use our imagination and experiment a little," she said.

"I don't need a book to know I want you."

"With all that expensive education of yours, I figured you'd be in favor of analyzing every angle first."

"I'll take you whatever way I can get you."

She gave into one small fantasy before moving on to the biggie. The almost obsessive desire to muss his already unruly mass of hair. Everything about him was neat and clean and pressed. Now he had the hair of a mad scientist.

The silky strands slipped through her fingers. "I vote we try the live version."

"I'm all yours, lady. You lead. I'll follow."

The blank ticket was her dream. "So, I'm the boss?"

His hands traveled up her back and pulled her tight against his erection. "And I'm your humble follower."

Hot damn.

"Let's try this." She reached up and grabbed the handcuffs hanging loose above his head.

His sexy smile faltered. "I'm not much into bondage."

"Me either. But then again, I'm not into sex rooms, one-night stands, or sleeping with men on the job." She treated him to a quick, hard kiss. "I plan to break all those rules tonight."

"Don't forget about tomorrow."

She wasn't sure she'd survive the next hour and he was talking about a second day of lovemaking?

"Right. And tomorrow."

She slipped the handcuffs over his wrists and clamped them shut. He shook his fists, as if testing the metal's strength. Then he swore like a drunken sailor.

"Uh, Hannah—"

"I'm the boss."

His nostrils flared as he dragged in a breath. "We have a problem, though. You see, if my hands are bound I can't touch you."

Her confidence growing, she slipped her fingers beneath the waistband of his creased pants. Air hissed out from between his lips when her knuckles brushed against his bulging crotch. Just as she planned.

Small clicks echoed in the room as she unzipped his pants. When her hand slid inside the cotton material to cup him, a tremor shook his large frame.

"The important thing here, Whit, is that I can touch you."

"Damn, Hannah."

She pumped her hand up and down in a slow tortuous movement.

"Jesus."

"Tell me what you want."

"Squeeze me." His chest rose and fell in rapid pants. "Harder, babe. Hold me harder."

She thought he'd never ask. Her fingers traced his length, overflowing her fingers. "Since I'm the boss, you should beg."

"Whatever you want."

His head dropped back. The chains holding his arms jangled as he pulled down hard with his biceps in what she guessed was an involuntary reaction. A slight sheen of perspiration moistened his skin when she tightened her hold on him, banding his width with her fingers.

"You are so smooth and hard." Her finger traced the tip of his penis until his broad shoulders shook.

"Damn it, Hannah," he grounded out. "Tighter."

"Like this?" Her palm traveled up and down, growing bolder with each stroke. When his hips bucked against her hand, she pulled back.

"Hannah!"

"You don't need to shout. I can hear you."

"What are you doing? Damn it, don't stop."

"But you're not ready for me, Whit. Not yet."

Four

What in the hell was she waiting for? He wasn't going to get any bigger. That would be biologically impossible. And he couldn't possibly want her more than he did right now.

The minutes blurred until he could no longer think of anything but her. He prayed for death. Begged her to let him come. Swore at her to end it and put him inside of her. Pleaded with her to show some mercy as her small hands caressed him and shaped him.

She made him wait.

He thought about gnawing through the handcuffs and escaping to freedom. But that would mean leaving Hannah and there was no way in hell that was going to happen, not when her sexy feminine side showed up to play.

Finally, when his energy drained and his control hovered on the edge, she stripped him naked. Dropped his pants to his ankles and dragged his gray boxer briefs down his legs with her teeth. His knees nearly buckled when her eager fingers toured his ass, caressing and tracing, before dipping into the crease.

He had spent frustrating weeks imagining how good her tight sheath would feel as he slipped inside her. How her body would glove him. He figured she would end his agony quickly. Be overcome with shyness and let him take the lead.

Wrong.

The little minx was enjoying herself too much to give him peace. Oh no, she delayed his gratification as long as possible. When she decided to drop her rules, she dropped them all.

Twenty minutes later he stood naked, chained to the ceiling, legs spread wide apart and his backside leaning against the chair. With Hannah sitting at his feet.

Her tongue roamed over his lower body, taking his eager cock into her slick, wet mouth. He was seconds from bursting, from spilling into her, when she pulled back again. His hips jumped in protest.

Sweat beaded on his forehead as he watched her stand up. She shook out her hair, letting it fall against her shoulders. With his mouth already watering, she pulled that tiny tank T-shirt over her head, exposing creamy breasts to his view. Her soft pink nipples stood at sharp points against her flushed skin. She was round and firm and perfect for his hands.

"Jesus, baby. Unlock me so I can touch you."

"Not yet."

Again with the "not yet" bullshit. He made a mental note to work on her vocabulary as soon as he could speak again.

He tried to convince her by describing the image forming in his head. "Think of how good it will feel when I run my tongue over your nipples. When I strip those pants down your legs and caress every inch of your skin with my mouth and hands."

She shivered but didn't bend. "I like you like this, Whit. At my mercy."

He'd be on his knees if the handcuffs reached that far. "Hell, you don't have to tie me up for that. Anything you want."

"Anything?" Her husky voice licked at his erection.

"Let me make you come like I've fantasized about. Let me kiss you. Everywhere."

"Soon." Her brown eyes sparkled with mischief. "What I want is to strip for you."

He couldn't agree more.

Then she added to her ingenious plan.

"After I'm naked and wet"—she whispered the last part—"I'm gonna climb on top of you, put you deep inside of me, and ride you until we both come."

He gritted his teeth to keep from exploding right there.

She walked around his nude body, trailing her fingers over his bare skin as she went. "Or maybe I'll make it last. Rub my body against yours but not let you inside me. Make you come while I watch, then start again."

Her words were going to kill him. The touch got him there faster. His head fell back as he tried to count to ten. Shame he couldn't remember what came after number two.

"Or I could take you in my mouth. Give you some release. Then I'll use my hands."

He swore, using every word he knew in one inventive sentence that would have made the old Hannah blush and his mother smack him silly.

"That was impressive." She stopped behind him, her body leaning against him so that her mound pressed against his ass. "So is this." She reached around and gave him one last squeeze.

His body trembled and his muscles grew weak from the tension. He had two, maybe three minutes, before he lost control.

"Honey, please. Get me down or jump on top of me. Just do something."

"Not yet."

He officially hated that phrase. "The hell with waiting. Get protection."

"But—"

"Now, Hannah. No more games."

She cocked her head to the side and stared at him, her eyes clouded with need. "From where?"

Whit took her momentary brain cell loss as a sign of just how interested she was in him. The feeling was mutual. After all, he had planned this scene for weeks. Without the handcuffs.

The room had every sexual toy in history. Condoms were right at home here in sex land. At least they were once he planted them two days ago. His uncle and aunt were way past the point of needing protection. He wasn't.

"On the counter, honey."

"Over there?"

Now she had to be playing with him. "Hurry!"

She was gone for less than a second. She reappeared before him, her eyes glazed with pleasure and dark as night. He reached for her until the clanging chains stopped him. Her petite form stood just outside his grasp.

He opened his mouth to beg one last time but closed it again when she reached for her jeans. One by one, she loosened the buttons on her fly then eased the baggy pants down her slim legs. The slow striptease topped every fantasy he had ever had about Hannah.

So did her amazing body.

Her thighs were muscular, yet soft. Her legs were long, the perfect length to wrap around his waist while he plunged inside her. She stripped until the only scrap of clothing separating them was a pair of thick, bulky socks on her feet.

His gaze traveled back up her exquisite body, stopping to linger on her thighs and on the soft tuft of blond hair shielding her mound. Past her thin waist, up to her ample breasts, before settling on her lovely face.

"Damn, you're beautiful." His mouth watered. Actually watered, something that had never happened to him before. "Stunning. If I ever see you wearing one of those man shirts again, I'll burn it."

She melted into a great big puddle of need.

His husky voice crept past her defenses and walked straight into her heart. His erection, plump and long, showed his patience had expired, but he rattled off her nonexistent virtues as if they really existed.

"You are one amazing woman, Hannah Bridges. Sexy and smart. Driven and talented."

She lunged for him.

She kissed him with a wild passion she didn't know existed. Her tongue snaked between his lips and plunged inside to rub against his. She was wet and ready to take him. Her hands roamed free over his body. Sliding down his smooth chest to his pulsing penis.

She rolled on the condom and sent a little thank-you to Uncle Calvin for his boy scout-like preparedness. One bare leg slid up his thigh until it hitched on his hip. Whit scooted down, lowering his body under hers as far as the chains would allow. The move gave her the advantage she needed. She wrapped her other leg around his waist and lowered her body onto his.

By inches, she slid her slick channel around him, bringing him deep inside. Tiny internal muscles clenched and tightened. The snug fit brought every nerve ending to life inside her in a white explosion.

"Holy shit." His head dropped onto her shoulder.

"I want you. Now."

"Can't tell you how happy I am to hear that." He huffed out his words between some very flattering pants. "I'm not going anywhere. Just breathe in, then push your hips down. Hard and fast."

She wanted to prolong the feeling but he had other ideas.

He gritted his teeth together near her ear. "Now, baby."

Her body didn't need any other encouragement. She pressed down on a sigh, pushing his penis inside her to the hilt. His body pulsed. The tight, full feeling was extraordinary.

His tongue swept out and licked her nipple. "I need you to move. Really move."

Lost in the moment, she almost didn't hear his desperate plea. "What?"

He arched against her until she squealed. Her lower body vibrated, the knot inside her pulling and tugging into a tight little ball. She squeezed her insides, pressing against his length as her body rocked up and down against his.

With one last squeeze of her thighs against his narrow hips, her body let go. Her chest heaved from the force of the air trying to escape through her windpipe.

Beneath her, Whit's solid body stiffened. His arms stretched to full length as she raked her nails across his back and tightened her legs around his waist.

"Come for me, Whit."

"Fuck me."

"No, fuck me. Now."

"Jesus, Hannah."

"Come."

He threw his head back and shouted as a shudder raced through him from neck to calf. His hips bounced and shifted as his body continued to move in and out of hers.

His body went limp and his knees started to bend. The chains held his body in place as he exploded inside of her. Heavy breathing drummed in her ears and hot breath tickled her neck.

Her muscles turned to liquid but he managed to balance both of their bodies on his, a feat worthy of a place in the Olympics. She wanted to stay there all night but took pity on him. His muscles had to be as squishy as hers.

She lifted off and slid down his body, earning a rumbling growl from somewhere deep in his chest. She leaned against him, afraid her jellied muscles wouldn't hold her up. "I'm not sure I can stand."

"You're amazing." He leaned down and placed a soft kiss on her lips. His piercing green eyes focused on her. "I'd love to curl up on the floor with you, but I'm locked up." He clanked the cuffs together to prove his point.

This time she did giggle. She thought about dancing around in a circle. Her body felt light and free. All her tension disappeared, taking her sexual hang-ups along with it.

All thanks to Whit. He was gorgeous and funny. A little controlling and difficult, but all man. Hell, even the boring khakis turned her on. And without them, well, he was even hotter.

He laughed. "What are you thinking about? That little smile is almost evil."

"Not evil. Interested."

"That's my girl. This time when you come, I want my hands all over you."

His words made something flare to life in her belly. "I'm not arguing. I might even be willing to try that chair."

"Now you're talking." He pressed his lips behind her ear. "We can get started as soon as you set me free."

She'd bite through them if he promised to do that thing with his mouth again. "Sure. Tell me how to take them off."

"Right."

"Right," she repeated.

"I'm serious, Hannah." And he suddenly looked it too.

"I guess that's a good thing."

His body stiffened and not in a good way. "Are you kidding?"

"I don't even know what we're talking about."

His eyes narrowed into tiny slits. "Hannah, please tell me you have the key to the handcuffs."

"There's a key?"

Five

Whit inhaled, trying to calm his anger.

"There's nothing here." Hannah scurried around the room. She picked up a particularly large dildo then dropped it as if it were on fire.

"Not your favorite toy?"

"Let's just say your aunt must have been a strong woman. Or very large. Was she actually able to walk after spending time down here?"

"I've asked you never to talk about my uncle and aunt and whatever they did in this room."

"Hey, you're the one with the porno relatives."

He wondered if Hannah even realized she forgot to put her clothes back on. "Yeah, no inhibitions at all."

Every time she turned away she flashed him a centerfold shot of her bare ass. Round and perfect and creamy milk white in color. Not that he didn't enjoy the view. He did, but being restrained was not in any of his plans. With every second that ticked by he lost an opportunity to touch her.

"Check the drawers," he called out.

"No way."

"Why the hell not?"

"Do you know what kind of crap could be in there?"

"You mean crap like the key?" He shook his arms until the chains started jingling.

"Whit, get a clue. How do I know the stuff in there is even clean?"

His head fell forward, his chin against his chest. "You're killing me, babe."

"You look pretty healthy to me."

He slowly lifted his head. He wasn't sure when she had moved but she stood right in front of him, her gaze focused on his growing erection.

"How did you do that? It's only been a few minutes."

He was two seconds from chewing off his arm to get loose. "I didn't do anything. You did."

"Aren't you supposed to need some time to revive? You know, before you can do that." She pointed at his cock.

"That? Good lord, woman, show the instrument some respect. That part of my body happens to worship you."

"Will it do so again soon?"

When her pink tongue slipped out to lick her lips, he lost his cool. "Hannah, you have five seconds to find the key."

She slammed her hands on her hips. With her legs wide apart and her brown eyes gleaming, she looked ready for battle. Naked battle with a telling wetness between her thighs.

"Don't boss me around, Whit. I'm not your slave girl."

"No, as of five minutes ago you're my lover. My very naked lover and if you don't get me down soon, we're going to have a second round of stand-up sex."

Her voice grew sexy, as if the devil himself sent her up to torment him. "That doesn't sound so bad."

"And you're dressed for it."

The blood drained from her face.

Well, damn. He wondered if the word *lover* got those tiny wheels spinning in her head again. Well, she'd have to get used to it. They were lovers now. Finally. Now that they'd made love, he had no intention of going back to last names and icy stares.

"Honey?"

"I'm naked!" She shouted the obvious right before she started racing around the room ranting about someone being an idiot. He was pretty sure she meant him.

Hannah knocked against a stack of his uncle's more racy books. They tumbled off the shelf and landed with a sharp crack on the floor. Papers flew. Condoms flipped through the air. A box of scented oils crashed and the sweet smell of strawberry filled his nose. When a stream of jelly-like liquid squished under her foot, she squealed.

She finally grabbed up his shirt and started to get dressed. He tried to protest but the evil eye she shot him convinced him to keep quiet. Crouched over, her breasts pressed tight against her knees, she slipped on the button-down oxford with a speed that both impressed him and made his blood boil. The only problem was that the twisting circus move hid her beautiful body from his view.

"Now why are you doing that? There's no need for formal wear down here."

"What do you think, you idiot? I can't waltz around without any clothes on."

Back to name-calling. Great. That probably said more about his lovemaking skills than he cared to admit.

"No one is dancing, and no one can see you but me."

She bunched the sleeves up past her elbows. She stood up, her spine stiff and her chin up.

"So?"

"So? Did you forget what just happened in here?"

"Hardly."

"I've seen you. Every bare inch. Fabulous, by the way."

Her hands dropped to her sides and her mouth fell open. She was so damn adorable with her hair all mussed and her lips swollen from his kisses. His shirt skimmed the tops of her delicious upper thighs, revealing miles of delectable leg and hinting at the treasures underneath.

He vowed never to dry clean the oxford again.

"You let me walk around without any clothes and never said anything?"

"Absolutely." And he'd do it again in a second, this time keeping his mouth shut so the show would last a few minutes longer.

"I looked ridiculous."

"No. Never that."

She sputtered. "A decent man would have reminded me."

"A stupid man did."

"Whit—"

Time to get this hunt back on track. "The key."

"What?"

"Unless you want to spend the rest of the weekend feeding me and helping me whiz—"

"That's just not going to happen."

"—we need to find that key."

Interesting. Her mouth was all over him but she couldn't feed him a granola bar? "Just trying to be practical, honey. A guy's gotta go sometime."

"Speaking of that. I need to use the bathroom. I never expected to be locked in a basement when I drank twenty ounces of coffee this morning."

Funny how she thought going to the bathroom was more important than releasing him from the cuffs. Now he knew how frozen meat felt.

"Could you wait until we find the key?"

"No."

Of course not. He nodded in the general direction of the small bathroom in the corner. "In there. It's nothing special. Just a toilet and a small sink."

"I'm not choosy."

The bathroom door clicked shut just as the banging started. Whit jumped a foot. He whirled around, twisting his arms, and nearly strangled himself with the metal chains hanging above his head.

He could hear the furious shouting on the other side of the

door. The visitor's identity wasn't a big mystery. Cole. A man with possibly the worst timing in the world. No way was Cole going to see him trussed up like a turkey.

Whit yanked down hard on the restraints, trying to break their hold. He'd either be free or bleeding to death from his flesh wounds in the next few minutes.

The outside door creaked.

Whit pulled harder, his muscles straining. When the door swung open, he began to pray. Where was a giant sinkhole when you needed one?

Cole stalked inside. And he wasn't alone. Adam followed close at his heels, his blue eyes sparkling with mischief.

Whit dropped his chin to his chest. "Shit."

Cole looked at Whit then stared at the floor. "Damn it, man. Where the hell are your clothes?"

"If I'm not mistaken, they're scattered all over the floor," Adam said.

Cole's tan skin blanched white. "Give me a reason not to kill you. Both of you."

"What the hell did I do?" Adam asked.

Whit had a more pressing question. "Why are you here?"

"Adam told me about your plan to set up Hannah."

"Adam did what?"

"I didn't use the word 'plan'. I said—" Adam shook his head. "Really, Whit, how am I supposed to have a conversation when you're naked? And is that a condom?"

"Get out." Whit hissed out his suggestion.

"Oh man, this makes my day. Except for the part about seeing my baby brother naked." Adam bent over double, hands slapping his knees. He laughed until he choked.

Whit thought that was fitting.

Cole clearly didn't find the situation as amusing. If the way his cheeks puffed in and out was any indication, he was furious. "What are you doing, Whit? I want an explanation. Now."

Adam gestured at Whit then took off in another fit of

laughter. He finally calmed down enough to choke out a sentence. "What the hell do you think he's doing? The guy's naked and tied up."

"I'm trying hard not to notice that part," Cole grumbled.

"Can't you see he made a pass and Hannah dumped his sorry ass?"

Whit shot a worried glance at the bathroom door. Through some blessed act of intervention, it stayed closed. He only hoped the tiny room was soundproof, too. They had to shut up before Hannah walked out.

"Look, Adam—"

"So, I guess you've finally lost your touch with women." Adam launched into his smart-ass diatribe. "All those years of playing sports, doing anything to score, those must be behind you. Hell, you can't even get a woman to stay with you in a locked room."

"He's lucky Hannah didn't kill him," Cole muttered. "I still might."

A man could only take so much. "What the hell's wrong with you, Cole? I'm the one staked to the wall."

"Hannah's my cousin. You used me to get to her. I thought you were asking about her for work reasons."

"I was!"

"Do I look like a damn imbecile?"

"Cole, calm down. Let Whit explain." Adam walked around his brother, shaking his head in mock disapproval. "What happened? Hannah figure out about your planned seduction and decide to humiliate you instead of falling at your feet?"

Whit tried to figure out how long he had before Hannah stalked out of the bathroom and belted him. "Adam—"

"If I had known you were asking all those questions about Hannah so she could become your next conquest, I would have flattened your ass."

"Oh, leave the poor guy alone, Cole. He's had a rough night."

"She doesn't have anyone. I feel protective of her," Cole said.

Adam snorted. "Then why'd you give Whit the lowdown on her?"

Definitely time to stop this conversation. "Guys—"

Cole interrupted again. "I thought he was interested in giving her a job."

Adam smirked. "Looks like he was trying to."

"I meant the house job, you ass."

"That was a front. He saw Hannah, all cool and aloof, and decided to teach her a lesson."

"Adam!" This time Whit shouted to shut Adam up.

Cole and Adam both looked at him. Cole spoke first. "Why are you yelling?"

"Shut the fuck up." Whit gritted out the words through clenched teeth.

"Well, well, well. Aren't we moody when we don't get laid." Adam chuckled at his joke.

Whit tried to figure out a way to bang their heads together with his hands tied, or at least make them shut up before Hannah overheard and ripped his balls off with her fingernails.

Cole nodded in Whit's general direction without giving him eye contact. "As far as I can tell, he deserves it."

"Not to state the obvious but you're the one who set Whit on her tail." Adam chuckled again then stopped. "Damn, Whit, put some clothes on."

Cole added his two cents. "Yeah. That's not right."

"Don't you think I would if I could," Whit hissed out. "I have to get down first."

"Where's the key?" Adam asked.

Whit was pretty sure he could kick Adam in the head from this position. It would be worth the risk of landing on his ass to get these two to be quiet.

"Do you think I would still be hanging here if I had the damn key?"

"All I'm saying is that there's no question I got the family jewels. Maybe Hannah ran after she saw you naked."

Cole growled. "Damn, Adam, you're looking at him there?"

"Both of you. Shut. Up." Whit's locked-jaw growl did the trick. They both stared at him again. This time their mouths stayed closed.

"Listen, we have a problem," Whit whispered.

"That's an understatement." Hannah's angry voice echoed in the small room.

At the sound of her husky voice, Whit's stomach fell. He got a look at her face and the blood froze in his veins. Her skin was pulled taut over her cheekbones. Her beautiful brown eyes were flat and lifeless. Somehow her body shrank five inches in each direction while she was in the bathroom. His shirt hung like an oversized curtain from her slim shoulders. Whatever warmth she felt for him five minutes ago had frozen into a solid block of ice.

"Uh-oh." Adam's quiet whisper was the only noise in the room. The wary look in his eyes said it all. Hannah was furious and they were all potential targets.

Cole tried to soothe her first. Poor bastard. He reached out but Hannah shrank away.

"Don't touch me, Cole."

"Hannah—"

"Be quiet." She snapped at Cole but never broke eye contact with Whit. Her frosty glare ate right through him. Whit knew if she had the power to make him evaporate, he'd be nothing but a trace of moisture on the floor.

"We didn't know you were here." Adam, one of the tallest and most domineering men Whit knew, actually shrank back when Hannah glared in his general direction.

"No kidding." Her icy voice made him shiver.

"Let me explain."

"What's to explain, Cole? I guess it's a good thing I was here, that I overheard your testosterone-fueled chat, otherwise I might never have known Whit's true intentions. That he set up this little scene to humiliate me."

Whit swallowed his pride. How else could a man hold a conversation in a roomful of people, wearing nothing but the skin God gave him?

"Hannah. You've got it wrong."

"Really?" she screeched.

Not yelled. Not screamed. Screeched.

"Adam and Cole were just playing around. Talking shit. It doesn't mean anything."

She stalked over to Whit and stood just inches away. If his hands had been free, he'd have been covering his balls.

"From what I heard, you were the one playing around," she said.

"That's not true."

"With me."

"No, I—"

She sneered at him. "You set me up. You lured me down here to have sex with you."

"Damn it, no."

"What was the point, Whit? You wanted to tell all your male buddies, my employees, that you bagged the ice queen?"

"Better not or I'll kill him for you." Adam's gaze was full of awe and something Whit suspected was respect for Hannah's command of the room.

"You actually slept with him?" Cole choked out the question.

Hannah was on her cousin in a second. Whit enjoyed the brief reprieve. He'd never seen a person look that angry. Her body vibrated with it.

"How the hell is that your business?"

Cole went toe-to-toe with her. His very furious cousin. Whit gave Cole points for guts. No brains, but plenty of guts.

"Whether you like it or not, you're my business."

Hannah shoved against Cole's chest. "Really? Is that why you gave me up to a guy who only wanted to humiliate me?"

Oh, come on. He was the naked one and *she* felt foolish? "Now, wait a second—"

Cole and Hannah shouted at Whit to shut up. Whit was smart enough to do it even though he mumbled a few words under his breath about being the injured party in the room. The very cold room.

"Whit told me he had a job. That you'd be perfect. I knew about your deadline so I thought the arrangement would work." Cole scowled. "I never thought you'd actually sleep with him."

"Look at him! What did you think would happen if we were locked in a room together?"

"Thanks. I think." Whit was sorry he spoke the minute the words left his mouth. Him talking only made the flush on Hannah's cheeks brighter.

"I didn't know about the room. That was Adam's genius idea. Adam and Whit. When I found out about the plan, that Whit had arranged for you to spend time with him, I dragged Adam over here to get you free." Cole still couldn't look in Whit's direction. He threw out his arm in a wide arc. He could have been gesturing toward Whit or the dildo on the floor. Hard to tell.

"Besides, I didn't force you to sleep with him, you know. What's up, Hannah? He's not your type."

"What does that mean?" Hannah demanded to know.

"Yeah, what the hell does that mean?" Whit asked.

"He's rich. Successful. Annoying as shit."

"Is successful a bad thing?" Adam mumbled the question under his breath so only Whit could hear.

"The only reason I met him was because of you." She whipped around and glared at Whit again. "And you. What kind of man sleeps with a woman as a joke?"

He was getting ticked off. His character had taken enough knocks for one night. "That is not what happened."

"Well, I have a joke for you, Whit."

"Does it involve a gun?" Adam tried to bring a little lightness to the tense situation.

"No. The key."

Whit felt a spark of relief. "You found it"

Hannah smiled. Not one of those warm, loving smiles. No, more like the diabolical about-to-pluck-your-chest-hair-out-one-by-one kind of smiles.

"Oh yeah. I found it."

Whit's shoulders relaxed. "Thank God. Get me down so we can have a normal conversation."

"And then he can put on some damn clothes and spare us all the agony," Adam said.

Hannah started walking toward the door. Her narrow hips swiveled in an unconscious swing beneath his conservative shirt. The problem was that the sexy walk headed in the wrong direction.

"Where are you going? I need the key and we need to talk."

"It's too bad for you, Whit."

A chill moved back into the air. "What is?"

"That I flushed the damn key while I was in the bathroom."

Six

"You have to forgive me."

"Actually, I don't." If Cole pleaded his case one more time, she was going to belt him.

"But we're related. Think of the holiday dinners. You not talking to me. My mom crying." He shook his head in mock despair. "A very sad scene."

"We've never had a family dinner. I wasn't invited, remember?"

"You're killing my heartfelt apology."

"Gee, what was I thinking?"

"My guess is you're too busy being angry with Whit to think."

Hannah slashed open a cardboard box and stared at the stacks of shiny new tile inside. She'd spent the morning ripping up the old floor in Whit's house. Broken ceramic squares littered the room and a fine sheen of chalk dust covered every surface. The appliances were gone. The room was little more than a shell. The physical work revived her.

She wandered over to the home project early Sunday morning in the hope of finding quiet. Some solitude in which to forget all about one Whitman Goodard Thomas. She needed the bone-crushing work. Sweat running down her face with not a male in sight. A few hours of escape in which she didn't have to deal with Whit's image or the memory of his blinding kisses.

Cole had other ideas, including groveling at her feet until her head exploded.

"He's a good guy, you know." Cole had made that astonishing statement three times in ten minutes.

"Uh-huh."

"If I didn't know better I'd say you were ignoring me."

"I'm certainly trying."

Cole exhaled loudly. "Whit made a mistake. Okay, make that a big miscalculation, but that doesn't change who he is at base. He's a good man. Honest and decent."

"Not in my experience."

Cole leaned back against the counter. "You're not making this easy."

"I'm not trying to." She was trying to forget. Not remember and certainly not forgive.

"Whit isn't the type to use a woman for sport."

"If you say so."

"Well"—he drew out the sentence—"you liked him enough to sleep with him."

She dropped the box she was holding and let it crash against the floor. A plume of dust puffed up off the floor, making her cough.

"I love you like a brother but if you say one more word about Whit and his supposed virtues, I'll smack you."

Cole held up his hands in surrender. "Right. Got it. Woman scorned and all that."

She tugged on her slim white T-shirt. She'd abandoned her usual flannel tent and enjoyed the freedom. She wasn't accustomed to worrying about whether or not her tiny top covered all the important female parts that needed covering.

Cole stayed quiet. She enjoyed a few beats of silence but

knew it wouldn't last. She counted to ten in her head, just waiting for the next argument.

"All I'm saying is that I've known Whit for a long time. He's not the type to scam a woman."

"Uh-huh." She busied her hands reopening a box she sealed earlier to return to the manufacturer.

"It started out innocent enough. He asked about you. About the company."

"I said 'uh-huh.' That's the universal sound for I don't care and find another topic."

Cole ignored her. "He wanted to know all about you."

Her solid wall of control crumbled. She whirled around, her vulnerability showing. "And why did you tell him? That's what I don't get, Cole. You're supposed to be loyal to me. Why talk?"

"Because I insisted."

At the sound of Whit's low, even voice she froze. Slowly, steeling her nerves, she turned. He stood leaning against the doorway, one ankle balanced over the other, with his arms folded across his stomach. His brown hair wore the track marks from his fingers.

"Don't blame Cole. If you want to be mad, which you clearly do, then be mad at me." Whit's usually vibrant green eyes were flat and wary.

"Oh, don't worry, I have enough anger right now for both of you."

Whit's lips curled in an empty smile. "Nothing new there."

Her traitorous heart did a little jig at the sight of him. Gone were his usual pressed khakis. In their place, a pair of blue jeans, faded nearly white, hugged his impressive frame. A blue polo shirt pulled tight across his broad chest, highlighting every indentation of his muscles. A body she now knew by heart.

She wanted to be cool. To toss her hair back, say something witty, and act as if his stark betrayal meant nothing.

She prayed her severed heart wouldn't flip over. But that's just what it did. Flipped, then clenched as if a hand had slipped into her chest and was squeezing the life out of her breath by breath.

Good thing Whit looked as bad as she felt. If he'd smiled she might have thrown a box at him. "What are you doing here, Whit?"

"Working."

"On a weekend? Since when?"

"As you keep reminding me, this is my house. I can drop in at midnight and dance in the dining room naked if I want to."

The vision was all too easy to picture. "I don't have time for this today."

"Hannah, for God's sake, give the guy a break."

Just what she needed, Cole rushing to Whit's defense. This house was her last solace; now she was losing that, too. "I can handle Whit without your help."

"Yeah, you're doing such a fine job so far," Cole muttered.

Whit's gaze bounced between them. "You two can carry on without me. I'll be upstairs, working on the plumbing in the hall bathroom."

Whit tried to stage a graceful exit.

She wasn't feeling that generous.

The anger simmering inside her stomach needed an outlet. A target. The rage caused a wave of sickening dizziness to run through her body. She stored up all the useless energy and aimed it square at Whit.

"I get it now," she said.

Whit stared at her over his shoulder. "Get what?"

"You're here because you want this job finished. The sooner the house is done, the sooner you move on to the next project and a new and unsuspecting woman. It's easier for you to run away now that you've been found out for the fraud you are."

Whit's hand dropped from the doorknob. "Do you honestly believe that?"

Her brain insisted but her heart rebelled. For the first time since she'd walked down to the basement with Whit, she led with her head. She learned the hard way there was no other way to proceed with Whit and survive.

"Yes."

"Hannah, don't do this," Cole said.

Whit held up a hand to stop Cole's defense. "No, Cole, it's okay. Hannah's obviously made up her mind about me."

"I have."

How dare Whit sound as if he were the injured party in all of this? He created this mess. Lied to her. Embarrassed her. Used her. *Slept with her as part of his warped ego trip.*

She saw a brief flash of something that looked like pain cross in his eyes. "I'm not going to fight with you, Hannah. If you want to have a rational conversation, fine, but I'm done with the blame game."

She kept her defenses up, afraid to let him in for even a second. "Or is it that shoving me out of here as fast as you can will help you deal with what happened. Let you go back to being Mr. Nice Guy."

"Since when do you think of me as nice?"

The man had a point. "I guess I was right to be wary of you and your lame promises."

Whit stared right through her in deadly silence. She started to squirm.

"Whit, why are you here?" Cole asked.

"Because she has a deadline."

Her breath caught in her throat. He remembered. She had poured out her heart, took a risk, and talked about what drove her so hard at work. And he remembered.

Random thoughts and images bombarded her brain. She careened from hope to fear and back again. Trusting him was out of the question. Impossible, really. But the fact that he focused in on her deadline meant something. What, she wasn't sure, but something.

"I suppose you want me to thank you." She forced out a harsh whisper.

His eyes softened for a second before his face washed blank again. "Wouldn't think of it."

Then he turned and stomped out of the kitchen and up the stairs. Unfortunately, he left Cole behind.

"I hope you at least have the grace to feel like shit after that."

She thought about playing dumb but decided against it. "I guess you think I should."

"Absolutely."

"Yeah, well, I think so, too. For some reason Whit brings out the worst in me."

She felt worse than shit. If there was such a thing. Her insides felt empty and hollow. If this was love, it certainly sucked. As soon as the thought popped into her head it popped out again. But it was too late. The seed had been planted.

Love.

Damn it.

Had she really been stupid enough to fall in love with a guy who tricked her? With a guy so totally wrong for her?

"You could apologize," Cole suggested.

"After what he did to me? Get a clue." She wanted to shout in frustration, to curse the unfairness of the situation, but some of the steam behind her anger had evaporated.

"Tell me what you think he did again."

"Better yet, I'll tell him. Person-to-person."

She dumped the rest of the ceramic tiles on the floor and stalked out of the room toward the massive staircase in the hall. If Whit were dumb enough to wander into her lair, well then, he deserved whatever he got.

"Hannah?"

"What?" She snapped out the question.

"In case you need it, the key and the handcuffs are on that fancy chair by the window in the library."

Her insides froze. "Why in the world do you think I'd care about that?"

He winked at her, his smile wide and stupidly simple. "Call it a hunch."

Seven

Whit shimmied on his back under the toilet bowl and used his handy wrench to take out his frustrations on the unsuspecting drainpipe. The steady clanking noise stopped the dialogue raging in his brain. If he concentrated for even a second, Hannah's insults and accusations echoed in his head.

What the hell was he thinking slinking back into this house? To Hannah?

She obviously hated him. Not that she didn't have a good reason, but she made him sound like a complete ass. Sure, he had seen her photo at Cole's house and felt an immediate and unexpected spark. He'd heard about her in construction circles and admired her work and perseverance. After all that, he decided the idea of spending a few hours investigating what she had hidden under that icy reserve sounded damn good.

He never intended to use her. Never that.

"Did they teach you plumbing at Vanderbilt?"

He jerked forward at the sound of Hannah's husky voice and banged his head on the bottom of the ceramic toilet bowl. The unexpected shot to his temple sent him reeling. A second bounce when the back of his head smacked against the floor didn't help either.

He started swearing like an obnoxious drunk. A state that sounded good at the moment. He let out one final expletive. "Damn it!"

"Very smooth."

He struggled to a sitting position, rubbing his head and mumbling under his breath about interfering women the entire time. "Your bedside manner needs work."

"Ask anyone. I'm not known for my charm."

No way was he touching that.

He tried to steady his swaying body by holding onto the toilet bowel. Unfortunately, he forgot about the wrench in his hand. The metal whacked off the bowl then bounced off his knee. His second stream of profanity was even more clever and long-winded than the first.

"Good grief, Whit. You're going to kill yourself." She rushed over and slid onto her knees beside him. "And that's not fair."

He rubbed the sore spot on the back of his head and the new bruise on his leg. "Why is that exactly?"

"Because it's my right to kill you."

"Well then, use the wrench and make it quick. At this rate it will take days to finish me off."

Being this close to her creamy skin, close enough to smell the fresh scent of flowers that hovered around her and feel the soft puffs of air against his cheek, was like coming home. Being with her felt right.

Shame she wanted him dead or, at the least, castrated.

"How's the head?"

Better by the second. "I'll live."

She scooted away from him, putting a safe distance between their heated bodies, but stayed on the floor beside him. At least she'd stopped screaming at him. That had to be a good sign.

"Tell me why you're really here, Whit."

With that, the tentative peace evaporated. He exhaled. "I

wasn't feeding you a line. I came to help with your deadline.
I have extra time."

"You have time because under your original plan you
thought you'd be seducing me right now."

True, but he wasn't about to admit that. Not when
Hannah was within five inches of a wrench and more than
capable of swinging it at his fat head.

"You're determined to be angry."

She pushed up to her feet and walked to the window in
the bedroom next door. The room was empty except for a
desk and some paperwork she stepped over. "I figure I'm en-
titled."

Fine, if she wanted to clear the air, then so be it. They
could exchange jabs all day for all he cared. He hadn't slept
anyway. Couldn't. Spent most of the night tossing and turning, trying to figure out a way to win back Hannah's trust.
The idea of being without her, of never having another night
together, rubbed his insides raw.

Somewhere along the line Hannah went from being just
another worker to a beautiful woman he wanted, to . . . his
woman. She worked her way into his brain and was slowly
creeping her way into his heart.

He never thought of himself as a forever kind of guy. Until
Hannah. Now she filled up a large part of his world. At first,
he wrote off his feelings for her as lust. A mixture of attraction and hormones. Now he knew better.

He was falling in love with the ornery woman. Just when
she started falling deep into hate with him.

"I'm here to help."

"Uh-huh. Help."

His back teeth snapped together. Hannah was determined
to make this moment as hard as possible. And he was determined to find a chink in that mile-thick armor.

He continued over her dismissal. "Not because I think
that hanging around will win points or work an angle. The

bottom line is that your grandfather's offering you a raw deal. Thanks to spending time with me this weekend you're behind in work. I owe you."

Her chin lifted another inch. "Sex wasn't my payment?"

She was trying to piss him off. Damned if it wasn't working.

"Making love with you is another issue and you know it. One we better not talk about right now."

"Why not? This seems like the perfect time to me."

"Because I'd like my balls to stay attached to my body." He hoped he'd need them again someday.

"I don't need charity."

"Really? What do you need?"

Her brown eyes darkened. "Space."

"Wrong. Space is the last thing you need."

"I suppose you think you're smart enough to know what I need."

Hell, yeah. "Maybe you need a reminder."

In one step, he was on top of her, his arms locked around her waist and his heated body snug against hers.

Her eyes widened in surprise as he swooped in and treated her wet mouth to a scorching kiss. For a few seconds, her soft body stiffened and her hands pushed against his chest. When he deepened the kiss, sinking into her from chest to knee with every fiber of his being, she relaxed. Her muscles loosened and whatever resistance she planned on showing melted.

Before his mind turned to mush and his control took a hike, he pulled back. His brain managed to function long enough to send a message to his hands to let her go.

"You're not so tough." He soothed her swollen lips with his thumb. "This act you try to pull off, all hard and disinterested, doesn't fly."

"Our attraction is pretty undeniable. I admit that."

That was something. "More than a sexual pull holds us together."

"I have responsibilities."

He nodded. "I get that."

"Abandoning everything I've worked for and tried to build over a roll in the sack isn't an option. You are a diversion I can't afford."

Her icy words settled in the pit of his stomach. She wouldn't let him in. That blue-collar barrier she liked to throw up between them was back in full force.

He dropped his hands and stepped back. "You just can't put down the shield."

"I don't need a fancy education to know I need to be wary of you."

"Right. Not when you've got all that baseless indignation to keep you warm and toasty at night."

"You've got nerve calling me names, demeaning me."

"Don't you get it? I don't have to belittle you. You do that all by yourself."

Her jaw dropped open. "That doesn't make any sense."

"Sure it does. You walk around with a chip on your shoulder, just waiting for a reason to discount what other people say. If people have too much money or too much education, you decide they are unworthy of your time."

She pulled back as if he'd slapped her. "That's not fair."

"It's true."

"Is this a piece of wisdom from your freshman year psych class?"

She didn't even know she was proving his point. "You're always ready with a comeback."

Her chin kicked up another notch and her eyes clouded with anger but she stayed silent.

"Pushing people away is so easy for you."

"Some people. A certain architect, for example."

"Must've been a huge relief when I messed up so badly. I saved you from having to find a lame excuse to keep me at a safe distance or trying to come up with an excuse for why you enjoyed our time together in the basement so much. Now you can just tell yourself I'm a bastard and that you were right to shut me out in the first place."

Silence followed his outburst. His anger exploded out of nowhere. And ruined any chance of having a civilized conversation with Hannah. His stomach felt as if it were scraped empty. He welcomed the headache because the pain drowned out every other feeling humming through his body.

"Kiss me again."

His head shot up. He must have heard her wrong. Maybe she meant to tell him to kiss her ass.

"What?"

"You heard me. I want you to kiss me."

This had to be a test of some kind. Some twisted attempt to confirm how much of a bastard he was. She stood stick straight, her arms flat against her sides and her hands balled into fists. No exactly a welcoming stance. More like the look of a woman ready to strike.

"Why?"

Those fists were on her hips now. "Just do it."

His dick swelled to attention. "You aren't going to slap me or anything are you?"

"Since when do you play hard to get?" She sighed. "Just forget it."

She turned to leave but he beat her to the door. No way was she leaving this room before he had a chance to imprint his body on hers. He'd grab whatever opportunity she offered; he craved her that badly. Simp that he was.

"Not so fast, honey," he whispered as he stared down at her, his eyes glazed with need.

"I thought you weren't interested."

"Honey, I'm always interested when it comes to you."

Without touching her, his body looming, he backed her up until her thighs hit the desk. He leaned in, easing her body down until she balanced her upper body on her elbows behind her.

"What are you doing?"

If he were doing it right, that should have been obvious. "Making us comfortable."

"I said a kiss." Her breathy voice ate at him, making his insides flame with desire.

"But you didn't say where."

He lowered his body over hers, fitting his erection in the heated seam of her thighs. He nibbled at the corner of her mouth, stoking the fire burning in his gut. He ached to take her. To spread her legs and plunge deep inside her, wiping out all of her fears and doubts.

But right now she needed something else. Something gentle and reassuring.

His lips hovered above hers as his fingers speared through her silky hair, holding her head still. He nipped and licked, driving them both to near madness.

"Kiss me, Whit. Now."

When he felt her thighs clench tight against his hips, he gave into the need coursing through him. He lowered his head and pressed his lips against hers. He grabbed her wrists and stretched her arms above her head. When she moaned, he deepened the kiss. His tongue swept into her mouth as his erection hummed to life against her stomach.

"God, yes, Hannah."

He transferred both of her small hands into one of his. His free hand cupped her breast, teasing the nipple to a hard little nub.

"You are so beautiful."

"Whit, please . . ."

The door opened but they were too far gone to even notice. "Whoa! Jesus, Whit, try locking a door."

Adam's voice washed over him like a bucket of ice water. "Damn it!"

"Oh my God." Hannah pushed against his chest as she struggled to sit up.

This wasn't happening. Not now. "Get out, Adam."

"Right. I'm gone." Adam started to back out of the room

with a stupid grin on his face but Hannah's shout stopped him.

"No! Don't move."

Adam shrugged. "I'm not really one to get off on watching, but if that's what you need—"

"Shut up, Adam."

"Stop! Don't go." She shoved hard against Whit's chest. "Whit, move."

The sensual mood slipped away and there was no way to get it back. He reluctantly slid off of Hannah, letting his hand trail down her slender stomach until he lost contact and stood in front of her.

He turned his frustration on his brother. "What in the hell are you doing here?"

"Last time I checked I owned the place." Adam shot a quick look at Hannah as she tucked in her T-shirt. "But I guess I should have called first."

Hannah jumped off the desk and moved away from them. She might separate physically but he did not intend to let her separate on any other level.

"Your timing was fine," she said.

Amusement danced in Adam's eyes. "I bet Whit disagrees."

"You can leave now. Hannah and I have unfinished business."

"Whit, knock it off," Hannah warned. "We were done here anyway."

"Didn't look like it to me," Adam said.

Hannah's eyes narrowed. Whit felt lucky Adam was the subject of her wrath. This time. "Really? Did I ask you?"

"Um, no."

"Hannah, stop threatening Adam. Adam, get lost."

"Not before I figure out how I'm supposed to work without any men," Adam said.

Whit felt the tension spread across his shoulders. He had

two seconds to stop this conversation before Hannah realized his plans. "Adam, we'll talk about this later."

Hannah shook her head. "We'll talk about this now. What's going on?"

"Adam," Whit warned.

Adam centered all of his attention on Hannah. "Whit sent some of our guys to work on projects. Projects I've never heard of."

"Where?"

Whit jumped in. "This is a private business matter, Hannah. It doesn't concern you."

Hannah's mouth dropped open. "You didn't."

He had nowhere to hide. This time he was fully clothed but he felt just as naked. "It's not what you think." That was his refrain every time he talked to Hannah these days.

"You're unbelievable. I'm outta here." She left before he could grab her.

"Damn."

Adam stared at the empty doorway. "She can be nasty. I think I'm in love."

"Yeah, well, get over it," Whit growled as he wiped a hand through his hair.

"This isn't just about wanting her." Adam made the question a statement.

"No." Not anymore. He had passed that point before the basement door ever locked them in.

"Not to state the obvious but you've got a lot of work ahead of you. That's one angry woman."

"No kidding."

Adam whistled. "Good-looking as hell, too."

Whit wondered if beating the crap out of his brother would kill off his pent-up arousal. "You wanna die?"

"Not especially."

"Then make yourself useful and help me put up the chair rail."

"The good news is she looked pretty willing."

Clearly, Adam wanted to pursue his own topic. Not work. Whit dropped the hammer and leaned back against the wall. "Willingness isn't the problem. Letting go of her fears is."

"Need help with her?"

"No, I've screwed this up on my own. You showing up didn't help either."

"Okay. Then how about telling me what's going on with our business. If I'm going bankrupt over Hannah, I may as well know why."

Eight

Exactly nine days later Hannah walked up to the historically accurate wooden staircase of the Victorian house in search of Whit. Confused as ever.

The kiss was a mistake. She wanted to prove she could be close to Whit and stay unaffected. Instead, she landed on her back and was two seconds from ripping his shirt off when Adam strutted into the room.

She had tried ignoring Whit. Showering him with degrading comments, in her mind anyway. Nothing worked. His image never left her mind and his betrayal seemed less important as the days went by.

He refused to stay out of her head and her heart.

And her business.

"Returning to the scene of the crime, so to speak." Adam stepped out of the kitchen and caught her at the bottom of the stairs.

"Adam." A sharp pain settled in her abdomen. His mannerisms were so like those of Whit, just seeing him was a reminder. "What are you doing here?"

He sat down on the step in front of her so they were eye to eye. "Trying to keep Whit from working himself to death."

Her insides stilled. "What does that mean?"

"Just what I said. On top of his architectural and business duties, which are considerable, he's helping out with internal construction on this house and some others. He hasn't slept in days."

"He's working on my other projects when I'm not there."

Adam looked down at his folded hands then back up again. "Yeah."

"Replaced one of my project managers without telling me."

"Guy was a fool from what I can gather. Whit did you a favor. Then again, that's all he seems to do lately."

Her grip on the banister tightened. "You're blaming me? I didn't ask for his help, Adam."

"You didn't have to. That's the point." He sighed. "Look, if the plan is to yell at him or tease him then walk away without looking back, don't bother. Turn around and leave."

Anger swept through her like wildfire. "Give me a break. Whit's the one who—"

Adam raised a hand to stop her. "Save it. I know about the basement and his plan to get you alone for a few days. Hell, I helped him since he was so insistent and desperate to be with you."

She opened her mouth to protest but Adam talked right over her. "I know he wanted to get you alone. I also know you didn't fight him when you had the chance, and not because he bragged about being with you, so wipe that thought out of your head. That's not Whit's style. I know because I know him."

"He didn't force me. He never would." She knew that from the beginning. The confined space hadn't destroyed her because Whit was there. Right where she wanted him.

"Then what's the problem, Hannah?"

She jumped to the defensive. "He's trying to take over my life."

"He's trying to help you."

"I don't need his help."

His eyes narrowed. "Really? What do you need?"

"Him!" The word came out of nowhere and hung in the air. "Just him."

The second phrase seeped out of her, making her wish the floor would open up and swallow her whole. Adam's sly smile didn't help. "Well, I guess that settles that."

She thought about knocking the satisfied smirk right off his face. "It doesn't settle anything but I plan to do that right now. Where is he?"

"Upstairs."

She nodded, then walked in the opposite direction, toward the library.

Adam scrambled after her. "Wait."

"I can handle this from here."

"I said upstairs." Adam spoke slowly, as if she were a toddler.

"I heard you." Hell, the whole street probably heard him.

"Then why are you going the wrong way?"

She grabbed the handcuffs off the chair and started for the staircase, brushing right past Adam and ignoring his startled expression. He knew enough about her private life. She wasn't about to share more.

"What are you doing with those?" he asked.

She narrowed her gaze.

"Oh." Comprehension dawned on his face. "Oh, damn, I get it. Whit's a lucky bastard."

"Uh-huh. Get out."

Adam broke into a wide grin. "Welcome to the family."

"And lock the door behind you."

One down, one to go.

Whit woke from his brief nap. An uncomfortable wooden chair substituted for his soft bed. He hadn't slept much. Hadn't had the time or desire. Not without Hannah.

He moved his arm to look at his watch and nearly ripped his shoulder out of its socket. His eyes popped open.

Handcuffed . . . to the chair?

"What the hell?"

"We're going to talk," she said.

He looked up and saw Hannah sitting across from him, holding him in his tracks with those sexy brown eyes. She wore blue jeans and a form-fitting white T-shirt. Gone were the oversized flannel shirts. She didn't seem to need a shield now.

He wondered if he did.

She had turned a chair around and now sat with her arms resting over the intricately carved back. He tried to assimilate all the clues. Her shiny eyes and determined look. The handcuffs. What her presence meant. None of the clues made sense.

"Okay." That seemed like the only safe word at the moment.

"You sent your men to my jobs."

He closed his eyes briefly in pain. She had found something new to be pissed about. "Look, Hannah, I can explain."

She shook her head before he finished the sentence. "No. We're not going to do it this way. I'm going to ask a question and you're going to give me a simple answer."

"You're in charge." He rattled the handcuffs to prove his point.

"Right. Now let's try this again." She leaned in closer. "You sent men to my jobs."

"Yes."

"Do you think I can't do my job?"

His teeth clamped together. "No."

"Do you think I'm incompetent?"

"Damn it—"

"Answer me."

He pulled on the handcuffs but they would not budge. "Of course not."

"I don't need a baby-sitter."

"I never said you did."

"But you thought I couldn't finish the three jobs without your help."

Then he saw it. A fine trembling moved through her hands.

Her control hovered on the edge. She deserved the truth. That was the least he could do for her.

"Your grandfather gave you an impossible task, Hannah. No one, I repeat, no one could have met that deadline. He set you up to fail, probably so you'd come running back to him."

"And?"

"And I couldn't let that happen."

Her eyebrows inched up in question. "Why get involved?"

"Because the situation wasn't fair."

"Uh-huh."

He tried again. "Because I owed you."

Her lips twisted in a sneer. "For the sex?"

Wrong conclusion. That line of thinking would get his ass kicked. Hell, he'd never get free at this rate.

"I didn't mean it that way."

"Smart man."

He exhaled, trying to find the right words. He knew this was important to her. To their future. She was waiting for the right answer. He just didn't know what that was.

"You are extremely talented and competent. No one can take that from you. But your grandfather could take your company for no good reason. I wasn't going to let that happen. Not like this."

"Why?"

"I told you."

"Why?"

He snapped. "Because I'm falling for you. Okay? Are you satisfied?"

"Falling?"

He went for it. "In love. With you."

She blinked. "What did you say?"

His head fell back and he stared up at the ceiling.

"You don't want to hear the truth, I know. It scares you to death. I get that."

"Whit?"

He heard the shock in her voice and kept on talking. "I'm pretty shocked by the whole thing myself, but there you have it. I wanted you and tried to get some time alone with you."

"But only for sex."

He lowered his head and looked deep into her wide scared eyes. "Maybe it started out that way but not now. Now it's something else."

"Something like love." She talked as if she were in a trance.

"Yes. Maybe even a forever kind of love."

Her head started spinning. *He loved her.* Or was well on his way to being there. He had turned his life around to help her behind the scenes and without expecting anything in return. For the first time in her life, someone accepted her for her.

"You love me." She repeated his words.

His intense green eyes sparkled. "Yes. I'll give you whatever time you need to adjust, but I'm not going away."

"Where would you go?"

It was his turn to look confused. "Huh?"

"Forget it." She got up and moved the chair aside. When she straddled his lap, placing a knee beside each firm thigh, his muscles flexed across his chest.

"Hannah?"

She slid her arms around his neck and pressed her breasts against his chest. "Say it again."

He didn't pretend to misunderstand. "I love you."

"You said you thought you loved me."

"Yeah, well, I thought I'd better ease you into the idea first."

She kissed him then, with all the passion and desire she had stored deep inside her. When she pulled back, his mouth curved into a shy smile.

Her finger outlined his perfect mouth. "Some people will tell you I'm difficult."

"Say it isn't so."

Her fingers trailed down his chest to caress the bulge in his jeans. "Some people even think I'm a bit, shall we say, chilly."

He groaned. "Honey, there's nothing cold about you. Not in that shirt."

"It was too hot for flannel."

"It's October."

"I didn't mean outside." She tried to kiss him again but he pulled away. "What?"

"We're jumping a few steps here. Ten minutes ago you were furious and demanding answers. Now you're on my lap, not that I'm complaining."

"I tried to stay mad but I couldn't."

He frowned. "Don't you have something to say to me?"

She always thought the words would be hard to say out loud. But then she hadn't counted on Whit. On having a handsome architect in perfectly pressed khakis stumble into her life and never want to leave.

"I love you," she said, the words coming out with ease.

He smiled.

"Only you."

The smile grew.

"With all that education and all that arrogance, how could I not?"

"You're a sweet talker, honey."

"And I have an even sweeter suggestion."

A lazy arousal settled in his eyes. "I'm all yours."

"Good, because my plan involves those handcuffs and a little room in the basement."

He threw his head back and laughed. "Throw in a hard-hat and you've got a deal."

How could she say no?

Two lovers. And an unforgettable passion
that transcends time in
AGAIN
by Sharon Cullars.
Coming in May 2006 from Brava . . .

Inner resolve is a true possibility when temptation isn't within sight. Like the last piece of chocolate cheesecake with chocolate shavings; that last cigarette; that half-filled glass of Chianti . . . or the well-defined abs of a man who's had to take his shirt off because he spilled marinara sauce on it. Not deliberately. Accidents happen. At the sight of hard muscles, resolve flies right out of the window and throws a smirk over its wing.

Part of it was her fault. Tyne had offered him a shoulder rub, because during the meal he had seemed tense, and she'd suspected that his mind was still on the occurrences of the day. After dessert, he sat in one of the chairs in the living room while she stood over him. Even though he had put on a clean shirt, she could feel every tendon through the material, the image of his naked torso playing in her mind as her fingers kneaded the taut muscles.

As David started to relax, he leaned back to rest his head on her stomach. The lights were at half-dim. Neither of them was playing fair. Especially when a hand reached up to caress her cheek.

"Stop it," she whispered.

He seemed to realize he was breaking a promise, because

the hand went down, and he said, "I'm sorry." But his head remained on her stomach, his eyes shut. From her vantage, she could see the shadow of hair on his chest. She remembered how soft it felt, feathery, like down. Instinctively, and against her conscious will, her hand moved to touch the bare flesh below his throat. She heard the intake of breath, felt the pulse at his throat speed up.

She told herself to stop, but there was the throbbing between her legs that was calling attention to itself. It made her realize she had lied. When she told him she wanted to take it slow, she had meant it. Then. But the declaration seemed a million moments ago, before her fingers touched him again, felt the heat of his flesh melding with her own.

He bent to kiss her wrist, and the touch of his lips was the catalyst she needed. The permission to betray herself again.

She pulled her hands away, and he looked up like a child whose treat had been cruelly snatched away. She smiled and circled him. Then slowly she lowered herself to her knees, reached over, unbelted and unbuttoned his pants. Slowly, pulled down the zipper.

"But I thought you wanted . . ." he started.

"That's what I thought I wanted." She released him from his constraints. "But right now, this is what I want." She took him into her mouth.

She heard an intake of breath, then a moan that seemed to reverberate through the rafters of the room. She felt the muscles of his thighs tighten beneath her hands, relax, tighten again. Her tongue circled the furrowed flesh, running rings around the natural grooves. She tasted him, realized that she liked him. Liked the tang of the moisture leaking from him. And the strangled animal groans her ministrations elicited.

There were pauses in her breathing, followed by strained exhalations. Then a sudden weight of a hand on the back of her head, guiding her. She took his cue, began sucking with a pressure that drew him farther inside her mouth. Yet there was more of him than she could hold.

He was moments from coming. She could feel the trembling in his limbs. But suddenly he pushed her away, disgorging his member from her mouth with the motion.

He shook his head. "No, not yet," he said breathlessly. "Why don't you join me?" Before she could answer, he stood up, pulling her up with him, and began unbuttoning her blouse, almost tearing the seed pearls in the process. The silk slid from her skin and fell to the ground in a languid pool of golden-brown. He hooked eager fingers beneath her bra straps, wrenched them down. Within seconds, she was naked from the waist up, and the current in the room, as well as the excitement of the moment teased her nipples into hard pebbles. His fingers gently grazed them, then he grazed each with his tongue. Her knees buckled.

"How far do you want to go?" he breathed. "Because I don't want you to do this just for me."

Her answer was to reach for the button of his shirt, then stare into those green, almost hazel eyes. "I'm not doing this for you. I'm being totally selfish. I want you . . . your body . . ." She pushed the shirt over his shoulders, yanked it down his arms.

"Hey, what about my mind?" he grinned.

She smiled. "Some other time."

They undressed each other quickly, and as they stood naked, his eyes roamed the landscape of her body with undeniable appreciation. Then without ceremony, he pulled her to the floor on top of him so abruptly that she let out an "oomph." His hands gripped the plump cheeks of her ass, began kneading the soft flesh. She felt his hardened penis against her stomach and began moving against it, causing him to inhale sharply. His hands soon stopped their kneading and replaced the touch with soft, whispery caresses that caused her crotch to contract with spasms. One of his fingers played along her crevice as his lips grabbed hers and began licking them. His finger moved to the delicate wall dividing both entryways, moved past the moist canal, up to her clitoris, started teasing her orb just as his tongue began playing along hers. She grounded her pelvis against him, desperately claiming her own pleasure, listening to the symphony of quickly pumping blood, and intertwined breaths playing in her ears.

He guided her onto his shaft. Holding her hips, he moved her up, down, in an achingly slow and steady pace that was thrilling and killing, for right now she thought she could die with the pleasure of it, the way he filled her, sated her. She felt her eyes go back into her head (she had heard about the phenomenon from other bragging women, and had thought they were doing just that—bragging. But now she knew how it could happen.)

"Ooooh, fuck," she moaned.

"My thoughts exactly," he whispered back, and with a deft motion, changed their positions until he was on top of her. Straddled on his elbows, he quickened his thrusting, causing a friction that drove her to a climax she couldn't stop. Her inner walls throbbed against the invading hardness, and she drew in shallow breaths as her lungs seemed to shatter with the rest of her body.

She put her arms around his waist and wrapped her legs around his firm thighs. His body had the first sheen of perspiration. She stroked along the dampness of his skin, then reciprocated the ass attention with gentle strokes along his cheeks.

"I want . . . I want . . . " he exerted but couldn't seem to finish the sentence. Instead, he placed his mouth over hers until she was able to pull his ragged breaths into her needy lungs. The wave that washed over her once had hardly ebbed away before it began building again. Now his pace was frantic, his hips pounding her body into the carpeting, almost through the floor. Not one for passivity, she pounded back just as hard and eagerly met each thrust. The wave was gathering force, this one threatening a cyclonic power that would rip her apart, render her in pieces. She didn't care. His desperation was borne of sex, but also she knew, of anger and frustration. He was expelling his demons inside her, and she was his willing exorcist . . .

Blood was everywhere. On the walls, which were already stained with vile human secretions; on the wooden floor, where the viscous fluid slowly seeped into the fibers of the wood and pooled between the crevices of the boards. Soon, the hue would be an indelible telltale witness of what had happened, long after every other evidence had been disposed of. Long after her voice stopped haunting his dreams. Long after he was laid cold in his grave.

He bent to run a finger through one of the corkscrew curls. Its end was soaked with blood. The knife felt warm in his hands still. Actually, it was the warmth of her life staining it.

He turned her over and peered into dulled brown eyes that accused him in their lifelessness. Gone was the sparkle—sometimes mischievous, sometime amorous, sometimes fearful— that used to meet him. Now, the deadness of her eyes convicted him where he stood, even if a jury would never do so. The guilt of this night, this black, merciless night, would hound his waking hours, haunt his dreams, submerge his peace, indict his soul. There would now always be blood on his hands. For that reason alone, he would never allow himself another moment of happiness. Not that he would ever find it again. What joy he would have had, might have had, lay now at his feet in her perfect form. Strangely, in death, she had managed to escape its pall. Her skin was still luminescent, still smooth. If it weren't for the vacuous eyes, the blood soaking her throat, the collar of her green dress, the dark auburn of her hair . . . he might hold to the illusion that somewhere inside, she still lived.

He reached a shaky hand to touch her cheek. It was warm, soft, defying death even as it stiffened her body.

He bent farther, let his lips graze hers one last time. Their warmth was a mockery. Her lips were never this still beneath his. They always answered his touch, willingly or not.

He saw a tear fall on her face, and for a second was confused. It rolled down her cheek and mixed with the puddle of blood. He realized then that he was crying. It scared him. He hadn't cried since he was a child. But now, another tear fell, and another.

Through his grief, he knew what he would have to do. She was gone. There was no way to bring her back. Her brother would be searching for her soon. She wasn't an ordinary Negress. She was the daughter of a prominent Negro publisher, now deceased, and the widow of a prominent Negro lawyer. She had a place in their society. So, yes, she would be missed. There would be a hue and cry for vengeance if it were ever discovered that she had been murdered.

Which was why he could not let her be found.

He knew what he had to do. It wasn't her anymore. It was just a body now. Yet, he couldn't resist calling her name one last time.

"Rachel."

Then he began to cry in earnest.

Tyne pushed through the sleep-cloud that fogged her mind. The dream-world still tugged at her, reached out cold fingers to pull her back. But her feet ran as fast as they could, ran toward the name hailing her, pleading with her to hurry. The name reverberated around . . . *Rachel* . . . *Rachel* . . . *Rachel* . . .

"Rachel . . . Rachel . . . "

The sound woke her. She slowly opened her eyes, lay there for a moment, not remembering. Gradually, disorientation gave way to familiarity. Shaking off sleep, she became aware of her surroundings. Recognized the curtains that hung at the moon-bathed window, saw the wingback chair that was a silhouette in front of it. Sometime during the night or early morning, he had retrieved her clothes and laid them neatly on the chair's back.

He was shifting in his sleep, murmuring. Then she heard the name again, just as she had heard it in her dream. "Rachel." He strangled on the syllables, his voice choked with emotion—with . . . grief, she realized. She sat up, turned. His back was to her, shuddering. He was crying . . . in his sleep. Was calling to a woman—a woman named Rachel. Someone he'd never mentioned before. And obviously a woman who meant a lot to him, and whose loss he freely felt in his unconscious state. So he'd lied about never having been in love. But why?

A pang of jealousy moved through her, pushed away affection, gratification. She didn't want to be solace for some lost love he was still pining for. Didn't want to be a second-hand replacement to someone else's warmth in his bed. She looked over at the clock. It was almost four anyway. She might as well get home to get ready for work.

She shifted off the mattress delicately, grabbed her clothes from the chair and started for the door. She would dress downstairs to make sure she didn't wake him. She turned at the door to look at him. The shuddering had stopped. There was only the peaceful up and down motion of deep breathing. She opened the door, shut it lightly and made her escape.

Here's a scintillating look at
Alison Kent's,
DEEP BREATH.
Available now from Brava!

While Georgia had holed away in the suite's monstrous bathroom to shower, shave, shampoo, and pull on a clean pair of undies, her T-shirt and jeans, Harry had been busy. Busy doing more than getting dressed and ratcheting up the who-is-this-man-and-where-did-he-come-from stakes.

He wore serious grown-up clothes as beautifully as he wore casual, and as well as Michelangelo's David wore his marble skin.

She'd walked out of the steamy bathroom and only just stopped herself from demanding what the hell he was doing breaking into her room before she realized her mistake. He was that amazing. And her heart was still dealing with the unexpected lust.

The man was the most beautiful thing she'd seen in forever. Her first impression, made from Finn's truck when looking down from her window, had been right on the mark. But he was so much more than a girl's guide to getting off.

His smile—those lips and dimples, the dark shadow of his beard—was enough to melt even the most titanic ice queen. Not that she was one or anything . . .

Sitting as she was now in the hotel's salon, having her hair and makeup done, she kept sneaking looks over to where he sat waiting and reading a back issue of *Cosmo*. Every once in a while he'd frown, shake his head, turn the page. If she hadn't been ordered not to move by her stylist, she might never have stopped laughing.

When Harry told her he'd arranged not only this appointment but another with the hotel boutique's personal shopper for jewelry, shoes, and a dress, she'd asked him if he thought she was made of money.

He'd pulled out his wallet, handed her a five to pay back the tip, then reminded her she was the one donating to General Duggin's Scholarship Foundation tonight.

Making sure she arrived looking the part of wealthy collector rather than pack rat was the least he could contribute to the cause—a cause he'd then started to dig into, asking her questions about her family and the importance of the documents Charlie had sent her to find.

Since she'd been stuck on the pack rat comment, frowning as she ransacked her duffel for the sandals she knew were there, thinking how she really *had* let herself go since being consumed by this quest, she'd almost answered, had barely caught herself in time.

The story of her father's wrongful incarceration and her determination to prove his innocence had been on the tip of her tongue before she had bitten down. If Harry knew the truth of why she wanted the dossier, he would quickly figure out she had no intention of delivering it to Charlie Castro.

Then, no doubt, they'd get into an argument about the value of her brother's life versus that of her father's name, and he'd want to know why the hell they were going through all of this if not to save her brother.

She really didn't want to go there with Harry. She was having too much trouble going there with herself. Finn would understand; she knew he would. As long as he was alive to do so when this was over . . .

At that thought, she groaned, the sound eliciting the stylist's concern. "What's wrong, sweetie? Too much color? Not enough? The highlights are temporary, remember? Three washings max, you'll be back to being a brunette."

"Oh, no. I was thinking of something else," Georgia assured the other woman, meeting her reflected gaze. "I hadn't even looked . . ."

But now she did. And she swore the reflection in the mirror couldn't possibly be hers. "Wow," was the only thing she could think to say, and so she said it again. "Wow."

"Yeah. I thought so, too." The stylist beamed at her handiwork—and rightly so. Georgia had never in her life looked like this. The highlights in her hair gave off a coppery sheen. Her layers, too long and grown out—she was desperate for a new cut—had been trimmed, colored, and swept up into an intricate rooster tail of untamed strands.

And then her face . . . Was that really her face? The salon's makeup expert had used a similar color scheme, spreading sheer terra cotta on her cheeks, a blend of copper and bronze on her eyelids, finishing off with a gorgeous cinnamon-colored glaze on her lips.

And all of it matching the beautiful ginger-hued polish on the nails of all twenty fingers and toes. She could go for this girly girl stuff. Really.

Especially when she lifted her gaze to meet Harry's in the mirror. He stood behind the stylist, his shoulders wide in his designer suit coat, his hands jammed to his lean waist, his smile showing just a hint of teeth.

She had no idea when he'd moved from where he'd been sitting to her chair, but the look in his eyes, the fire in his eyes, and the low sweep of his lashes were enough to make her swoon.

It had been so long since a man had shown *that* kind of interest in her that she didn't know what to do, how to react, to respond. Except the truth was that it wasn't the men. It was her.

She had refused to let any man get close enough to do more than notice her skill for ferreting out valuable antiques for years now, longer than she could remember.

But now, here came Harry into the middle of her personal catastrophe, a veritable stranger who had the body of a god and a killer smile and eyes that were telling her dangerously sexy things about wanting to get her naked. He was helping her in ways that went above and beyond.

And she still had the night to spend in his room. "Can we charge the makeup to the room? I'll pay you back."

"Sure." His eyes sparkled. His smile grew wicked. "And it's my treat."

The stylist swept the cape from around Georgia's shoulders and Harry offered his hand to help her from the chair. It was a Cinderella moment that she had no business enjoying, but she couldn't help it.

She hadn't done a single thing for herself in so long that it was impossible to brush aside this feeling of discovering someone she'd thought lost.

She was well aware of why she and Harry were together, the full extent of what was at stake. But it had been years, literally *years*, since she'd considered herself attractive—not to mention since she'd felt confident that someone of the opposite sex found her so.

Harry did. She didn't doubt it for a minute. Even if it did up the nerve-wracking factor of the long evening ahead in his company.

While Harry tipped the stylist and settled the bill, she took the bag of cosmetics from the cashier, absently noticing how the attention of every woman in the salon, whether overtly or subtly, was directed toward the check-out station and the fit of Harry's clothes.

She wanted to laugh; here she was, panicking over sleeping near him when he could crook a finger and have any of these women in his bed.

And then she didn't want to laugh at all.

She wanted to grab him by the arm and drag him out of there, leaving a battlefield of bloody cat scratches in her wake. Like he belonged to her or something, and how ridiculous was that? He was nothing but a man who happened to be in the wrong place at the wrong time, who was going out of his way to get her out of a jam.

Finn would have done the same for a woman in need. Her ex, hardly. They'd been married, and he wouldn't have done it for her. Unless there was something in it for him . . . Hmm. Too bad she hadn't snapped to that before.

Harry scrawled his signature across the bottom of the ticket then handed the pen to the cashier. Georgia cocked her head and considered what he could possibly hope to gain from helping her out. He was going to a lot of expense . . . and sex was the first thing, the only thing, that came to mind.

Turn the page for a sneak peek at
Dianne Castell's
THE WAY U LOOK TONIGHT.
Available now from Brava!

Callie lay back against the headboard staring at the computer propped against her knees; the moon and the glow from the monitor were the only lights in the room. After her little groping session with Keefe on the front porch that ended in total humiliation, how could she sleep?

She checked her email again looking for a message from M. Perry but still no reply. She clicked back to solitaire to start another game.

She was furious with Keefe, the bastard. Getting her to respond to him just to puff up his male ego was something she never dreamed he'd do. She knew the soap set, at least she thought she did. There were the actors who were self-absorbed and thought they were the second Tom Cruise on their way to the top; the playmates who were in it for the glam, and the press hounds who loved seeing their names and pictures everywhere. But Keefe never fit into any of those categories. He seemed . . . real. Till tonight. Guess that put him in the Tom Cruise category. She lost at solitaire again, checked her in box again and there it was . . . a reply from M. Perry.

She sat up and took a deep breath, then opened the e-mail. M. Perry said the meet was a go. "Holy cow," she whispered into the darkness. "We really did it."

This was a big step closer to finding Mimi. If Perry didn't know something about Mimi the people he worked for had to have a hunch where she was, why else would they be advertising for her in Memphis? She should tell Keefe. No matter what their differences he needed to know about the note even if it was the middle of the night, actually almost morning. He should make plans and she needed to know what to write back to Perry.

Callie slid from the bed, pulled on her robe and tip-toed into the hall. She looked both ways to make sure Rory wasn't around to get suspicious, then she opened the door to Keefe's room and went in.

Moonlight fell across Keefe's bare back. Did it have to be bare? She tried to resurrect her thoughts of him as a bastard, but it didn't help to see his . . . skin. Lots of it. Didn't the man ever hear of a T-shirt? The sheet just covered his butt. Eyes closed, breathing slow and steady. There was not one thing slow and steady about her right now. She should have never come. What was she thinking? She turned and started for the door and he said "Enjoying the view?"

See, bastard! She spun around. "You are the most arrogant conceited, self-important, smug, high and mighty, stuck up, vain, arrogant—"

"You already said arrogant."

"Well, I'm saying it again because it's doubly true." He rolled over onto his back taking the sheet with him. Thank the lord for that! She didn't need any more maleness to distract her; this was enough. "I came to tell you we heard from M. Perry. The meeting's on. I thought you might like to know and what do you want me to reply?"

"So what the hell are you doing up at this hour?"

"What do you think, waiting for the darn e-mail, like I said. This is important. I need to reply."

"Tell him to look for three guys in Atlanta Braves baseball hats. Now, what else do you need?" He winked.

"I need to beat you about the neck and shoulder." She

yanked the door open and resisted the urge to slam it as she left and crept back to her room. Her stomach churned and she ground her teeth. She was angry enough to spit nails. How could she be attracted to such a jerk? She wasn't, it was over. Two years of ogling and daydreaming about the man officially ended tonight. Common sense had prevailed over primal lust. In fact, common sense should always prevail, especially in important matters.

And by late the next afternoon as she and Bonnie entered Slim's, Callie was more convinced of that than ever. Sally waved her over to a table where she and Georgette sat and Callie pushed the stroller in that direction. Dinner customers occupied about half the tables including Eleanor Stick sitting in the back. Well, what brought that on?

Callie lifted Bonnie onto her lap and Sally leaned across the table. "Did you see who's graced our presence for dinner tonight? Eleanor's working at the hardware store. Can't seem to find babysitting jobs anywhere, now that Keefe made a point of telling everyone on the Landing she's way less then a great babysitter."

Bonnie started to fuss and Callie rocked her but it didn't help. She stood and paced and ran smack into Eleanor Stick. The old bat smirked. "Taking care of young'ns isn't as easy as you think, is it, city-girl?" she harrumphed, then strolled off toward the door, nose in the air, shoulders back.

Bonnie yelled louder and Callie said, "Now look what she did. The woman brings out the worst in this baby."

Georgette sighed. "Oh, good grief." She stood and lifted Bonnie into her arms. "Crying babies make me nuts. Let me have a go at this. I worked my way through college at a daycare." She put Bonnie to her shoulder, her cries gradually decreasing by several decibels.

Georgette slowly grinned, a real grin as if she truly enjoyed the moment. "She likes my earrings. One of my cousins was the same way, into the bling even at this age."

Bonnie cooed as she played with the silver and gold dangles

at Georgette's ears and Sally said, "Georgette, you're a baby genius."

Georgette sat down. "Just doing what needs to be done."

Callie felt her heart soften toward Georgette. This was a genuine side of her Callie hadn't seen before and she liked it. "Bonnie wins everyone over and maybe after tonight we'll be a step close to getting her mama back."

Sally huffed, "Well, I doubt it. Three men in baseball caps? What the heck kind of disguise is that? That's what happens to men—they never play dress-up when they're growing up. The don't get the fantasy concept. Perry's going to recognize Keefe, someone's bound to know Digger, and Demar reeks cop. The man might as well have 'I am the law' written across his forehead. The meet's never going to come off."

Callie said, "But what if Keefe and his merry men don't do the meeting. What if someone else does . . . like us." Her gaze fused with Sally's and she sat up straight.

Georgette sat down. "The guys already said it's them and only them and we weren't invited to the party." Callie bit at her bottom lip. "Well, that was before I sinned."

Georgette whispered, "Sinned as in little-white-lie or as in hold-onto-your-butt?"

"The butt one. I told M. Perry to look for three women in red boas at nine o'clock at Kerby's. I had to keep the time the same because I mentioned it in the first note and I didn't want to do anything to scare him off."

Sally put her fingers over her mouth to stifle a laugh then said, "Honey, if three red boas don't scare him off nothing will."